Items should be returned on
shown below. Items not alrea
borrowers may be renewed in
telephone. To renew, please q[....] on the
barcode label. To renew online [....] required.
This can be requested at your local library.
Renew online @ **www.dublincitypubliclibraries.ie**
Fines charged for overdue items will include postage
incurred in recovery. Damage to or loss of items will
be charged to the borrower.

Leabharlanna Poiblí Chathair Bhaile Átha Cliath
Dublin City Public Libraries

Baile Átha Cliath
Dublin City

Date Due	Date Due	Date Due
0 9 JUL 2015		
1 1 FEB 2016		
1 4 JUN 2018		

'Invested with a weighty, parable-like intensity.'
The Times Literary Supplement

'Spectacular.'
Sunday World

'Deeply funny about the absurdities of human behaviour.'
Irish Examiner

'Prose that could be described as musical … Elegant and thoughtful,
often funny, never dull or repetitive.'
Irish Echo (Australia)

'A powerful, passionate novel.'
Books Ireland

'The strangeness of McGuinness's novel, the offbeat atmosphere
and the narrative motility, certainly make it an intriguing
piece of work … Defiantly unusual.'
Literary Review

Arimathea

Frank McGuinness lives in Dublin and lectures in English at University College Dublin. His internationally acclaimed work includes *The Factory Girls*, *Baglady*, the multi-award winning *Observe the Sons of Ulster Marching Towards the Somme*, *Innocence*, *Mary and Lizzie*, *Someone Who'll Watch Over Me* (New York Drama Critics' Circle Award, Writers' Guild Award for Best Play), *Dolly West's Kitchen*, *Gates of Gold*, *Speaking Like Magpies*, *There Came a Gypsy Riding* and *Greta Garbo Came to Donegal*. Frank's widely performed adaptations of classics include Lorca's *Yerma*; Chekhov's *Three Sisters* and *Uncle Vanya*; Brecht's *The Threepenny Opera* and *The Caucasian Chalk Circle*; Sophocles' *Electra* and *Oedipus*; Euripides' *Helen*; Ostrovsky's *The Storm*; Strindberg's *Miss Julie*; Ibsen's *Rosmersholm*, *Hedda Gabler*, *The Lady from the Sea*, *A Doll's House*, *Ghosts* and *John Gabriel Borkman*; Molina's *Damned by Despair* and most recently James Joyce's *The Dead*. TV screenplays include the award-winning *The Hen House* (BBC2) and the celebrated BBC drama *A Short Stay in Switzerland*. He has published five volumes of poetry with The Gallery Press, the most recent being *In a Town of Five Thousand People*.

FRANK McGUINNESS

Arimathea

BRANDON

This edition first published 2015 by Brandon,
an imprint of The O'Brien Press Ltd,
12 Terenure Road East, Rathgar,
Dublin 6, Ireland.
Tel: +353 1 4923333; Fax: +353 1 4922777
E-mail: books@obrien.ie.
Website: www.obrien.ie
First edition published 2013.

ISBN: 978-1-84717-766-7

1 2 3 4 5 6 7 8 9 10
15 16 17 18 19

Printed and bound by Nørhaven, Denmark.
The paper in this book is produced using pulp from managed forests.

DEDICATION
For Mary Finn

Chapter One

Euni

He came from out foreign and he spoke wild funny. All the older girls thought he was the last word from the day and hour they set eyes on him but they were stupid, and he would no more look at them than if he was the man in the moon. I don't know where that shower got the notion that he was the kind of fellow listened to the likes of them. Was it because of the way some of them sprawled in front of him, were they expecting him to draw them? I doubt if he even noticed they were making a show of themselves. He certainly didn't breathe a word in front of me if his stomach was turning at the sight of those eejits. Maybe he was blathering to himself in his own language, so we would never make out what he thought of them.

It was hard to know what he thought. My mother said, he

keeps himself to himself, and will you let the poor stranger alone? He has his work to do, he wants to do it and get home. Like the rest of us, he's missing his own bed. Making all the beds – his as well – that was one of my jobs about the houses, the upper and the lower. We owned two houses down the lane. We weren't swanky, just that one belonged once upon a time to my Granny and Granda. Anyway, I was saying about his bed, it smelt like none of the rest. It was just always fresh. Mammy changed our sheets once a week and his sheets were washed at the same time, but there was a scent like himself on them, and it was nice, I thought. He must have cleaned himself very thoroughly.

I know he did, for I saw him once. The man is meticulous, my mother told her sisters, my two aunts. In fact, to tell the truth, if I were being honest, I'd say he was pernickety, she whispered. I left them to their whispers but they didn't know I'd seen him soaping himself at the basin in his room. He was browner than anybody I'd ever seen. And even though he didn't know I was watching him and I didn't want him to know, I nearly asked him out loud if all the men were as tanned as he was back where he came from, but I didn't. Here the sun turns everybody beetroot – especially our ones with our red hair to a man and a woman, especially my mother.

He said to me he liked red hair. Not like his own, that I saw on his chest, wet from the water in the white basin, the hairs black as your boot, and fine as the ones on his arms. Yes, he was meticulous in the morning but by evening time he was anything but. Then he was stained with the colour of the paint.

His clothes were stinking to high heaven by the weekend. Mammy fetched them herself down from his room come Friday night, so they could be soaked and the dirt got out of them by Saturday evening, for it is a sin to wash clothes on a Sunday. A venial sin. But to iron on Sunday – well, that is mortal, and if you do and you die, God will brand your bare back with the mark of a red hot iron. Imagine the squeals out of you suffering that. And the smell of your skin burning. So the Sunday was not a day for work, but plenty of times he did. He would lock the door to stop anybody coming in to annoy him. Not that I did so after he lost his temper the first time I juked my head round to see how he was doing. His face turned the most awful shade and he just roared at me. What did he say scared the living daylights out of you? Mena Kiely asked me. I told her I couldn't tell because I didn't understand one word. Mena said, God forgive him, he must have been cursing in his own language. Well, he was very angry whatever he was saying, he put the heart crosswise in me, Mena, I thought I was going to die, honest to good God, I told her. But you didn't, did you? Mena whispered. And my cheeks burned scarlet. That was because, well, Mena was expected to die at any minute, God rest her. No – no, I mean, God love her. She wasn't exactly my best friend, but you had to mind her all the time at school, or out playing. She was very delicate and she couldn't run fast. If you hit her hard she would lose her breath as if she raced all the mile from Cockhill cemetery to the town. We all took a turn to give her a wallop to hear how she panted. She didn't care the first time you did it because the noise of it was a good laugh, but if you kept hitting her then she'd tell your mother or the nun. Nobody minded her being a tittle-tattle because she was sick, but it meant you couldn't trust her.

You could trust me though. I'd say nothing to anybody about anything. I had eyes in my head and ears that could listen but that doesn't mean I would let the world know my own or my family's business. That's why it was really stupid for him not to let me see his old paintings. God strike me down dead for saying that because it was holy pictures he was doing. That much I knew for sure from the start because it was Fr O'Hagen brought him to us in the first place. I thought Mammy was going into a fit when she opened the door to see a priest standing there with a smile on his face, and he wasn't looking for money.

–Good day to you, Mrs O'Donovan, how are you?

–I'm well, Father O'Hagen, I'm very well.

–Isn't it biting cold for the month that's in it?

–It is. This June is like an October.

–May I come in? I have to ask you a favour.

She let him in. She even offered him tea. And he took it. I was watching her hands shake as she lifted the boiling kettle from the black range to scald the silver teapot. He was still standing as she put in the tea leaves.

–Sit down, Father. Excuse my manners. Sit down. The tea will be soon ready. Do you like it strong? I'll just fetch you a cup to drink it out of.

The good stuff was put on the table. White china with gold at the edges we didn't eat off even on the Christmas. She poured out for him and he sat at our table, Fr O'Hagen, drinking our tea with our milk and our sugar in his mouth. I thought she would offer him a piece of treacle scone with raisins, yet she didn't. I had already staked a claim for it if he left it or any of it lying on his plate, but it was not to be. He had a big face and I was sure he had a long tongue. I thought he looked like a cat, a black and white cat, but then he came to the point. Would we be able to put up a visitor, an artist, a painter that was coming to the town? A painter all the way from Italy, where the Pope lives, he instructed us, as if we didn't know where the Pope lived. I could see the shock on Mammy's face.

–Will he not be wild fussy, Father? All airs and graces – would he not look down his nose at the like of us?

His eyes were scouring the kitchen, catching every speck of dirt as if it were mice droppings. Then he started to lower his voice. He assured her she kept as clean a house as any he'd ever witnessed in this parish, or any other for that matter. She was renowned for her cooking and baking. And the Italians, if they were fussy about anything, it was about their food. He knew that from his own stay amongst them.

–But how will we understand him? Does he speak our language?

There was nothing there to worry about. The painter's father was a distinguished professor of languages. He would surely have taught his son how to master at least the basics of English. Fr O'Hagen himself still could recall a fair smattering of Italian. Between the lot of us we would make a fist of the words to get us all by.

—I still don't understand why you don't ask Anna Boyle, or the Ferguson woman in Ludden. They have houses big enough to take in lodgers. We would be very squeezed—

—If he were to stay here, Mrs O'Donovan, that would be the case. But I was hoping you might let him have the use of your empty house down the road. He could work there as well, uninterrupted. And come here for his grub.

I mentioned to you about my grandfather's house eight doors down from us. We lived next to the forge where my daddy worked. It was bigger than the lower house because there were rooms above the smithy. That's where I was born. In the biggest room in the house. Since he died two years and three months ago Granda's house was empty. That broke my heart. I hated the priest and the painter already because I didn't want strangers traipsing through where he lived. My mother told Fr O'Hagen that house hasn't been lived in since the death.

—Then surely it's perfect.

I'd never heard that word said before. I must have seen it written down, because I knew exactly what it meant, and I was certain as well that Mammy would let this boy from Italy stay. You couldn't refuse a priest. It's bad luck and bad manners. He was asking if her husband, our Daddy, would be agreeable to his request also? Where was he? Out walking the greyhounds. She would tell him when he came in. There was one other thing – she was sorry, but she was obliged to ask.

—Look around you, Father. We are poor people–

—It will not matter–

—I'm thinking of his keep. We couldn't afford–

Fr O'Hagen assured Mammy there would be no question of this family being out of pocket during the lodger's stay. The priest himself would provide a weekly rate to cover bed and board. The visitor would expect nothing fancy. He'd never set eyes on the man before, so he didn't know what size of an indi-vidual he would be. As a race, the Italian people, they did tend to be thin and lithe, so he doubted if we would be entertaining a glutton to devour us out of house and home. Mammy was glad to hear that. So, have we a deal? We have.

That's the way he landed in with us. As the priest was leav-ing, Mammy asked what was it this boy was coming to paint? A new Stations of the Cross, in the chapel. It was time we had one. Wasn't that right?

The lower house was always locked to us after Granda passed away. I didn't mind because without him it smelt like the taste of sour milk. I think Mammy thought the same. That's why she scrubbed the place room by room, me coming after her giving her a hand. She said you're never too young, girl, to learn how to clean a house from top to bottom. That will be your job for life.

—But I'm going into the factory when I leave school–

—You'll leave there when you get married. Every man expects his wife to have his home shining like a new pin.

She was emptying dirty water down the sink. It splashed against her hands. They were rough red, hard as the floors beneath our feet. She was sweating a bit from the work and she used a blue towel to wipe her face. I told her I really didn't want to go into the factory. She stopped and looked at me. Then she took the soaking floor cloth and rinsed it dry. She asked me what would I do instead? I told her I would love to be a nurse. I was a bit breathless because it was a big secret, so I didn't see her shoot the cloth at me until it stung my face. It was the shock of it made the tears spring into my eyes, because it wasn't that sore. Then she just said, how in the name of Jesus would the likes of us get to be nurses? Tell me how, you stupid bitch? You'll step through that factory door and you'll earn your pay making shirts. That day will be coming soon enough. You're no different from the rest. You have to rough it. Learn that. Get on your knees and help me put a shape on that scullery.

I did as she bid me. I never looked at her. I knew not to when she was in a temper. Eyes boring into her always drove her mad. I still managed though to sneak a look and here's the strange thing – she was doing something she very rarely did. Standing still, looking straight at me, saying nothing.

The painter, he used to do that at times as well. Stand still, looking. Looking at the stupidest things. Leaves, his hand, the table beneath his plate. I asked him what was he looking for? He said one day he'd tell me. I said, go on, tell me now, go on, tell. He said not to be nosy. He didn't say it – he just touched my nose and he laughed. I went all red because I never as much as touched his hand before that. He laughed his head off when he saw me blushing and I couldn't understand why there was what felt like tears in my eyes because I wasn't sad or it wasn't as if he hit me. I got very quiet and he asked me was I all right?

I didn't answer him. I just kept on making his breakfast. Mammy trusted me to do that much. I watched his egg boil in the saucepan. I knew exactly how long to keep it in the water for him to like it. I don't know why this day I didn't take it out when it was ready, but for some reason I let it stay in longer there and didn't lift it out. I put it in the eggcup and carried it to the table. I didn't watch him when he cut the top off, for I was buttering his toast with all my might. I expected him to give out to me, but he said nothing. When I looked over I saw him putting a giant knob of butter into the yolk and mix it all through. He still barely looked at me as if he didn't notice I gave him a hard boiled egg on purpose, so then, for badness, I said, butter costs money.

He rose up from the table. He took the egg in his hands. He put it on the floor, he put his boot down on it and smashed it into a million pieces. He looked me straight in the face. I pay you money, he said, good money. I get nothing from you, from your family – I get nothing from you for nothing. Do not forget that, because I do not, nor will I let you. Do you remember?

I nodded. I was broke to the bone. And the yellow mess

on the floor was like dog skitters when the greyhounds had the runs. I think he believed I was going to cry but I would not give him the satisfaction of that. He might think he was a smart alec from Italy but I wasn't going to let myself or my breed down in front of him by blubbing over what he did to a stupid egg. Let him go hungry. I'm from Donegal. We don't let anybody walk on us, no matter what they are or where they're from. Anyway, wasn't I in the right? Butter does cost money.

Only eejits waste it. During the war in England and across the border in Derry people were panting for a pound of butter. I said that to him. Do you not know the shortage of the stuff there was and there still is, mister? We had a war here, you know, maybe it didn't happen in Italy. Jesus, his face was a panic. I thought he was going to beat me. He took the spoon from stirring his tea. He started to beat it on the table. He said, you know damn all about the war. Do not dare to say you suffered during it. Italy did. Ireland did not. Do not ever talk to me about the war.

He walked off, not touching hardly a bite of his breakfast. I said to him he'd better put something inside his belly. He would faint maybe if he didn't even have a sup of tea. That's when he started to laugh. I thought it was because the word belly slipped out of my mouth. Then he said, I will die if I don't drink tea, is that so? I said, he might. Nobody could survive without tea. He said I was right. Nobody could. Pour – pour. I did, and he drank the mug down in one go. He said, are you content now? I eat.

I nodded, but I couldn't care less. All I was worried about was he'd tell Mammy and she'd be raging I hadn't done my job and she liked people to carry out what she asked them to do. That comes from being a forewoman in the factory before she had wains. I didn't hear that from her, but the whole town knew she was the youngest woman ever to be made that high up in all the years they made shirts in this place. She wasn't one ever to show off. She hated big heads as much nearly as she did liars – and by God she hated liars – so she never talked a lot about what working there was like, but it was well known she was wild fair to each and every one working under her. All hands were fond of her.

She wasn't of course always that fair to me. It still came as a big shock when I was lying on the bed one summer's day and she must have wanted me out of the house because she shouted at me, asking why nobody my own age bothered with me? I wanted to say, that's just not true, but it was in a way, and I've been wondering why. Here's my answer. It's because I'm friends with Mena. And because she's not well, people must think the same about the two of us. That we're not right in the head. She has something wrong on the outside – everybody can see that – but they notice nothing untoward about myself so they can imagine something's wrong inside of me, that in some way I'm just like her. I suffer because I don't turn my back on her, like the rest of them laughing, calling her gimpy or pegleg or humpyback, God forgive them.

The painter didn't laugh at her. He was very good to the poor soul. Always asking her questions and listening carefully

19

to what she'd answer. I couldn't believe the way he'd sit talking to her about everything under the sun – school, her Mammy and Daddy, what she wanted to be when she grew up. She said a nun – everybody says a nun – and he told her she would look beautiful. That's when he gave her a lovely drawing of her face. Well, I think it was her face, but you wouldn't know for sure. He said it was of her. I heard him saying that. But she looked more like – she looked more like – I can't say for sure, but Mena, she said, that's not me. Don't say that's me. He said nothing as she hobbled away, leaving the lovely drawing behind. I picked it up and asked him for it, but he said nothing. Just put it all rolled up in his pocket. I said to him that it was a pity he destroyed it like that for even if Mena didn't want it, her mother and father would. A present, a bit of thanks to them for all they put up with her. She has a wild bad temper at times, flying off the handle for no reason. She is a handful, in her own way. He'll learn that, as I did, and I'm her best friend. Her only friend, as I've said before, and I'm paid back for it by nobody else wanting to play with me unless there's not another being in the lane – then I'm made welcome to join in.

That night I had a dream about me and Mena. We were standing at the very edge of the pier. We were holding hands. I could see our parents – her ones and my own – standing a good bit away from us. The next thing I knew we must have fallen in because we were stuck in the water not panicking. Our mammies and daddies though, they were roaring and crying and calling at us to come back to them, to leave the sea. It was as if we weren't listening, for we did nothing to reach them. Then I let go of Mena's hand and I could see tears tripping my mother, so I tried to get back to them on the pier, and my da's hands, they grew like a giant's, and they caught me miles out in Lough Swilly and carried me back. But Mena, she never looked at us, safe as if she was walking on the earth. She just kept floating, and in the dream I could see why – the painter was waiting for her in a white sailing boat. And the strangest thing of all about this is that Mena couldn't swim. She wouldn't put a foot into the water for all the money in the world.

But he could swim. And he did, first thing in the morning, every day of the time he was staying in the town, no matter what the weather was like. He'd brought a black swimming costume with him. Black with red stripes. I know what it looks like because my mother washed it when she did his clothes along with the minister's and his niece's garments. I never spied him take his dip because it was always so early I'd still be asleep in my bed. And he bathed only in the men's bay where ladies weren't supposed to watch fellows walk half-naked into the sea. And anyway what is it to me seeing him like that? Didn't I give him his breakfast and see him in his singlet, white as an angel next to his brown skin?

I asked him once did he believe in guardian angels? He said he did, and that he'd seen his own. I said that was an awful lie. Nobody was allowed to do that, but he insisted he could when the mood took him. I said I don't believe you – if you did, tell me what the angel looked like. And I bet him he couldn't. What will you give me if I can? I'll give you nothing, I say, because I'm going to share my great secret – I can see them too, I can see them.

That stops him in his tracks. He asks me what do they look like? I say I'm not allowed to tell him. He says he understands. Nobody should reveal things like that. I think to myself that is just jealousy on his part. I'd be dying to know. So I tell him I can reveal only this – girls have a guardian angel dressed in pink, boys have one dressed in blue. He looks straight past me, as if there's somebody listening to us. He nods and says, I'm sure you're right, yes, you're right, but in that case I have to ask you a question, why is your angel dressed in blue? Only sometimes, I say.

It just slipped out. I nearly run out of the room. How did he know that? This boy might be too smart for his own good. I don't know why it is I am breathing funny, but I am and I can say nothing. He takes advantage of that, knocking the wind out of my sails.

–Why are you sad? It is a most beautiful blue. It is the right colour for your red hair.

–Do all red-haired girls have a blue guardian angel? I asked him.

–No. It is very special.

–Does it happen in Italy or only in Ireland? I wanted to know.

–It does not happen in Italy.

–How often have you seen it?

–Not that often. You are special, he said.

But I'm not. No more than Mena is beautiful. I've wondered since I met this man, what was wrong with him? Now I know he's a liar. And I'm feared of liars, for as I've said, Mammy hates liars. Above all else, she hates liars. I'm not cruel and I'm not stupid, she always declares, but I would hang all liars. It's why we've always told the truth. And it may be why nobody likes me. Somebody asked me once – it was Peggy Jennings who sat beside me in third class – she asked did I like her new brown shoes? Because I said no, she turned against me. I did say as well they would look better on a horse. I said it for a joke, but she turned her face from me. That's you all over, she hissed back. You'd sicken a goat. Is it any wonder nobody can stick you. At least I don't smell.

I told Mammy Peggy Jennings said we smelt. Our house smelt, our clothes. She said our house was like a byre. And Peggy's mother, she wondered often if the people who let Mammy do their washing and scrubbing knew the state of her own house, they would lock the door on her. I should have known there was going to be bother when she said not one word. Just listened and listened. Letting me blabber on. And I couldn't stop until she asked me, is this the truth? Honest to God, it is. All right, she'd heard enough, she would call round to the Jennings and sort this out. I went green.

Why in God's name had I picked Peggy Jennings? Why had I not spun that smell yarn about another girl, any other girl, for there is one saying in this town that everyone agrees on, it is God spare us from the Jennings. What had I started? What would Mammy do? She asked if I would go with her and confront Peggy. I said I didn't want to and I hope she wouldn't either. Why would that be? Surely I'd want Mammy to stand up for herself. Peggy Jennings had insulted this family. We needed to show that breed we would not take it lying down. Give me my coat, and get your own, I'm not letting them away with that. I didn't move. She said, what's wrong with you? I was holding my stomach because there was a pain in it like a stick down my gullet. Why are you saying nothing, why has the cat got your tongue, wait a minute, we don't have a cat, you must be silent for another reason – what is it? My stomach is wild sore, Mammy, I don't know what's wrong with me. Was it something you ate? Did you have a feed of sour apples? Were you progging fruit in Louis O'Kane's orchard? No – no – I wasn't, I swear. Then why should you have an ache? I told her I didn't know. Maybe I was in need of a dose of syrup of figs, she wondered. Would that clean me out?

I could smell the syrup of figs through the glass of the bottle in the press. I could feel the stickiness of it on my face still after I spat it all out the last time they tried to choke it down my throat. She knew it was the worst thing she could threaten me with. I told her it wasn't that bad, I didn't need medicine. Was I sure? I was positive. Absolutely positive? Absolutely certain? No doubt in my head. She had a look in her eyes that I knew better than to answer her. So I just stood there but could not face her, keeping my eyes to the ground.

–You don't have a wild pain, do you?

–No, Mammy.

–In your stomach or anywhere else, do you?

–No.

–That was a lie, wasn't it?

–Yes, Mammy.

–And so was everything you told me Peggy Jennings said, wasn't it?

–Yes.

–A lie?

–A lie.

–A lie?

–A lie.

–A pack of lies?

–A pack of lies.

I was expecting the worst clout of my life to knock me into a corner. But it didn't come. She just left me standing looking at the kitchen floor. Then she sat down in her chair. I couldn't bear to watch what she was going to do. And she still did nothing. Nothing at all. She just left me standing there. The two cheeks on me were burning. I was on fire with shame. And she kept on sitting, even though she should have been getting the tea ready, but she did not stir.

I thought about Daddy coming in from the forge, starving, wanting his food. The younger ones were roaring. They must have been getting hungry. But Mammy just sat as she was, not bothering about anything. I think if I say I'll give her a hand, she might be less cross – that is if she is cross for I don't know what mood she's in. I've never seen her not moving like this. Will I put on the kettle? Will I draw the tea? Should I butter some bread? Is Daddy having eggs? She doesn't answer. I ask the same questions again and at long last she just says, you stay where you are. My wee brothers are now squealing like stuck pigs but she doesn't seem to notice. The crying brings Da in from the forge next door, all smelling of the fire. He looks about him and listens. He asks what's the commotion for? Has there been a murder? Mammy stands up. She puts her two hands on my head. She turns me round to face my father. He doesn't know what is happening. He says, so what in Christ's name is going on in this kitchen? She lets go of my head. She points her finger at me. I hear the words she's saying to Daddy. Look at her, look at our daughter, we have raised a liar. That's when I burst into tears and tell Mammy I'm sorry. Tell Daddy I'm wild sorry. And that's why to this day I'm feared of liars.

A couple of days after that Daddy got me a ribbon – a white one, really long, and he said when Mammy had forgotten all the bother about Peggy Jennings I should get her to tie it in my hair. So I asked that Sunday and she did. She kissed my hair again, as she kissed it every Sunday. The Italian painter asked me why didn't I wear it every day? I said, are you simple or something? I can only wear it on a Sunday. Why don't you wear your nice suit every day? Same reason, isn't it? You have to keep your good clothes to go to Mass. He was walking up the lane with me to the upper house for our Sunday dinner. I could smell it as soon as we opened the front door.

First we started with soup after Daddy has cut the sign of

the cross on himself and so did we all before eating. Mammy always put any flowers she found on her walks in a wee vase on the table for the big dinner, and Daddy always cracked the same joke – I'll just remove the whin bush from the table before we start eating. Mammy raised her eyes up and called him a gulpin of a man. Those flowers came from no whin bush. She knew better than to bring gorse blooms into a house. She'd always heard it was considered unlucky. What is whin please? What is gorse? Gianni asked this one week after hearing it repeated so often. Explain it to him, Daddy told me. Gorse – whin – they are the flowers of the mountain. Our mountain is called Fahan Hill, I spoke slowly. Fahan Hill, he said after me, and for some reason we all burst out laughing, even the little ones, because we were looking forward to a lovely feed as Mammy ladled out the soup, smelling of beautiful vegetables and milk.

I love to stir them all around in the plate, the carrots and leeks, the barley and lentils, the wee bits of spud and white parsnips. Eat your food, Euni, it will grow cold, your soup. Mummy's voice is polite when Gianni is around us. Soup, he says, and points to the plate. We all nod. Soup, yes. Slap up your sloup – there's plenty more in the slaucepan. Daddy roars laughing when he says this because our old neighbour, Maggie McFadden, she would always say that when she drank soup. That's what he tells Gianni, and Mammy says, how would this man know who Maggie McFadden is. Slap up your sloup, there's plenty more in the slaucepan, he says it again just to annoy her.

But she's not annoyed. She goes to get the beef out of the oven. The spuds are roasting pure gold. The meat smells like the best taste in your mouth, and she cuts big slices for the two men, leaving it to wait for the green cabbage and soft potatoes that her giant spoon puts so delicately in front of them to eat. That's fit for a decent man to eat, Daddy smiles and takes his pile of dinner from her. So does the Italian painter, and he has the same amount of roast as Daddy has. Mammy has the next most – I have a fair share – enough to stuff me – and the baby boys get their bit as well. Before she starts to eat, Mammy will open two bottles of stout, giving one each to the lads. It is the only drink that is allowed in our house, and Daddy never ventures into pubs because he is good-living and wouldn't thank you for getting fluthered like some, no names mentioned, as Mammy always says, and then mentions the name of every drunkard in the town. Daddy asks the Italian, does he enjoy Guinness? Guinness, the painter says, raising his mug, and him and Daddy hit their mugs together. You boys would drink wine, wouldn't yous, in Italy? Gianni nods. Mammy takes a sip of her milk, eyeing them both. She says the only whiff of wine you'll get in this place is on the chapel altar. And Fr O'Hagen doesn't share it, Daddy says. That's enough, Mammy gives him a cross look, more than enough.

We all eat every bit of the delicious dinner. Gianni takes a bit of bread and wipes the gravy that's left on his plate. Daddy does it too – the first time I've seen him do that. Mammy says to go easy on the bread – leave room for dessert. She has made a red jelly. She loads it into bowls. I ask Daddy does he want to hear a joke. He asks me to tell it. I say, would you like to come to my party? Go on, Daddy, tell me – would you like to come to my party? He says, yes, we'd all like to go. Do you know what you'll get to eat? What will we get? Custard and jelly and a punch in the belly. Mammy's sitting beside me, and just for a joke I punch her in the stomach. Mammy lets out a big roar. What are you doing, girl, what do you think you are doing? Daddy is shouting at me. Are you trying to kill the baby?

I don't understand what he is chatting about. The two babies are sitting at the table. I haven't touched them. And Mammy is saying, I'm all right, Malachy, for Jesus sake I'm all right. She doesn't know. Euni knows nothing about these things, she was only playing. Daddy walks Mammy slowly outside. The bowls of jelly are sitting in big red lumps. Gianni hands me one of them. He nods at me to tuck in. But I can't. I just shake my head. Then he asked me something I'll never forgot – not to my dying day and they lay me in the clay at Cockhill.

–Did you not know your mother is having a baby soon?

–What do you mean?

–You will have a little sister or brother.

–Why?

–Where do you think your mother and father got you?

–The coal boat. It comes into the pier to deliver all the babies as well. Nurse Kelly goes down and collects them. Then she has to wash all the dirty dust from them and bring them home. Everybody knows that. Maybe they do it different in Italy. Do they?

—Yes, they do.

—How?

—It is not a coal boat.

—Then what kind of boat?

—No kind. It is a bird brings them. It carries them in its beak.

—Where?

—To the baby's parents.

—How does the bird know where they live?

—The baby has its name and address written on its wrist.

—Are you telling me birds can read? Do you think I'm a complete eejit? What kind of stupid people are they in your country? Believing that nonsense. Have you ever heard the like? You shouldn't tell Irish people that kind of thing. They'll all think you're not right in the head.

—So I should tell them in Italy about the coal boat?

—Why shouldn't you? It's the truth.

—How do you know?

—My mother said so, she never tells lies.

—Maybe not.

—No maybe about it. You have to believe me.

—I do.

One thing I notice about Gianni. He speaks English a lot more around me when I am on my own than he does when he's with big people. He's always putting questions to me. I give him as best an answer as I can. It never contents him though. Daddy and Mammy walked in then and that stopped our conversation. Mammy told me to eat my jelly. Everything was grand. Daddy said my hair looked really nice with the ribbon in it. He said it was the best bargain he'd ever bought. And he told me I was a good girl. He said to Mammy as it was Sunday maybe we should have a wee dram, the three of them. She looked funny at him. He asked Gianni would he like a dram of whiskey? His treat? He went up to their bedroom and came back with three glasses smelling of the strangest stuff. Him, Mammy and the Italian started to sip it. Best of health to the company, Daddy saluted them. Mammy said, don't let this be a habit – no harm in a drop at Christmas or Easter, but certainly not every Sunday. Not in this house.

Daddy laughed. He said he was married to the worst wife in the world. The Italian was a lucky man to be single. Mammy didn't seem too pleased. Then out of the blue Daddy said, the painting, how is it going? Are you starting to make a fist of the job? When can we see what you're at? Little did I ever think there would be any man drawing the last journey of Our Blessed Lord through Jerusalem to Calvary in the big room of my parents' house. Well, come on, let us in on the secret – how is the painting coming along? Gianni said he could not tell. Too early to know. But he did have one thing to ask. Fire away, boy. Could he come and watch Daddy in the forge? He needed to see horses close up – for the Roman soldiers. Daddy just looked at him and shook his head. Mammy must have noticed how the Italian was taken aback. Daddy was very silent all of a sudden. She said me and her had a fair bit of washing dishes and cleaning up to do. Would you lads not like to stroll down to the football pitch? There would surely be a match on a Sunday.

Gianni said he would like to but Daddy told a lie. He said he wasn't much of a football man. Not his game. Anyway, he fancied a wee snooze after a big dinner. No, not much interest in football. Boxing – that's what he'd choose if he had to pick his sport. Boxing. Did they have much of it in Italy? Gianni said there was quite a bit, but he'd never been a fighter. Then we'll have to train you, won't we? Daddy told him.

Chapter Two

Margaret

Custard and jelly and a punch in the belly. God love my Euni, but the child thought this was the funniest joke in the world. I'll never forget her face when she saw the reaction to her thumping me in the stomach. Now I'm not saying it wasn't sore – Euni is like her father, always the blacksmith's daughter, not knowing her own strength at times – but still and all I think we should have watched what was said. Especially in front of the Italian stranger. Christ knows what he must think of us.

Not that he'd ever let much out of him. That's all for the best. He's here to do the job Fr O'Hagen is paying him to do. Let him do it. No distractions from the curse of drink or of women either, for that matter. It wouldn't do, would it, for a man hired to do the painting of Our Lord's agony to be out gallivanting with the smart girls in this town. Not that I think any of them would touch him. They would run a mile if he went near them. There's nothing wrong with the way he looks – he knocks the like of our specimens into a corner, that's for sure. Dark eyes, jet black hair, beautiful skin – I even think our wee Euni has a notion of him in her innocent way. But Jesus Christ, the women hereabouts would hardly look at a man from Derry, let alone marry him, if it meant hoofing the fourteen miles to live away from their mammies' firesides.

But then, I should talk. Look at myself. Am I one to talk about upping and outing and seeing the world over the railway bridge? What did I do? I married Malachy O'Donovan. He was reared six doors down the lane from our own house. I was born a McCarron. The middle girl in a house full of three daughters and two sons. I went to school until I was fourteen. Then went to the shirt factory with the smell of the books and chalk still on me. Got married when I hit nineteen and had our Euni by the time I was twenty-one. What age must she be now? Twelve, or is it thirteen? Wouldn't you think I'd know the age of my only daughter? The two boys came soon together, one after the other, a while after Euni was born. She'd been the only one for too long. She got too used to it, and I admit we did dote on her, Malachy especially. Naturally enough she liked him spoiling her. Maybe without our knowing it she heard us too often talking to her like an adult and not a wain. That's why she is what some call advanced for her age but I call being a right wee granny at times. Maybe it's why she has so few pals except for that unfortunate Mena one.

She is not long for this world, but then who is, God spare all belonging to us?

Malachy says I'm worse than Maggie Mourn, the ancient woman all in black who makes her living washing the dead of the parish. I think that might be exaggerated just a bit, but I am inclined to look a little on the gloomy side. Always have, always will. And I did warn him when we were courting that if he thinks I can be relied on to dampen proceedings, then wait until he knows my sisters Tessie and Seranna. I once was boiling an egg for my dinner – it was a Sunday, I wasn't rushing in and out from and to my work – and didn't I lose track of time entirely? Just sitting there, doing nothing. I thought that egg must be ready. When I sliced the head off it, it was as raw as if it never touched water. I made the mistake of observing to Tessie, look at that egg, it's not cooked, is there anything more annoying?

Tessie didn't take her eyes out of the *Irish Independent* – she's a born Blueshirt, worships Michael Collins – she kept on reading and she said, what about Marie Goretti? What was done to that little saint was a bit more annoying, God forgive me for even referring to it.

–What has Saint Marie Goretti got to do with me not boiling an egg right?

–Am I saying it has anything to do with it? I am merely pointing out for my own information as much as it is for yours that what you describe as the most annoying thing that could happen might be open to question. I for one believe that being held down, as Marie Goretti was, being held down by a filthy brute who wants his dirty way with you and won't stop until he cuts you to ribbons and then leaves you battered black and blue – that, as far as I'm concerned, is a lot more annoying. But of course what do I know? I take it for granted I am wrong. Maybe your egg is more important in the eyes of God than a child protecting herself from the disgusting devil that would destroy her. When I hear they're canonising you for the sacrifice of going without your dinner, I'll be on my knees saying my prayers to Margaret McCarron, saying I'm sorry for your trouble that you had to go hungry for five minutes.

I should mention that she kept up this stream of abuse while all the time keeping her eyes glued to the *Independent*, turning the pages occasionally. I felt like putting a match to it while she was still reading but I resisted the temptation because, to be honest, our Tess does have a lifelong attachment to the child martyr and she did even take Marie Goretti for her confirmation name when she received the sacrament at the age of eleven. We thought as she got older she might lessen a bit in her devotion. We thought the cure had been found when she started to admit she would never miss a picture that James Stewart acted in, but when it came to the crunch even he could not hold a candle, though he might be the last word as a film star, according to Tessie herself – no, he couldn't get within an ass's roar of her perpetual devotion to the Italian saint.

So you can see she would be mad with excitement when she heard about the visitor from Italy. She nearly knocked down the door to my house after she heard Fr O'Hagen has asked us to put him up. She arrived out of breath, her coat flung open to the four winds and her hair like a whin bush, all mad with excitement, even dragging our youngest sister, Seranna, in tow behind her. Seranna rarely leaves the darkness of her own house. She believes in sitting in silence with the mount of misery that is her husband, Richard. He never believes in wasting electricity – that's why the house is nearly always pitch blackness. You're only allowed to plonk your arse on one of three chairs they use to save the wear and tear on the rest of them. Malachy is more or less barred from entering their place since the one occasion he was offered a cup of tea. The shock nearly killed us till we tasted the tea. It must have been made with leaves they'd been re-using since the Christmas before Jesus was born. He took one smell of the mess in the mug – taste it and it would poison a normal human being but Richard and Seranna must have had stomachs like elephants – and Malachy asked Richard is this tea or is it shite? I normally have no time for rough language, but on this occasion he took the words out of my mouth.

Anyway, there's the two of them trotting in my door, Tessie leading Seranna as always, while I'm in the scullery rinsing the minister's sheets, steam all around me like your breath on a winter's day, only today I'm roasting. As always it's Tessie who's first to open her mouth, and she thinks she's being as funny as Laurel and Hardy. Seranna does, now it strikes me, look a bit like Oliver Hardy, but I shouldn't say that. Tess looks me in the eyes and says, I wonder could you explain to me what is the connection between us?

—You're my sisters, as far as I know.

—Well, that's news to me. Is it to you, Seranna? Sisters are supposed to share their news, what little there may be of it. I have to rely on strangers to find out what's happening in this house. Who's this Italian that I'm told is coming to stay down in the lower house? It was Susie Gallagher let me in on the secret — where she learned it from I don't know, so don't ask me. You didn't think it worth your while to confide in me or Seranna. Did she, Seranna?

—I won't wait for her to open her mouth. I might be waiting till the cows come home before that one gets into her swing, and I haven't got the time. I'll tell you straight now since you have the cheek to cross-examine me. I was asked to take him in only yesterday. How Susie Gallagher knows I cannot tell you. Maybe Malachy mentioned it to someone when he was out with the greyhounds. Maybe Fr O'Hagen himself met her and gave her the word. Ask her how she found out if you're that keen for gossip. I barely know a thing about him. That's why I haven't told you. Now, will you let me get on with my washing?

—Is he a painter?

—He is.

—Is he going to do the Stations of the Cross in the chapel?

—As far as I know. You'll get all the information you need on that score from the priest.

—So he's definitely a painter?

—Are you deaf as well as stupid, Tess McCarron? Didn't you hear me say that's what he is?

–And he definitely is staying in the lower house?

–I am not repeating myself anymore. Get out and let me get on with my work.

–Hold your horses, big lady. I'm not finished with you yet.

–Tessie, would you kindly tell me what you want – what exactly you want? And why Seranna is standing beside you like the bloody Rock of Gibraltar?

At long last Seranna opens her mouth. I have a handful of suds, and I swear to Christ I feel like letting her have it in the gob. In fact, I do. Let her have it though right in the big eyes and she lets a squeal out of her. I'm blind, I'm blind, she's shouting, I'm blind. Well, you live in darkness already, I shout back at her, now Richard can lead you about on a rope. He has you chained to him every other way. God forgive you, mocking the afflicted, Seranna wails. The afflicted can kiss my arse, I tell her, and so can the two of you. Now, what is it exactly brings you here? It's not to see how I'm doing and I think it's for something other than to give off that I don't let you know all my business. You find out everything anyway. Tell me what do you want? Is it to put in a good word for you, Tessie, with the Italian? Maybe he'll take you off our hands at long last. Malachy says a man will be the life of you. I get a look from her that would sour milk.

–Is that what Malachy says? Well, I suppose I should listen carefully. Right enough, it's not everybody he sneers at, is it? And he knows everything – he knows all about me, doesn't he? Tell him I said thanks for the advice. That will improve my lot in life. He's done it for you. There you are scrubbing a Protestant minister's dirty sheets. Jesus, I should be on my knees begging I be sent such a man to mind me.

   –I threw suds into Seranna's face. You watch yourself it's not a hot iron going into yours. What is it you want? Jesus, wouldn't life be sweeter and simpler if my sisters would just say out straight what they're looking for?

   –Show her your prayer book, Seranna. Show her.

   Seranna takes a missal out of her blue shopping bag. The black cover is well battered. I know that prayer book like the back of my hand. Our Mammy gave it to Seranna for her twenty-first birthday, and we were glad it went to the youngest of us girls, though Tessie and myself, we would have loved and treasured it, because it belonged to Mammy's grandmother, and for all we know could have been passed down from even earlier. I always imagined I could feel my mother's hands on it, and so I lost the rough voice when I saw it since it was the nearest I would ever get again in this life to my dead mother. Show her what we're wanting her to ask, Tessie said.

   I stop my washing to watch. Seranna starts to sort through the cascade of memorial cards and holy pictures falling from the missal. How do I know for sure which one she is going to pick up for me to see? Of course it is of Marie Goretti. There she is, and with the prayer painted in the shape of a lily coming out of her hand, the child already looking like a grey ghost, her eyes the size of saucers and her hands permanently encased in rosary beads, begging for release from the torture of this world as I am from the torture of these two women. I would like to shake them, but I don't, for, God love her, Seranna handles the picture as if it were made of gold and as delicate as dust. Seranna explains that this particular litany painted on the card is one you recite to protect your purity with the aid of Marie Goretti. And I have to say the saint has certainly listened to my sisters in that respect, even if one of them is a wedded woman. It's tempting to laugh in the face of them, but it would break your heart the way they believe. I ask again what it is they want me to do?

Tessie explains her long devotion to this particular picture. She says it would be the happiest day of her life if she could find one to hang on the wall of her house. She'd heard that a neighbour did have it hanging above her bed, but when Tessie managed to wangle her way in to have a look on the excuse that she was visiting the sick while the woman was laid up with a bad leg, she discovered it was no such thing, for the picture had no lily. Tessie had practically ransacked every shop in Donegal to find it. No luck. Then she started looking through Derry. Not a sniff of anything similar to what she wanted. Some smart boy directed her to a place in the Waterside. She should have smelt a rat, because that was where the Protestants lived in Derry. When she got to the shop all she saw in the window was Orange regalia. Shitting herself with fear, she ran like the hammers of hell away from there. Next time she met the bucko who tricked her, she let him have the full blast of her tongue, but he just mocked her mercilessly, singing 'The Sash My Father Wore', till she stopped ranting at him. Next she found out one woman on the collar section in the shirt factory, she had a sister-in-law who helped clean the chapel in Letterkenny – they claimed she did the flowers but Tessie's inquiries proved she was a cleaner pure and simple, never mind how she found that out. Jesus, the airs and graces people give themselves. Anyway, the woman was good enough to investigate as far away as Bundoran but she had no luck locating it. Tessie was so set on getting hold of this picture that she determined to do what she had never done before – take a bus as far away as Strabane. She got word there was a fanatical loyalty to Marie Goretti in that part of the world, so who knew what you might find? The twenty-six miles were the furthest she'd ever been away from home before. She'd never taken two buses in the one Saturday morning either, and when the second one left Derry, from that minute on her heart was in her mouth. People would know for sure she was a strange woman in a strange place, so she thought better, in case they robbed her, not to ask where she might get her hands on what she was looking to find. Instead she wandered down every street and examined every huckster of a shop in Strabane, but not one of them could oblige her with what she wanted. Only that she knew Strabane was definitely in Tyrone, and that Tyrone was definitely a Catholic county, she would swear from the lack of religion she found there, no hand nor finger was ever dipped in a holy water font. But here is the most unusual thing. The more she wandered through that town that she was such a stranger in, the more she was convinced she could see Marie

Goretti's face contained in the rough features of all the young women rushing, roaring past her, ignoring her completely as if she was not there – Tessie was not there no more than Marie Goretti was there in the shops of Strabane. It dawned on Tessie that if she were to drop dead at that instant, if the hand of God were to touch her heart and stop it, not one being would know who she was or where she came from. They might bury her in the Finn River for all they cared about this corpse that she now would be. She started to shake and decided to get home to Donegal – to walk there if necessary. To give her strength she prayed that if she got back safe and sound she would make all the more effort to find that picture. This was why she had come up with the idea she was about to tell me. This was why she and Seranna were standing looking like two children in front of me, wanting something, as the sweat poured down me washing sheets in the scullery. Would I ask the Italian to paint Marie Goretti for them? Would he put the long lily and the rosary beads in it? Did I think he would at long last grant their dearest wish to have her hanging on the wall protecting them against all badness and evil?

I said, what harm in asking him? Of course I will. There is a chance he might do it, there is a chance he mightn't, we won't find out till we put it to him straight and see if we get an aye or a no out of him. Since I was never bird mouthed about settling things one way or another, I took the responsibility of putting them out of their agony. I did warn them you could not expect the man to work for nothing. He would charge and it might cost a pretty penny. They said they didn't care. They'd pay. He can't beggar us, can he?

So after a few weeks when he'd been here and I knew him a bit better and was sure he could understand me, I put the holy picture of Marie Goretti in front of him. I explained to him about my sisters' devotion. I told him they'd like a painting done of the saint if he would be kind enough, and they were willing to pay good money. He didn't smile. He didn't say anything except no. No. No excuses, no pardons, no palaver. Just no. I have to admit I was taken aback and my face showed it. But it made no difference to his decision. It was no, and he continued to eat the slices of bacon I'd fried for his midday meal, neatly dividing them with his sharp knife, cutting them in small pieces, not bothering to say, sorry, I can't do you this favour. I couldn't help saying they will be disappointed, wild disappointed, my sisters. He only said he did not understand – what was disappointed? What did it mean?

I could tell from the way he eyeballed me he knew damn well. I came to the conclusion that he knew an awful lot more than he claimed he did. And I have to admit I thought it was a very useful trick. And when he refused Tessie and Seranna – I had witnessed that look before. It's when the Reverend Sewell has shut out the world to everything but himself and what he's reading. I've been doing bits and pieces about the rectory for long enough to never go near him then and so does Martha, his niece. We've sometimes nodded in the direction of his study, and the nod says it all. Not to be disturbed. It would be a brave man or woman to knock on that door till he decides to set foot outside of the four walls he's locked himself into. The library, that's what he calls it. Martha once let slip that there's days when she has to leave his meals on a tray waiting at the top of the stairs – when he's hungry, he'll fetch it himself and eat. Could be any hour of the night. Isn't it the oddest way to conduct yourself? Who could live with the like of that? She does – she comes down in the morning to get herself ready for work in the Protestant school, and there's the dirty dishes waiting for her to wash. Strange animals, men – that's what she whispered to me. And I nodded, for I agree. Don't I live with one?

When I told Malachy the Italian has said no to my sisters, the brute said he was delighted to hear it. Best news he'd heard all month. Enlighten me why? I demanded. Why should he bother his hole doing what the like of those two mad women want him to do? Why be at their beck and call? That's our Tessie and Seranna you're referring to, show a bit of manners, I said. He laughed and told me that was good coming from myself.

–What did you call them only the other day?

–Never mind what I called them – what has that to do with him turning his nose at their offer of work?

–You called them Simey and Dimey – by the way who are Simey and Dimey?

Only wee Liam, my youngest, was lying in the bed between us I would have broken his mouth for being so smart, but instead I just said, tell me why are you on his side? Didn't he come here to finish one job? he says. Isn't that what he's being paid for, money agreed, time to do it in agreed? The deal he struck with Fr O'Hagen, that's the deal he's going to stick to, Malachy argued. He could see nothing whatsoever untoward with that. The man clearly knew what he was doing. There was no doubt about that. I asked him, how did he get so pally with him? Why take his side against his own? Your sisters are not my own, thanks be to Christ, that was his answer, give my head peace, woman. With that he turned on his side to sleep. If that bugger thought I would let him slip away into having a quiet kip he was much mistaken. I nipped the child, dead to the world, between us. He started roaring like a bull, strange from his sleep. Jesus, do I get no rest morning, noon or night? Malachy was shouting, that Italian git has the right idea, running off to here. I swear to God, I might follow his example and clear off to Italy. You do that, I say, and I can follow you, me and the three wains. That will put a stop to your gallop. Come here to me instead, he whispered. And he grabbed me. Malachy, for the love of Jesus, mind the child, mind Liam, I warned him, but he wouldn't be warned – he never is when he is in that mood, a pack of wolves would not have dragged him from me. They have their uses, men.

And I said the same to Martha Sewell when she was vowing to me once never to marry. I know I might have been taking my life in my hands risking an opinion about anything other than the running of the house, but she was sitting in the kitchen with her face like long after the old man had given her another tongue lashing over something or other that had not been done to his rigorous high standards. Save us from all men, Mrs O'Donovan, she sighed in a whisper to me so himself wouldn't hear her. Well, Miss Sewell, I said, but there's times they have their uses. And out of the blue she laughed heartily.

It was a lovely sound, Martha Sewell laughing, for, by Christ, you didn't hear that often. Not that it was her fault this should be the case. There was little in that silent rectory she lived in with the uncle to amuse man or beast, let alone a young one barely hitting her twenties. I know I'm beginning to sound as mournful as our Seranna – you'd think from listening to me I was Martha's granny's age rather than being ten years older – but even though myself and Malachy might have next to nothing compared to the Sewells with their library, my heart did go out to that poor girl.

Not that to her credit she looked for sympathy. Whatever hardships she had to bear living with that stern man, she endured all with next to no complaint. If I had been in her shoes, I would be swinging from the end of a rope in Mountjoy Prison for I would have strangled him. But thanks be to the crucified Jesus, when I finished my tasks I come home to a house full of children. She lived in that quietness where a body would be petrified to breathe a word out of place in case it offended the Reverend Sewell. I suppose she put up with it for this was all the shelter she'd known since she was orphaned. After her education finished, she came to live with her uncle here, and one thing I will say in his favour is that he made sure that at the very least she would be lovely spoken. I don't know how she put order on a class of pupils if any of them was as bad and rowdy a wee bitch as I was in my schooldays. Protestant children were probably quieter. But I do admit it now, I was a right handful.

If our Euni knew what a bold girl her mother could be when she was the same age as my daughter is now, I think she would be very shocked. There was one nun in particular – I was the bane of that woman's life. She loved Ireland with a passion. There was even a rumour doing the rounds that she was Padraig Pearse's sweetheart. Alice Timmons in our class said her da told her that when the English shot Pearse for leading the Easter Rising in 1916, Sr Kathleen then entered the convent. Everybody thought this was the most beautiful thing you could do, but it still didn't stop me from taking a hand at her. She asked us once a month to write a composition about patriotism. How it is noble to die for your native land. I got fed up with being asked the same question, so this time I wrote that I didn't think it was all that noble – Irish soldiers were good for nothing, if you listened to the women they were married to at any rate. They treated the same women like dogs most of the time, and if a wife was widowed, didn't everyone know fine well that she would be far better off with a British army pension? They look after the ladies left behind far better than the Irish government ever did, so I'd say you can forget being patriotic. I knew no more about the military than I did about China, but of course it didn't stop me from driving poor Sr Kathleen demented. I was expecting a clout from her, or at least a swish of the cane over my head, but no, that wasn't what she did.

Instead she did not hand back the copybooks as usual. For the last half hour of the school we said decades of the rosary out loud and at the end of each decade she had us sing as loud as our lungs could every verse of 'Hail Glorious Saint Patrick'. That was a hymn we only belted out on his feast day in March but today – I can't remember what month it was, May, likely – today we were poisoned hailing our patron saint. This kept on and on and on until the school bell rang at three o'clock and we were all dying to get into the fresh air and run home to play. I was reaching for my school bag to make a quick getaway, when I felt her bony hands on my shoulders and heard her telling me to stay behind.

I stood in the empty classroom after they had all gone. It smelt of each and every one of us. If I were to be struck blind, I could have used my nose to find exactly where we sat and put a name to every desk though I could see nothing. I was just wondering what it would be like to have no sight when she spoke, and she said it was more in sorrow than in anger. She had now given up on me. She had done her best but it was too late, for I would soon be leaving school and going into the shirt factory where they might put a semblance of manners on me or they would surely show me the door. I could see how upset I'd made her and I was truly sorry, for of all the old bitches of nuns that tortured us, she was by far the kindest. She never raised your skirt in front of the whole class to examine how clean your underwear was and to tell you to go home and get your mother to change it, if you had a change of underwear. One mad nun actually did that to Alice Timmons that I mentioned before. Alice wanted the ground to open and swallow her. Sr Kathleen would never do that. And I had proof of that because now she was saying she wished to give me something. It was a book called *Ireland's Heroes*. And it was about the scores, the hundreds, the thousands of brave Irish men and Irish women who shed blood for freedom. She told me she had received it many years ago from a very special hand. Now she passed it into mine with the hope that it would change my ways.

I was sorely tempted to ask was it Padraig Pearse's hand, but thought better of it. I'm glad I did, for she was in a very funny mood. The next thing she did I've never understood and I never will. She asked me to tear the book apart. Page by page. Throw them into the nearest bin. Her voice was very low. She wasn't angry – she was not joking – I was in no doubt she was serious. Go on, tear it, page by page, she repeated calmly to me, do it now, do it immediately, do as I order you. I wasn't going to insist I couldn't do that. She had given the book to me, it really was a present and there were no books in our house, so I really did want to hold on to it, but I knew I couldn't. There she was standing before me and even though there was neither strap nor stick in her hand – she was the gentlest of the nuns, Sr Kathleen, as I've said – I still was too terrified not to do what she commanded. So I ripped the book apart, page by page, and threw them away in the bin. Good, she said, very good, that's the right thing for you to do – that's what you've done, isn't it, with the sacrifice of all the generations that have gone before this one. You've danced in the blood they shed to win your liberty. And what have you done with that liberty? Laughed in the face of it. Mocked it without mercy. Search through these torn pages and you will find the broken bodies and broken hearts of the men of 1916, the broken heart of Padraig Pearse, and my broken heart – you will find it as well.

That's when she started to cry. I thought to myself, Jesus, it must be true. Sr Kathleen did have a notion of your man, Pearse. But I stopped all bad thoughts because she was now weeping sorely. I didn't know what to do next. I knew saying sorry was useless, for she would never believe me, and I'm not a good liar, not a convincing one anyway. So I did the stupidest thing I've ever done in my life. Well, one of the stupidest. What possessed me to start singing 'Hail Glorious Saint Patrick'? The nun mustn't have believed her ears, because she nearly choked on her sobs. For a minute I thought she was laughing, but she certainly wasn't. There was spit coming out of her mouth, and the only time I ever saw the like was when one of Malachy's greyhounds took a fit suddenly and died. If you pushed me to it, I'd say she was foaming, and it was now much more in anger than in sorrow.

–Do you believe I confuse a saint for a man? Do you think I do not know the difference between our patron saint and one of our great patriots? Do you accuse me of such blasphemy? Do you, you ignorant little peasant – do you know what blasphemy means?

–It's a sin against God, Sister Kathleen.

–All sins are against God, peasant. I am referring to the specific sin of blasphemy. Do you know exactly what it is you have accused me of? Do you believe I would love any man as much as I love God? I am a bride of Christ. It is to him I am wedded, and I keep my marriage vows. Do you understand that?

–Yes, Sister, I'm sorry.

–Get out, peasant, get out. I cannot wait to be rid of you from my class. I will not ask you to go on your knees and beg forgiveness, from God, from Saint Patrick, from Padraig Pearse, and from myself. We offer you none now and speaking only for myself here, I will never forgive you, ever. Go.

I went, as you can imagine. And I suppose the kind nun never did forgive me. But do you know what? I thrived, to hell with her. I told Martha Sewell that story once when I was doing a complete rid out of the cellar in the rectory. I have to say the girl wasn't afraid to dirty her hands. She would muck in. And she listened to every story I told her. She wanted to hear more and more. I often wondered why. But then I never did understand her. Just when I thought I had her number, she'd defy me. There were times she caught me off guard, not least the morning when for the first time in all the years working for her family she knocked on my door at dinner time.

I opened it, and you could have knocked me down with a feather to see her standing in front of me. As I say, we were eating, Malachy, myself and the Italian painter. She just stood there, Martha, and I didn't think even of asking her what she wanted. Malachy shouted out, who is it? I said, Miss Sewell. And he said, well, are you going to leave the girl out on the street? She was apologising while I was telling her to come in, come in. I noticed she was wearing the gorgeous blue dress that set off her green eyes to perfection. And she had a white cardigan tied over her shoulder. She was bare-legged, and her sandals were white as well, showing off her small feet. She was carrying a basket of apples, the greenest I've ever seen. I wondered where she got them, for the Reverend Sewell had no orchard. But then of course she might just have bought them in Fullerton's fruit shop for her own use, but there was something about the way she was standing at my door I realised she was bringing the apples as a gift to us. And I don't know why I didn't at all like the fact I was right.

The men got to their feet and stopped eating upon her entry to my kitchen. There was a silence in the room you could cut like a knife. I'd have expected Malachy to show his manners and offer her a seat and a cup of tea. But he made no move to act the gentleman. He was standing there, taking in who he was looking at, as was the Italian boyo. It was then I realised, like a total buck eejit, for the first time, that this was a truly beautiful woman. How in the name of Christ had I denied that before now? Was it because I'd never witnessed her in the company of any man other than that man of stone, her uncle? Did she know the shock of her effect? I have to say I think she did. It was the way there was no need for any to speak a word. It was how her right hand went to the cardigan, untied its sleeve casually from her neck, and then she folded it over her left arm, pressing its whiteness to her breast. I finally realised I had to say something. Is there anything wrong, Miss Sewell?

She assured me with a smile nothing was. Absolutely nothing. It was just that Mr O'Kane had kindly sent bags of apples to Fr O'Hagen, who had offered more than they could cope with to the rectory, so she had thought myself and a few neighbours could use the fruit. That was why she felt bold enough to call and deliver – but she really should have known it was dinner time, and here she was barging in on myself and the men eating, disrupting the feast – forgive me please, forgive me.

It was the way she asked forgiveness I will always remember. I knew she meant it. Did she have a vision or something? Did she see all that was to befall? Or was she just saying forgive me please, forgive me? What would I know, a working woman more stupid than I ever let on? As I said I could see for the first time she was beautiful, but I also knew she might be a dangerous girl. Still, I took the basket and the apples and thanked her very much. Malachy asked me if that was all I had to say. Offer the lady some tea. And all the time the Italian painter kept his mouth shut, looking through her. And as I took the fruit she'd come to offer us out of her hands, that's when she looked back at him. I knew they had seen each other before, and now they were making sure of what they had seen.

I thought she'd take the hand off me when I offered her tea, for they shared a hungry look, the Sewells. I've often seen what they would eat for their main meal, stark in the pantry –

two thin slices of corned beef, four wizened tomatoes they'd divided. We might have little but we don't stint on eating the way they stinted. Still and all, she refuses to wet her lips. Why did I say that? Wet your lips – it was like something my granny might have said. For some reason I wanted to sound like an old woman, warning a young one to mind her ways. But she was gone as quick as she appeared. And the kitchen felt empty. A bit of a rare one, isn't she? Malachy said after I'd closed the door behind her. What did you make of her, Gianni? he asked. Gianni shook his head as he did when he claimed not to understand. The girl that's just called, her name is Martha – what do you think of her? She's done us a great honour entering our humble abode. What would you say brought her to these quarters? I don't think it was me. I don't think it was the wife. No, we can rule that out. What would you say took her over here?

Gianni smiled at Malachy. He explained he must get back to work. He was busy. Would we forgive him? When he left us on our own, I turned to Malachy. I said, I smell trouble. He said I always did. He was going back to his day's labour in the forge, and if I had something more to do than brood about the house I would put such fanciful nonsense out of my brain. Not our business, any road. But I think it is. Minding other people. I can't help that. It's in me. It has been since the minute I walked out the school door leaving childhood behind and walked through the gates of that shirt factory the day and hour I was fourteen years old, and I thought I'd entered hell.

There was no fires burning – none that I could see – but

there was noise. Machines going mad, women sitting at them, women I knew from the streets of the town, neighbours, relations, girls a matter of months or even weeks older than me that I played with and were now settled in the factory – women with heads bowed, working like demons, stitching shirts that seemed to come forever and would never, ever, ever stop, swamping us all. Nobody looked up or looked at me, nobody told me where to go or what to do. I was lost, me who had been head buck cat causing bother in the school that had vanished forever from my life. There were a few older men standing seeing all was operating smoothly. One was fixing a machine, his hands black with thick oil, the woman beside him roaring to get a move on – how was she expected to earn a week's wage? Would he come and put grub on the table for her? How could she work if she didn't have a machine? He told her to hold her tongue – he was doing his best – she was a cross woman – Christ protect him from all cross women. That's when she turned and saw me standing watching them. In her temper she roared, have you nothing better to do with yourself? Stupid little bastard, make yourself useful. Fetch me work. You're not paid to stand admiring yourself in this hole. Leave her alone, the man said. Have you just started, pet? I nodded. Do you not know what to do, has nobody showed you? I nodded again. A sharp kick in the arse would soon show her what to do, the cross woman said. The man told her again to hold her tongue. Everybody has to start, Bid Flood, even you had to start. So that must be this one – this whitret's name – Bid Flood. I'd not forget that.

She didn't back down but was at me again, pointing her finger in my direction. At least I don't slump there, she said, mocking people like that stupid wee fucker. Get a move on and get me work. I said leave her alone, the man said, she's only a child. Not in here she's not, Bid Flood warned, she's left her playing days forever. No more toy boxes, no more crayoning books. The sooner she gets that into her thick skull the better for her. You do her no favours letting on it's otherwise. She'll have to learn soft words are no help when she's in this factory – that's if she stays here, which from the cut of her, I doubt. Who is she anyway? A McCarron, that's what I'd guess from the big beating red face. She has her mother's smig of a chin as well – sharp enough to open bottles. Bad breed on both sides of her – she'll never have the gumption to stick things out. You better not get on my bad side, lady – no matter how short you last – one back answer and I'll knock you into the middle of next week, do you understand?

No, I didn't understand. But I nodded again. I spent that whole morning nodding my head to things I could neither make head nor tail of. Bid's bad words and rough voice rooted me to the spot, and even though her machine was now fixed again, she had ordered me to fetch her work, but I didn't know where to go and do that. I didn't dare ask her. The next thing I felt was water all inside my body, and I didn't know what was happening because I thought at first it might be tears, but nothing came from my eyes. And then I knew it was pee and I didn't know where the lavatory was. Oh Mammy, Daddy, Mammy,

Daddy, I'm bursting and I don't know where to go, I don't know who to ask, oh Mammy, Daddy, Mammy, Daddy, God in heaven help me – don't let me shame myself like a wee baby. The noise in the factory is getting worse. I can feel my legs are ready to give way beneath me. If I faint, Bid Flood will kick me from here to Cockhill cemetery and bury me alive in the graveyard. The fella who fixed her machine, he must have seen I turned a wild bad colour for he asked me what was wrong. Was anything wrong?

I have to go to the lavatory, sir, and I don't know where it is. Come on, young one, he says, I'll show you. Jesus, what is this factory and the women who work in it coming to, abandoning a girl just in the door not knowing her arse from her elbow, and leaving it to a man to show the poor young one where the ladies is.

There it is, when you're finished your business, come and find me and we'll get someone to show you the ropes. I went in and was never so glad to sit down in that closet and empty myself. When I'd done what I had to do, I thought I really was going to bawl but I knew I shouldn't for if I started I would never stop till my heart broke completely, and I had to find the kind man and thank him properly, for no matter what Bid Flood said about us, we McCarrons were reared to be civil and modest. However, I wasn't sure how far civil and modest would get you in this factory.

Far enough as it turned out. Once that first month or so passed, I settled. Indeed I thrived. That is our Margaret, working every hour God sends her, capable of turning a hand to every job in making a shirt, they think the world of her, even the management – that's how my mother would show off about me to the neighbours. And wasn't she pleased as punch when I was made one of the forewomen before my twenty-first birthday, the youngest ever in the entire history of any factory in this town, an old one said. Now Bid Flood fell over herself to be nice to me, making a big laugh out of how I'd stood up to her when I'd first set foot in here. She knew that one day this cheeky wee bitch would be running the show. I listened to her, a smile on my sweet face, knowing the true story, what she was capable of doing and never, ever forgiving her. No, I don't forgive but I'm not going to use that as a stick to beat myself, because I am also fair. And I believe I was very fair in my dealings with all I worked with in that factory. Especially the youngsters. For I could remember only too well what it was like my first day. I know what it is to be a stranger in a place where you know not a soul, and that's why I tried my best to welcome Gianni, once the priest asked us to give him lodgings.

He did seem to be settling well. Him and Euni were great pals. Malachy, though, he is a quiet man. He'd take his time before trusting a body. But he too seemed to be warming to him. One Sunday morning after Mass, he even asked Gianni to go for a walk, each with a greyhound on a chain in his hand, dandering leisurely along the White Strand, or taking the opposite direction over the Hill Head and making for the Milk Town. That was where Gianni took to strolling very early every morning after his dip in the ocean before a soul was stirring from their warm beds. It would make you wonder if the man ever slept. Malachy and myself, we were out for the count, exhausted, before our heads hit the pillow. But maybe that's how it goes with Italians. They need less kip than us Irish people. He always carried a wee bag with him with pencils, coloured pencils and wads of paper. It was that bag he presented to me, stuffed to the brim when he called one morning as I was getting the wains ready. It was the last thing under the sun I needed to see, him standing, smiling at the front door. You're up with the lark again, I said to him, are you looking for Euni to run down and make your breakfast? She's washed and dressed so she's ready, I told him. No, he had a gift for us all, and so he handed me what was crammed into the satchel, pouring it all out on the kitchen table. A mountain of mushrooms, all different shades of white and yellow, brown and gold, some even speckled, arranging them neatly in piles, lifting one to his nose, smelling the soil in it, and still smiling. The young lady, she brings you a gift of apples – I bring you these, these – he hesitated trying to find the right word. Mushrooms, Euni said, these are called mushrooms, aren't they, Mammy? Yes, I nodded, this is a gift of mushrooms. When I see her bring you food, he said, we do the same to our friends in Italy. We hunt and bring birds and animals. We gather mushrooms and we share. May I cook these for you?

I let him. He asked for butter. He took the salt and pepper. He melted the fat in the frying pan and placed the mushrooms into the sizzle. Malachy came down the stairs and nodded towards him, asking me with his eyes what was the boyo doing? Mushrooms – can you not smell them? He's cooking mushrooms for the two of us. Because I knew Malachy was mad about them and would eat them till the cows came home, but they turned my stomach, and I was worried how I could refuse him. Boys a boys, Malachy sighs, how long since I enjoyed a feed of mushrooms? This woman refuses to cook them. I remember when I brought some back that time I went to see an All-Ireland final in Dublin. Nothing would do my pal Tommy Patterson, God rest him, but that we could comb Dublin for mushrooms. Didn't we find one shop open on a Sunday selling them? When I handed them to herself – Jesus, the face on her, you'd think it was a parcel of shite. He burst out laughing then at his own dirty language. I ignored it all, too busy combing Euni's hair into her ringlets, dipping the comb into water, her patiently letting me tear the scalp from her, knowing better than to say boo, while the two boys took over cooking in my kitchen.

I don't know where I got the scundering for mushrooms from, because it wasn't as if we were reared on them, but I do hate them. And I had never seen the like of these monstrosities Gianni had collected near the source of the Crana River. That's where we'd worked out he must have located them on his stroll. Some looked like a heart, some like a twisted eel, some like a dog's paw. As he fried them I first of all got the scent of the butter burning, but then it was the stench – and to me it was a stink – of mushrooms filling the air, going up my nostrils, churning my stomach quicker than I thought could happen. Eating them would be like chewing clay. I didn't want to alarm the youngsters, especially Euni who was a bag of nerves since the custard and jelly punch, so I did my damnedest to hold it for as long as I could and I stayed put curling the child's hair.

And I might have lasted if he had not put a full plate of the stuff in front of me. If I had warned him I couldn't stick mushrooms, it would have been better manners than saying nothing and leaping to my feet and nearly vomiting before them all. You'd think Malachy might have said something and I suppose he did warn him with the Dublin story, but Gianni couldn't have understood. I managed to get outside to the grating and vomited without stopping. If Gianni's brown tanned face could have turned white with shock, it would have, I'm sure, and I could hear Malachy's voice shouting, Maggie, Maggie, are you all right? What's wrong with you, Margaret? When he called me by my full name, he was either drunk or very worried. And I could hear poor Euni crying, starting the boys up squealing too, and her asking, is Mammy sick again? Daddy, did I make Mammy sick again? Did I? What's wrong with her?

There's nothing wrong, I said. Mammy is grand. Stop worrying. Stop crying, Euni. I looked at Gianni. I said to him what didn't need saying. I should have told you I didn't like mushrooms. He apologised, saying I am sorry, I am sorry, I did think everyone would eat such lovely food. For some reason, don't ask me why, that made me see red and I snapped back, well, they don't, mister, they don't. If you boys are going to stuff your jaws with that poison, do it outside. I pointed to Gianni and told him, don't bring them into my house again. With that, I turned on my heel and left them, shocked at the cheek of me, to their dirty feed. And for the first time in years, I started crying, for I didn't know what was happening to me and why it was happening.

Chapter Three

Malachy

She was never like this when she was having a wain before. I was expecting a bit of strangeness because of the two daft sisters – but she was always right as rain, and the three babies arrived safely. This time it's like her nerves are at her – it would be fair to say morning, noon and night. She is changeable in her moods, and we're definitely all more worried than we've ever been before. Margaret is a strong girl and will pull through everything. That's what I constantly tell myself, but I'll let you know this much for sure, I'm glad to get out of the bed in the morning, throw a quick bite into my stomach, leave the youngsters to her and get into the forge and work. Since I had to let my young helper go – I was fond of the fella and he did not shy from toil, but there just isn't the business for blacksmiths in this town since the war ended – anyway, since he went off to chance his luck with his brother in Scotland, the place is cold as the grave first thing in the morning, and I have to get a fire up and running by myself now.

I miss the lad's company, even though Christ knows we said little enough to each other. He was a bit tongue-tied, I noticed, in the company of older people, so there could never be much conversation between us at the best of times. I gave him a start because his father, Jamsie the Mechanic, was good to Margaret – very good she always says – on her first day in the factory, so she always would put in a word for anybody belonging to him. I told her when she asked me to give the boy a start that there was likely not the money to employ any man more than myself, but she did convince me he was still a youngster, we wouldn't miss the pittance of a wage he would be expecting. She didn't want to see the young fella walking the streets or standing about becoming a corner boy learning bad language from the wrong kind of lazy company.

Lazy he certainly wasn't, and he could learn quickly, for I did notice he had the one thing necessary to be a good black-smith. The boy had no fear of fire. When he shook my hand the first time we met, I thought to myself, feeling the softness of those palms, that this child would not last too long in the furnace of a forge, but he took to it from the word go and certainly proved me wrong. Of course there is so little work in this town, he and his family were desperate to get him in any-where. Hunger is the best sauce, they say, and he was hungry to do as well by me as he could. He was nervous at the start, though, near the horses.

That was to be expected. The boy had not been reared on a farm. I doubt to the day he stepped into the forge if he'd ever been beside the animals apart from the ones tethered by the farmers once a month in the Market Square, doing their deals over sheep and beasts of cattle. Christ, the smell of dung on the streets of the town those fair days, it would knock you down. Maggie's sister – the eldest, Tessie – she would give off. Honest to God, she'd whinge, could they not wash down the foot-paths at least? We have to walk home for our dinner through a midden – I can still hear her complaining – it's enough to sicken a dog, them dirty old brutes of farmers and their filthy animals soiling every inch beneath our feet. For badness, I told her she should grab one of those same brutes, one with a dying mother and a few fields. Some carbolic soap and a tub of boiling water – that's all she'd need to scrub the dirt off them and make them presentable to the world. She declined the offer, thanks very much. I must think she was very hard up if I believed she would sink low enough to lick her lips for any pigman or sheep farmer from the back hills of the Illies. She could do better. Well, get a move one, I said, or you'll have a full beard growing on you, before you know it.

That's not funny, not in the least bit funny, Malachy O'Donovan – she was miffed, very miffed, and rightly so because there was always a wee sign of a black moustache above her mouth. Maggie had told me Tessie was touchy about that, and I'd always resisted making a mock of it till now, but I couldn't help myself laughing at how raging I'd made her, because her voice got as high as a kite and sounded so comical coming out of her small body. She was like a puppet you squeezed to make a sound. The young lad working in the forge, he must have found it funny as well for he had the courage to laugh in her face. That was the red flag to her. Jesus, did she let him have it. I'm glad you're amusing yourself at my expense, she said with a twisted smile on her face, keep on having the best of times bursting your sides. That will not last much longer. The only reason you're working here is because our Margaret believes she owes your da a favour. Well now she's paid him back – you know the beginnings of being a blacksmith. You won't know too much more. I wouldn't get too comfortable. You'll soon be for the road. Have a good laugh at that now. And think of me as you throw up your guts sailing to bonnie Scotland on the Derry boat. They'll always need thick big bastards like you to dig their roads. That's put the smile on the other side of your face.

If she had kicked the young fella hard in the arse and he had a boil up it, Tessie couldn't have hurt him more. I never saw a human face change colour as quick or as often as his did while she was slapping him down. And if the boy was deeply shocked by her, to tell the truth I was equally as angry with her. Who the hell did Tessie McCarron think she was? What right had she got to dictate who or who not I could keep working for me? And of course I knew where she got her information from. It had to be from my wife, who should know better than to discuss our matters with anyone outside the four walls of our house. Little point in confronting Margaret though – she would never deny she had done it, the woman was incapable of telling a lie – but it made me wary of what it is you can confess to a person who does not know who to and who not to repeat anything to. Anyway, the poor young fella – Jack Shields was his name, or was it Michael? Once they're out of sight, you forget them – the long and short of it is through Tessie's big cruel mouth he got wind that he would be out of a job sooner rather than later.

I was surprised at how forward the boyo grew after getting this news. I had let sleeping dogs lie, never confirming nor contradicting what had been said in the heat of the minute by your woman, but from the way he started to carry on, it was clear he had believed what she said rather than take consolation from me saying nothing. I noticed he started arriving a bit later. Then he'd start shuffling his feet in the evening looking to be away a bit earlier. I insisted on keeping a clean premises and I expected the tools of the trade to be left ready for the next morning in impeccable order. He was falling short of the standard I would demand of a son of my own should he follow me into the forge, let alone what I would take from a stranger. By rights I should have hauled the little bugger over the coals, but I was sorry for him the way Tessie broke the hard lines to him and like a fool didn't I turn a bit of a blind eye to his misdemeanours? Always a mistake, and it was brought home to me how big a mistake after the Italian boyo came to stay with us.

Shields stopped showing up for work altogether. Strictly

between us, it caused me little grief. There was just enough work to be done for me to be kept on my toes. And it was a sweltering day with me shoeing two of Charlotte Divine's best horses when the father and mother landed in on top of me. Charlotte is a decent woman, but she expects the work she pays for to be done in the time I tell her the animals will be ready. One mare is a bit flighty and inclined to put the fear of God in you, the other one though is as gentle and sweet natured a creature as you could hope for. A fine pair they make together, one calming the other down − in fact Charlotte told me that even if she were tempted ever to sell, she couldn't let one go without the other, a chestnut and a black, beautiful together out in the field and now here in the forge, standing patiently, lit by red flames. I was enjoying just looking at the power of them when in, as I've said, walked the parents of Mr Shields.

I was in a bit of a panic because prior to the showdown with Tess, I hand it to the young fella, he'd never missed a day's work, through idleness or illness, so when I saw the two together I imagined the worst and believed something dire had befallen their son. But, no − not the case. They bid me good day, and I returned the greeting. I said I would offer them tea but Margaret was up the town doing the messages, I'd heard her slamming the front door shut about ten or fifteen minutes ago and she'd not come back yet. They thanked me kindly but no, they didn't mind about tea. So we all stood there, the two horses waiting as patiently to be shod as I waited for them to speak out what brought them to the forge. I had a solid enough idea what they'd come for, but I didn't think it was my place to start what conversation there should be between us. The mother, Janey Shields – she it was who got to the point.

–Well, Malachy, this is not the easiest visit for us to make to you.

–Is it not, Janey?

–It isn't. And you being kind enough to give our Jack his start, that makes it all the harder.

–It's decent of you to say so.

–I always hoped we were decent people.

–Well, of course you are. Who would say anything else?

–Then why are you giving our son the sack? Never in our lives has there been one of mine or one of his let go for not being able to pull their weight. What has Jack done to annoy you and shame us? We would be very grateful if you were to point out to us what's gone wrong. We thought we'd reared a hard worker. We thought you were content with him. What's gone wrong so suddenly?

–There's nothing as such wrong.

–Then why is this happening? Who are you taking on in place of my son?

–Nobody. What's put that into your head?

She said nothing to this, but turned her face away from me. She looked straight into her man's face, for it was now clearly time Jamsie Shields spoke out and declared what exactly this showdown was in aid of – what had brought them here? Jamsie started off saying how long we'd known each other, since Margaret set foot in the factory, that long. Will you leave that one out of this? Janey interrupted, she has nothing to do with it, nothing at all – spell out precisely what brings us here, why we have a right to be here.

I was going to let this lady know rather sharply I did not appreciate my wife being referred to as that one in my own forge, but I'd let the matter rest and allow him to get off his chest whatever was eating the two of them. He brought up again how long we'd all been neighbours and this time I thought the head was going to come off her shoulders with rage at him, calling him a stupid fucker, to my shock and, I'd say, to his own, demanding he get on with it. I like to think I'm a man who'd let a woman get away with plenty, but there's two things I do not like them doing. One is wearing trousers, and the other is cursing. Again, I kept my temper. I held my tongue politely, although politeness was not something this lady deserved. My silence was out of respect for Jamsie who after she said the bad word looked as if somebody slapped him hard on the cock and he was going to collapse. I think the man could barely speak, but he got his breath back and said out at long last, we hear you're hiring another man, a foreigner. A foreigner is what we've been told, she chimed in, somebody with no connection to these parts nor to yourself. He might not even speak English, might be some kind of heathen – but that's who you'll employ over our Jack, and you won't have luck for doing it. That's what we've come here to tell you to your face, and to say you've seen the last of our son, he won't be your slave any longer.

That was not just. I might not have paid the son much, but by the standards of anyone starting in a job in this town, it was a fair enough wage. To me, cheating a worker is stealing, and neither I nor any belonging to me is a thief. Janey Shields had a confounded cheek to imply it, and from the way poor old Jamsie Shields was shaking in his boots I know he could see a solicitor's letter coming through his door, but I imagine that being married to this rough piece of work, the man was no stranger to shaking. As I said, I kept my temper. I calmly asked where did they get this information? Fr O'Hagen's house-keeper, she hissed at me, was I going to deny it? Would I now think I had it in me to call the very priest a liar?

I have never prided myself on being a saint, but I swear to God I was showing this bitch of a woman a serenity I did not know I possessed. I asked her quietly but firmly who gave her the right to discuss my affairs with anyone, let alone the clergyman's hen wife? If she could not control her wag-ging tongue, maybe she was in the wrong profession, spilling out the secrets of the priest. I wonder would he approve of her gossiping and her big mouth? This did not shut Janey up. She felt obliged to say it was just as well the housekeeper did have a mouth big enough to let innocent people know when jumped up swanks like the O'Donovans think they can do the dirty on the ones gullible enough to do a day's work for them. Just who in hell did the O'Donovans think they were? Malachy espe-cially, showing off his fat arse once upon a time in his boxing drawers, fit only to batter down the wee boys he trains to show off what a big man he is. Christ, if he were to square up to a fighter his own size and age, the other man would flatten him, and she for one would pay good money to see that battle. I was informed that I was nothing but a useless big coward – and that is when she went too far.

There is much that can be upcast against me. I am not the smartest of men. Crying children drive me to distraction, and I demand they are taken from my company, no matter what is upsetting them. I also have a temper – a shocking terrible temper – and Mrs Janey Shields was about the find out how terrible, how shocking. The fire was by now roasting nicely, and the iron was melting red. I took the hammer in my hand. And the horses who had been watching this scenario as sedately as you please, this was when they started whinnying. That put the wind up her, I could see, more than the hammer, for a look of fear now passed from Jamsie onto her face. They were white as ghosts. I lift the burning iron, and I say to her, get out of my forge. Get out or this iron will be shoved as far up your high hole that it will burn the tonsils out of you. If you're as smart a woman as you think you are, you will get your narrow carcass out and take your drink of water of a man with you or I swear to fuck I will brand the two of you.

She didn't turn on her heel. She stood her ground. She said, well, now we're seeing you in your true colours. Now we're seeing what the sweetieball Malachy O'Donovan is actually like – a dirty-mouthed bully with the worst word in his stomach to hurl at a poor defenceless woman, standing here beside her man, who has never harmed a fly in his whole life, my Jamsie, as civil a being as God ever created. May the same God forgive you for what you've threatened us with because I will tell you one more thing before I'll give you the pleasure of going – I will tell you that God hears you, and you will never have luck for what you've said. You will have no luck if you let that foreign bastard into this forge, if you let him into your house, if he takes the bite from our son's mouth – I swear to the good Christ you will not have luck. Then she walked out leaving me, Jamsie and the horses to look after her. Jamsie takes his time till he follows her. Before he does so he whispers it's the lad, it's Jack, he's the apple of his mother's eye. If he takes the boat to Scotland or anywhere else for that matter – even if he hits the rocky road to Dublin – that will break her heart. That's why she spoke so rough and out of turn. She did not mean the half of it. She certainly didn't mean to curse you with bad luck.

But I think she did. I finished the horses, waited for Charlotte to come at the set time and regular as clockwork, she did. She was all set as usual for a long chat about the racing and we might get into the usual argument as to whether Jack Jarvis was the best jockey ever seen, but she noticed something was bothering me and had the good grace to excuse herself and lead the horses home to their stables. I could smell the dinner cooking in the kitchen – Maggie must have come back – the pink smell of the bacon boiling, the green smell of the cabbage, the white of the spuds. I didn't wait as usual for herself to call me. I left the fire as it was and went into the kitchen. Euni was sitting having her tea and two farthing cakes, shoving them into her mouth as usual. Stop devouring your food like a savage, I warned her, that's not the way you were brought up.

Sorry, Daddy, the child said, why are you here before one o'clock? Mammy hasn't your dinner cooked. Why are you early? Have you no work? What do you know about that? I snapped back. Who have you been listening to, saying I'm short of work? Jesus, the child is only asking you a simple question, Margaret chided me, stop taking the face off her. Give her a civil answer. What takes you in from the forge half an hour earlier than usual? That's my business, I said, can I not come into my own house when I like? Rush on back to school, Euni pet, don't be late, and I'm sorry I was cross with you. I didn't mean it. I have a wild sore head. Don't listen to me when my head's splitting. I'm like a bear. Give your old bear of a da a nice kiss. Make me better again.

When the child had gone to school, Margaret asked me what had happened. This fella we've taken in, I said, this Italian boy, what do we know about him? What do you think we know about him? She answered. Damn all – he's a stranger. All I did was say yes to the priest who asked me to put him up in a house of ours sitting empty. How could I refuse Fr O'Hagen? I'm taking it as given that if he brings him to Ireland then the Italian is hardly going to murder you in your bed and run away with me. Or maybe he is – maybe you heard different – what's put it into your skull to start questioning me about a man I know nothing about? And face it, neither do you.

–It's causing bad feeling.

–Among who?

–People.

–What people?

–The Shields.

–What have they got to do with it?

–They have it in their heads he's come to take Jack's job. They think that's why we want rid of him.

–That's what they think? Jesus, what stupid people are going this day. Do they actually believe a man is going to travel hundreds – thousands of miles all the way to darkest Donegal from the sunny shores of Italy to work with you in a forge? Is that what they think? Who told them anyway the man was coming to stay with us?

–The priest's housekeeper.

–Stella, Stella McKinney. Do you know what? That is an individual who cannot mind her own business. I swear she sits outside the confession box listening to the sins of people and starts spreading them in all quarters before you begin to bless yourself. That particular lady might be better off looking to her own life. I'll talk no more about this. Get your hands washed and sit to eat your dinner. The tea I made for Euni must be stewed by now. I'll make fresh. We're going to do what Father O'Hagen asks us. We're putting up the Italian painter in the lower house and let that be an end to it. He's staying.

Stay he did. And we made him as welcome as we could. A quiet being, he kept himself to himself when he came first, sticking to his own room, getting his stuff ready to start paint-ing the Stations of the Cross. We'd been told he had some Eng-lish, but there was little sign of that. He'd eat in silence with us, smiling occasionally, finishing whatever was put on his plate, bowing his head when he was done and going back to the house. Bit by bit, though, he started to come out of his shell. He built up a good trust with Euni, who we always thought a distant child but seeing the two of them together, I was struck by the notion she was lonely, and so was he, and it seemed that nature was minding the pair, drawing them together, her likely teaching him more about the language, him feeling surer about himself in conversation with a child. Maggie arranged Euni would get his bit of a breakfast ready – the girl was already a grand help about the house – and she was feeling all important to be given the task. Christ alone knows what it tasted like but he made no complaint, so she wasn't poisoning him at least. And as the weeks passed, he did start to talk more, or to sign and point more. He even started to venture outside a bit further, strolling through the town, still speaking to nobody but getting to recognise where he was living, its streets and laneways, the swanky parts of the town and the places where poor ordinary people lived. Then he started to wander further afield out into the countryside. I thought it would be the shore he'd turn to – it's where all the strangers say they like. But no, he swam yet he didn't spend much time there. It was the mountains and forest, the rivers that he walked by. Maggie kept on at me to ask him to walk the dogs along with myself. He did come on one outing, but the man clearly liked his own company, so I didn't force too many invitations on him. I took it for granted that he might want to be alone and figure out what he might paint next, without other people interfering on his privacy. That is why I was taken aback when out of the blue he asked if he could come in and work in the forge. It's also why I think he was so shocked when I refused point blank.

As I've tried to make clear I have nothing against the man. He was welcome in my home. We sat and ate with him like one of our own. But I have my trade and he has his. I don't believe in one cutting into the other. To put it straight, I did not want him footering round where I was slaving my guts out, getting under my feet. When I said to him on his own, what is it you really want to do there – is it paint the horses or what? He just shook his head. So what could it be you want to paint? And then he said, it is you, Malachy, I want to paint you. He had never used my Christian name before.

I do think once or twice he referred to me as Signor O'Donovan and we thought it a fine joke to receive such an unusual comical way of calling someone by that title, but this was definitely the first time he called me Malachy. I have to admit I was caught off guard. Yes, I was a bit flustered and might have delayed refusing him longer than I should have. Once he did not get a quick no to his request, he was talking nineteen to the dozen, a mixture of all languages to my ears, definitely trying to coax me into agreeing, his voice which admittedly was lovely now even lower and lovelier than ever, really soothing, really trying to win me over, sounding in a manner I had never heard one fellow talking to another fellow. I had to put a stop to this palaver, for it was time to come to my senses, so that's when I ruled out him setting up shop in the forge, or me standing without a bother in the world in front of him while he made a drawing of me. He didn't try to force me into changing my mind for he knew well there was no point, but he did laugh softly and held out his hand for me to shake to show there were no hard feelings. What could I do in all civility but offer mine to shake as well? When we did so, I noticed there was something strange enough about this boy's grip. You could feel the separate strength of every one of his fingers and thumbs. You could sense the power in his palm. It was as if he could use his wrist like a tongue to win you into his arms, and you would be hard pressed to get out of his grip for you knew he wanted you to stay at peace, gently holding his hand, happy in each other's company. I gave him a sharp punch in the ribs – not too hard – if I'd wanted, I could have sent him to kingdom come – and I said the forge was out of bounds to all but myself and my customers. If he wanted a bit of sore labour, we could troop out at the weekend to Carn Mountain and we could cut turf if the fancy took him and he could handle a spade. What is turf? He asked. I pointed to a stock neatly arranged beside the forge. There – that's turf, an Irishman's coal – what you burn in your fire. Fire, yes, we need fire in Ireland, he said, it is a cold country.

Cold country, my arse. We welcomed him, didn't we? Was he turning up his nose at us? Let him. I had enough on my plate.

For Maggie, it's fair to say, was not being easy at this time either. Now she had a bee in her bonnet about the Sewells, and it was no longer about the old man – she was upset over the niece, Martha, though the sun shone out of the same Martha's arse for many years, according to my wife. Something happened to make certain that was no longer the case. I'm not exactly sure, but it definitely had something to do with the young one knocking at our door. One thing I'm going to tell you about women – one and only thing I know for sure – they have a knack for getting to the point when they really want something. That's why they understand each other better than men understand anything on God's earth. It's why Maggie claimed she knew what Martha was up to when I asked why is she up to anything?

Maggie said she had eyes in her head and so had I, but she was using hers and I was blind to the obvious. You mean she's after me? I asked. Jesus, the vanity of men, the sheer bloody vanity, she squealed, no, she is not after a married man over forty with barely the nails to scratch himself. Christ, why would she be looking at the likes of you? I decided to roar laughing at her, but Maggie was in no mood for jokes this evening. That silly girl, Martha, she ranted, who would have thought her that forward and that foolish to be parading herself in this kitchen before a stranger that she knows nothing about? What came over such a sensible girl? Love makes us all go mad, I said. I wouldn't know, I've never been mad, she snapped at me. Surely you're mad about me, I teased her. Mad to stay with you, mad to have married, mad to have had three wains with you – aye, mad, I need my head examined. And with that she tried to clip my ear. I say tried to, but I was quick enough to dodge and grab her hand, so I could give it a quick peck. You eejit, she smiled, didn't I say you were mad? No, I corrected her, you said you were the mad one. Never mind me, she said, changing the subject, I'm talking about Martha. If she shows up at this door again, panting like a dog on heat, give her short shrift and get rid of the stupid bitch. I don't know why you're getting so worked up, I said, he barely gave her a second look. If she's after him, he must have left her broken hearted. He's given her no sign he's interested. He just went on looking at the table. He's not going to run away with her. We'll be hearing no wedding bells ringing for that pair. That's not what I'm giving off about, she corrected me. That's not what worries me. And you damn well know what I'm referring to. He is Catholic, one of us. She is the other side. And if Martha Sewell goes after him, there will be bother – serious bother. Something could happen. There won't be time for anything to happen, I reassure her, he'll do his work, get his painting finished and then he will be out of this town, safe from her Protestant claws. And do you think she might just have been delivering you cooking apples? That was all she was up to? I said. Trust me on this, she declared, that's not all she called here for. Why are you so sure? I confronted her. Because he is beautiful, she said, very lowly, very surely. Beautiful? He is beautiful? I asked her. She nodded her head. The last word, she said, better looking than many a film star, better looking than any man to hit this town since the Yanks came over the border from Derry during the war, and, God bless us and save us, most of them were only after their own sex. I don't think that's the case with the Italian. If it is, he might be after you, as well as Martha. Don't let me stop you.

She stormed off then, wetting herself laughing at her own joke. I would naturally not have noticed how handsome Gianni is, but she certainly did. She and her pals had entertained a fair few Yanks and most of them boys weren't after men I assure you. Of course, Maggie and the friends were decent girls all the time, having a bit of innocent fun. I doubt if there was even much of a courting session as far as my wife was concerned, but there is no doubt some of the ladies in this town entertained a few hopes for a happy life with soldiers from either America or England. Maggie herself never tried repeating the hard lesson that was learned by her old sparring partner, Bid Flood. Bid upped and left the factory in this town after war was declared. She smelt more money working in Derry for Tillie and Henderson making battle dress for the British army, earning a fortune doing all that overtime five days a week, sometimes six, covering the sorry arses of the British army after Hitler chased them back home to their mammies till the Yanks took them by the hand to save us all. It was a habit of the girls when they were making the trousers to stick a note into a pocket asking whoever wore them to write back and propose. Jesus, didn't the lucky man who found Bid's note do just that. They met and married on his next leave. A Scots man from Greenock. Married in haste.

By Christ, has she repented at leisure. He beats the lining out of her when he's drunk. And that seems to be all the time. First he took her back to Greenock. Life there must have been rough. She was home within months, him following her. Now, stuck with him, she's hitting the bottle to match her wee Jock. God love her, to the best of our knowledge she's fallen down twice on the street, blemishes on all parts of her to match the black eyes that they give each other, her as bad as him with the use of their fists when the two of them are well screwed. She's even hitting out now at anyone brave enough to pass comment on either her or her fighting man. One reckless individual had the neck to sing 'Still I Love Him' when Bid and Jock were staggering out of a pub.

> He stood at the corner,
> Shirt tail hanging out,
> He gave me a whistle,
> He hit me a clout.
> Still I love him,
> Can't deny him,
> I'll go with him,
> Wherever he goes.

No one will call me a prostitute, Bid roared, flatten the bastard, Jock. Jock, at this stage of the night, couldn't flatten a pancake. And Bid was not much better. So the song stuck to them. Now any smart alec who wants to annoy her croons it after she walks past, sober or drunk, sure they'll get a fine mouth-ful about minding their own business. Bid declares she herself knows a damn sight more about their breed and will take great pleasure in broadcasting it from here to Belturbet.

Maggie does not now and never will have sympathy of any sort for Bid Flood, but she would say you can learn something from the plight of the evil bitch. This town will punish you if you step out of line. The worst mistake Bid made was to come home and admit she'd ruined her life – ruined it through a ludicrous note put in a pair of soldier's trousers, believing in it as if it were some kind of magic. Well, maybe what happened was magic, but it was of a wicked kind. Now Bid was paying the price. The price was not worth it. I realise this must have been in the back of Maggie's head when she got so worked up about Martha and what might happen if she chanced her luck. You could have luck living in this town, but it was better not to believe too hard in chance.

I think that might be what Martha was hoping for in the Italian painter – luck, a chance, a chance to get away. I never believed she was as innocent as my wife believed. And it wasn't entirely without justification that I said she might be after me, not him, though of course making a laugh out of it took away the sting of any suspicion. If you'd ask me for proof, for chapter and verse, how I knew this for certain, I could not tell you. All I can say is that it was strange how our paths would cross. Three times, at the break of light, I met her as I walked the dogs and her sitting looking at the sea, as if it were talking to her, breaking her conversation with the waves to wish me good morning. And always I greeted her back. Twice she seemed to follow my steps as I made my way out to Porthaw beach, along a dirt track no grand lady would wander down if she were minding herself. And once as I passed her house, I saw her race along the walls – the low walls of her garden, and her feet were bare. That was the time she said my name, Mr O'Donovan, and I said hers, Miss Sewell. As I've said, it is no proof she desired me, but I could not get this out of my head. Or perhaps I am lying to myself and to the world. It was me pursuing her. But I do not credit that, for I am not free, while she is. I am tied to wife and children and the world can only see and hear my chains. They are what I wear. They are what I am.

And what was he, the stranger, my rival? Bit by bit he told me more. Bit by bit his tongue loosened, and I learned a little of what he was. He said next to nothing about the painting, very little about how Fr O'Hagen could contact him and bring him to Ireland, nothing about what and where he was before he came to us, for if he spoke it was to say very little. That very little made next to no sense, yet it was clear he was hiding an awful lot. Once he shocked me when we came across a shower of young boys playing cowboys and Indians, shooting pretend bullets, and your man, he ran away from the fight like a scalded cat. The speed of him silenced the lot of us, young and old. The lads asked me what was wrong with him, and of course I couldn't answer them. When I caught up with him I asked what in the name of Jesus was that escapade for? He was pure white still in the face, and he did not speak but he pointed to the sky and blessed himself, cutting the sign of the cross. I have to say that was one of the few times up to now I saw that he had any religion in him, even though we all knew his mission in the town, but the name of God or his holy mother to the best of my knowledge never passed his lips in any language within my hearing. I doubt deeply if Fr O'Hagen would have hired a pagan to do holy pictures, yet this man was not what I'd call Gospel greedy. But I'm talking about someone I knew little directly about. The only one he seemed to trust enough to risk talking straight to was Euni. And what good would it do to interrogate her about him? What does a child know?

I admit the man did intrigue me – but I had better things to worry me. He was not my concern in any respect. Not at all. I had a business that was not in the best of shape. The world was changing. Mine – I had to face this – mine was a dying skill. How was I going to keep a wife and three children – a fourth on its way – working at the trade my father passed down to me, one that had come from his father before him? We had survived the Famine because of the forge. Would it now be the end of us? Was that the fear eating Margaret? Was that why the infant in my wife's womb was panicking? Neither its mother nor indeed its father had any notion how they would survive.

Chapter Four

Simon O'Hagen

I suppose I should explain that he is here because of a letter. And in time I will read the same letter to you. But suffice to say that I do believe he will execute a fine job and that this church will boast an excellent set of paintings to convey Our Lord Jesus Christ's final trial, suffering and death on Mount Calvary, and that those who come to pray to God will give thanks for his efforts and for the sacrifices undertaken that allowed this parish to bring him from Italy and complete his task.

Well, truth be told, there wasn't much sacrifice involved. I inherited the money used to pay for his travel, his keep and his materials. Why not use what my mother left in her considerable will to fund a fitting memorial to her love of art in a place where the people are starved of iconography? She would have been well pleased to know this is what I did with part of my legacy. Not that she would have told me so, were she alive to inspect the project. And I'm sure she would have insisted on rigorous inspection. The formidable Mrs Freda O'Hagen – how often have I heard that accurate description applied to her by the tradesmen of Coleraine, all of them a little – maybe more than a little – intimidated, if not exasperated by my mother and her exacting standards. Trips to the greengrocer were a particular nightmare. She would inspect each tomato methodically – rarely allowing any with even the most remote defect to be bagged and carried to our meticulous home in Hanover Place. Potatoes she claimed to understand perfectly – as if by touching them she could detect the slightest flaw inside the vegetable. I can see through the skins, you know, she would threaten the shopkeeper, nothing is hidden from me. The unfortunate man and his wife – Mr and Mrs Dunlop – they had learned never to contradict her. They simply accepted she literally knew her onions, and her turnips, her cabbage, her carrots, her garlic, the fruits of the earth in all their profusion. They knew better than to question where this expertise might come from. It was certainly not from her knowledge of the soil. Dirt had never dared touch my mother's hands, fingers or nails. Her ability to select only the choicest of garden produce stemmed, she firmly maintained, from her finely discriminating eye. She simply could see what was worth the money – the exorbitant price she paid for the best of everything. And it was, in the long run, worth it.

Meals at her table were legendary. Not just the utterly delicious vegetables, but the meat as well. And if my mother fancied herself as a prime judge of God's green gifts, then she could match her exacting demands on the greengrocer with those she imposed on the butcher, Mr McGrail. The Dunlops were docile beings, capable of being silenced into submission by mother's stare of disbelief at the charge they'd dare suggest for the total of her purchases. Mrs Dunlop was known to cut the Sign of the Cross in grateful relief when Mother left the shop. Mr Dunlop was, I've known it whispered, once sorely tempted to suggest that Mrs O'Hagen might like to take her custom elsewhere, but the panicked look in his wife's eyes made him keep his counsel, for they both knew such a discourteous action could lead to dangerous consequences, for they had seen what happened when that woman lost her temper. The umbrella became a weapon – a lethal weapon – that could demolish, albeit accidentally, an arrangement that had taken hours to build. And naturally if fruit or vegetables fell on the floor, the simple rules of hygiene demanded that each single piece be put in the bin. You couldn't feed filth to human beings. So it all had to be got rid of – and my mother supervised the removal of each offending item. No, the Dunlops knew better than to cross her. This was not the case with Mr McGrail.

Coleraine was a town crawling with butcher's shops. The whole parish prided itself on the excellent quality of its meats. In that deeply divided place where every branch of every schism dividing the Christian world had its own place of worship, there was at least unanimity among the people that the beef was excellent, the lamb luscious and the pork a reason to fall on one's two knees and praise the Lord for his munificence. There was, however, one dissenting voice, and that was my mother's. The same voice was raised often in Mr McGrail's establishment. She avoided following the direct method of attack she used against the Dunlops. Her approach with McGrail was never to be predictable. I remember one instance when out of the blue she started to inform this man, whom the concerns of learning never bothered, about a book she was reading. A wonderful book, very enlightening, about the travels of Marco Polo. The inexhaustible amount of marvels he witnesses, the strange, even violent customs of Cathay – that's China to the hoi polloi. And yet despite this being a weighty volume, despite there being an unending sense of wonders that this Venetian adventurer encounters, not once in the annals of his wanderings did he mention the strange sight, smell or taste of green chops, green lamb chops. But she who rarely strayed from her humble abode in the little town of Coleraine, she had experienced such a delicacy last night. It was a pity that the Chinese didn't revel in such delights, for she was sure Marco Polo might have mentioned how they were cooked to make them edible, but he didn't, so they had defied her best efforts to serve them safely to her family, and she was obliged to hurl them into the bin. He took all this on the chin, barely registered any protest or defence, and when she had finished, he merely asked, Marco Polo, you say? He must be dead for years. Centuries, she informed him. Well, aren't you the great woman, he complimented her, to be able to contact the dead. I beg your pardon, what have you just accused me of doing? she asked him. He replied he made it a point of honour never to repeat himself and she heard fine rightly what he'd said. I am not in the habit, Mr McGrail, of contacting the spirits – she was affronted at the thought – when I say of those who have passed away that I hope God rests them, I mean it. Let them sleep in their graves till God wakes them and all of us for the Last Judgement. It's just that I am now in the whole of my health, and I would prefer not to join them beneath the earth, which I certainly will do if I eat the condemned meat in this shop. Good day to you and yours.

She walks with great dignity out of the premises, but he comes after her, saying hold your horses one moment, if you please, my good madam. She eyes him and lets him know she does not keep horses, but she is familiar with a few people who do and if he wants to sell their flesh to his unfortunate customers in the guise of beef she will gladly let them know there is a home for their nags when they are past their best days. He lets her know he himself would consider her the best judge of anyone or anything who'd seen their best days and he would be grateful if she kept her ancient relic of a face out of his butcher's. The last time he'd seen the like of such a face was on a camel he saw in a circus one summer when he was a child. It was an unfortunate choice of animal because she immediately leapt on his insult as an admission that he kept camels, and it was only one small step from there for her to assert that he clearly had a deal with Duffy's Circus to take their diseased beasts off their hands and sell them to the unfortunates who chose to buy their meat from his poisonous stock. Now that he had opened her eyes to his trade in disgusting creatures, she would avoid him and his wares like the plague, for fear she might catch it. It would be a rough plague put an end to the like of you, he shouted, letting the whole street hear his insults, for you are nothing but a jumped up snob, Freda O'Hagen. Get out and don't darken my door again. She informed him she was already out and there was no fear she would cross his door in the future. He called her an evil witch, and she took me by the hand, saying while the town listened, come along, Simon, don't listen to that bad man. Let him rant on, it's only to be expected, because at least, son, you know who your father is. Does he?

That was her parting shot, and I've never been able to forget it because it was the first time I saw a grown man cry. It was a mark of her triumph that she did not even need to look back at how she wounded him. It was not necessary. The look on other people's faces was enough. Of course they showed pity for the weeping butcher, reminded of his mark of shame, but there were definite signs of fear – fear that she knew all about them too, fear that she might tell it, fear that if pushed, she would tell it. That was how she worked, how she got her way – how she reared me. How I did what she told me. And I do believe she would have approved – she would have told me – to bring the Italian painter to Ireland. I'm sure that I was following her orders from beyond the grave, just as I had done all my life, and I did so because in important matters we agreed entirely.

Agreed I should become a priest, agreed that I should bow

to the privilege of hearing my vocation, and following it for the rest of my life. There are some men who embrace the sacrament of Holy Orders to please their parents – every Irish father and mother dreams that this blessing will fall on their families. I know of six brothers and six sisters who devoted their lives to Christ. As an only child, I couldn't obviously match that achievement, and neither would I wish to, for such a mass exit to the clergy smacks a little to me of the lunatic. The fanatic. And I was not a lunatic nor a fanatic. Neither was my mother. Despite her reputation, which she acquired after my father died in the way he did.

He fell down a well. He must have lost his balance. Had a wee turn, as our cleaner, Mrs McFadden says. Took weak. A true unfortunate – in the wrong place at the wrong time. Nobody knows for sure. He was missing for some days. They searched every highway and byway. They believed he might have strayed into the River Bann that flowed before our house. Maybe he had been watching it too long, from the day and hour of his birth, for this was his ancestral domain, this three-storey Georgian mansion, the only one owned by a Catholic family in that Orange town. Maybe it had been calling him into its deeps and maybe he had resisted the call. So to punish his disobedience, the gods of the river, thirsting for the end of his life, drove my father to his death, falling like a fool down a well.

My mother accepted this strange accident with remarkable equanimity. She had been running the family bakery more or less on her own for many years, since he took to walking the attic hour after hour, saying nothing, thinking of whatever it was he chose to think to block out what terrified him. Thus he confessed to us, one night at dinner, his terror was that he would be put away in either an asylum or a prison. We tried to convince him there was no likelihood, not the slightest likelihood of such an occurrence. He was a normal, level-headed man. He had done nobody any wrong in word or deed. He was respected as an honest man in all his dealings with his workers and the shops he provided with their daily bread. I should have made more cakes, he said once, I should have sweetened people's lives, more cakes, more sugartops, more iced buns, pink and white, more almond biscuits, more chocolate cherries, more raspberry and strawberry tarts, more apple pies, more gooseberry flans, more cream éclairs. This was the one time my mother lost her patience with him. How in God's name would we bake that scale of confectionery? she demanded. There's a war ready to start. Do you want to ruin us? People won't buy pastries in that amount. What are you thinking of? I don't know, he replied, I don't know what I'm thinking of.

Nor did anyone else, for after this he more or less stopped speaking to anyone, stopped going out beyond the trek to first Mass at eight o'clock on Sunday, receiving Communion but leaving before the last blessing and rushing home so he would not have to speak to a single soul. That's why when we couldn't find him in the attic, we knew there was definitely something wrong. Mother lit every blessed candle in the house, but it was to no avail. I remember it was a windy day, and if you opened a door the gusts would extinguish the flame. I'm sure we both thought that was a bad sign, but naturally we said nothing and comforted each other with the thought he would walk back through the door, healed of all his hallucinations, or else someone would find him and lead him back to us, earning a good reward for their bothers. It was not to be. We all hoped he had died instantly. That the fall was due to a severe heart attack. He wouldn't know what had happened, for the confinement and darkness of the well might have absolutely convinced him that it was the mad house or the jail. We never knew what did occur. He was fetched out, drowned. Mother refused to attend the scene of the accident. They could gawk at her to their cruel hearts' content at the funeral. She would, she assured me, not shed a tear. She would not give them the satisfaction. She knew that was all they were out to see. She warned me to do the same. And I gave her my word. We stayed dry-eyed through the funeral service and at the graveside, shaking their hands, accepting their condolences, agreeing it was a sore loss and that he was the best of men, God rest him. God rest him, indeed, my mother sighed as she climbed into the car and left me to deal with the grieving multitude. She had done her bit, now it was up to me as the man of the house to get rid of them all. I walked from the cemetery back to Hanover Place, where she was waiting, still dressed in black. We said nothing till she poured me out some tea, and I took my life in my hands and asked her out straight, why did he do it? How should I know, the man was a mystery to me, she admitted, a mystery to himself. Perhaps he was looking at something – looking for something. Looking for what down a well? I asked. His reflection, that was her answer.

It wasn't really an answer, but it would do me. And it would do her, for she was now a very content woman, as well as a very rich one after the will was read. I was not mentioned, which was a wee bit hurtful. The will consisted of three words, All For Freda. I don't know why I should have a face on me, because he was certain all would eventually pass on to me, and it did. She would never let him down on that score. But did he have any notion his son would, by choice, be childless? Did I ever tell him I had a vocation? Doubt it, for I blabbed it out in front of mother one evening during my final year at school. Where did it come from – this decision to go to Maynooth and study to be a priest? It was the most shocking thing I'd ever done, and it was my challenge to her – stop me, I will do what you tell me, you will know what my mad dead father would want me to do, tell me. All she said was, good, I am glad for you. And she left it at that. My future was decided. I would stick to it, as I had stuck to her and would always stick to her, come what may, till the day she left the earth.

Or so she would have liked to believe, but it was not true. Of course I respected my vows of celibacy, I am not a liar, but I have eyes in my head and a heart in my body, and those eyes can weep for joy at the beauty of women and that heart can beat as if it will break out through my skin at the thought of a woman's touch and the turn of her flesh. Yet I did not lay a hand on any, for it would have stained their souls with my sorrow – that I could not be theirs, could never be theirs, for I had nothing, nothing whatsoever to offer them, not even the sacrifice of my chastity. That same chastity was worth nothing. And whatever is worth nothing, then you should put no value on it. All my life I had tried to find what value is in me. Like my father, I have been looking for my reflection. Like him, I have never found it. And yet there were glimpses of it in painting. The painting of the beloved country. Of Italy.

As part of my studies in the seminary of Maynooth, I got to spend one summer at the Irish College in Rome. That was the time of Mussolini. Can you believe that tyrant held no fascination for me? We were well protected by the College from the everyday existence of the city with all its terrors and tremors, its veins of violence, its smell of shit beneath the scrubbed surfaces of the street. For that season it was as if I walked in a dream through Paradise, seeing what I chose to see, and what I chose to see was what Italy gave me. And I took it, devoured it, demanded more and got it. I was Adam and Eve in that Garden of Eden. Have you seen Masaccio's pair of them in the Santa Carmine?

It is worthwhile to go to Florence for many reasons, but if there must be a single one, it is this painting. The church it stands in is ordinary. At a small side chapel full of large paintings, some by Masaccio himself, the Expulsion is itself on a panel barely visible till you stand before it. The scenes from Christ's and the apostles' stories take precedence. It could be easily over-looked

– forgotten – in the concentration of great art that packs this small nook. But when I set eyes on it, I could not move, for it seemed as if it was what I searched for – as if our first parents were waiting for me.

Adam conceals his face behind his hands. He wants to hide it from the entire human race. The fingers of that hand seem carved from wood, from branches of the Tree of Knowledge. When he ate the fruit that grew on it, its germ entered his bloodstream. He became good and evil, sin and the hope of salvation, the delicious flesh of the apple tasting now like the serpent, winding around his innards, changing the very shape of all his features, twisting them into the age he would have been had he been born, and not created. His hair is tousled, as if God the Father possessed a heart, and the heart had broken at his children's defiance, he must pass judgement but he cannot help but touch the head of this gorgeous issue, feeling for an instant what was once so precious and now and forever must be punished, banished from the garden, from home. And Adam knows God will only be found in the emptiness that surrounds them in the panel. He has called out and heard nothing back in answer, where once there was a voice to keep him company. His naked flesh already shows the signs of wear and tear, the stains of toil – and there is from his brow, as there are tears beneath his concealed eyes, the sweat that must be shed to keep him fed and clothed – for now there is no more nakedness. For the first time in this human existence we feel the cold of air, the damp of morning. The world has been made anew by our disobedience, and we are responsible for its continuation and cultivation. All that was splendid is squandered. All that was light is now shade. They who were at the centre of the mighty universe, they are pushed to the side, screaming in loneliness, left to fend for themselves, and seeing each other, man and woman, for the first time as if they have made themselves. That's why Adam cannot look – he has done so, and the darkness blinded him. He cannot know what he will see when he removes those fingers smelling of hewn wood. It is his wife, in agony.

Eve in her suffering afflicted me, so that I thought I'd have to do as Adam did, and cover my eyes. From her open mouth I could hear the weeping that had afflicted all my species since the Fall. Her lips, I knew, were of the same colour as Adam's buried eyes, and there were tears tripping from them. I never knew before that a mouth could weep. When I looked at this woman, I realised her every limb was convulsed in sorrow, begging forgiveness, but here was the shock – who was it she was asking? God, or Adam? I began to hear a different story. She has been blamed for all that happened, and she admits to it. The woman takes on what she has done and dares to grieve alone. They know what it is like to stand separated, and in that instant her hair has turned red with shame, with sorrow. Her back is bent with the burden of what she carries, and it is inside her. I knew from the first glimpse of her, this Eve is with child. The dream of disobedience will end in a roar of pain, and she will deliver into the sour world the child that curves her spine, that is the shape of all that shall smite her through her banishment into her grave. Her bare flesh is mottled, blotched, scourged by the stings of God's reprimands. She is no longer his girl, but something dirty, something to be washed away, and if shedding her tears could do so, she would weep, as she does weep, for all eternity. She has been judged and found wanting, yet what can save her? From now on she will eat the dust of her dead. Whatever is stirring inside her though, it will not be content to pass meekly away, but will cascade from her in a terrible torrent, and for the first time she will see her own blood, blood already colouring her cheeks and feet, her arms and shins, blood that tastes now of the joy that's gone, joy that was his tongue, the taste of his flesh, the weight of him, Adam, Adam, his name the unheard sound she calls to the wind flattening the garden, ripping out its beauty, as she will be ripped apart by what she has done. That she knows she has done. Beneath her feet there are serpents coiled round serpents, all spitting poisons, saying her name, Eve, Eve, her eyes raised to the empty skies, begging for the mercy that she did not know the meaning of before they ate the apple and forgot God for a time. His direst punishment is to give them now the power to remember. And so once seen, this painting will always be remembered.

For years I sought the face of Eve, safe that I'd never find it. Then one day at Communion, holding out the host, I saw Margaret O'Donovan, her blue scarf covering her head as all decent women do at Mass, her red locks shining, tempting me to imagine Masaccio had painted her, glimpsed the future in her, and there she was – his, and my, Eve. The woman would have died with shock if I'd breathed a word of such nonsense to her. But I longed to tell her. I longed to talk to anyone, man, woman, it did not matter, about a world I had once seen in Italy, and that I longed to get back to. But the terrible years of the last war meant no one could travel there. My mother died during the savage winter of three years ago, giving the bitter '47 another meaning a century on from the darkest days of our Famine. She went as she would have chosen, that idiosyncratic lady, her death even more ludicrous than my father's. It is no exaggeration to say that the cause of her dying came down to a splinter she got in her finger bending to pick up from the floor a sixpence she had dropped in her own enemy McGrail's butcher's shop. She came to visit me in Donegal, constantly pining about her sore finger, nursing it under her arm, refusing to eat and eventually taking to her bed and never again rising from it. I could hardly credit that such a strong character should succumb so readily to such a small injury, but succumb she did, demanding constant nursing, insisting that Protestant girls make the cleanest helpers and have the most respectful bedside manner, so I was sent out to find a suitable candidate for my mother's deathbed. This is where the Reverend Sewell and his niece Martha proved the most invaluably useful of neighbours. Martha in particular knew of a ready supply, and her uncle's intervention ensured we got the best of a good bunch who proved herself capable of dealing with Mother's more complex demands. Such a little thing as a splinter had, she claimed, left her bedridden, so there was not a hope she would risk life and limb by venturing beyond the house again. I had better get used to her spending her last days in my company. I assured her it was my pleasure, and this amused her. She told me that since I'd first come into the world, she had never discovered what it was that really was my pleasure. It was not a condition she associated with me, and in that respect I was certainly my father's son. I protested that many things delighted me – my work, the people of my parish, my library, my paintings. No, these are mine, my dear, she corrected me, I think you'll find my money paid for them. It's paid for everything. Your house, furnishing, your car, your vocation as a priest. I have made all of this possible. And do you know why? To give you pleasure. Why is it then I feel I've not succeeded? Why do I believe you are incapable of feeling that? I insisted that I could, but she simply sighed and closed her eyes. I will never see this snow melt, she would observe and she was right. She didn't.

I buried her back in Coleraine beside my father. The funeral attracted fewer than she would have liked – not because she wanted a great show of sympathy, but she certainly did crave that those whose lives she had tormented would turn out to make sure she really was dead and buried. They did not oblige. All that attended were there, I thought, out of duty and no one, or very few, out of spite. Her passing left me completely alone, but as Mother rarely, if ever, listened to me, this was not a new sensation. And I cannot say, as she would have anticipated, I cannot say I took much pleasure in that familiar solitude. The absence of spring that year after she'd gone from me – I barely noticed it, but I was noticing the blacksmith's wife more and more.

I bade her the usual courtesies due to a parishioner. I made a point of attending local sporting events, for I knew her husband was a keen athlete and there might be a chance of glimpsing the wife. I endured the stench of boxing tournaments in which he excelled, and acquired a reputation as a bit of an expert in the noble art of fisticuffs. My enthusiasm was noted, and provoked sympathy, would you believe, among all sections of the populace. I was elected Chairman of the Boxing Association and President of the Football Club, titles I told them I was delighted to be associated with and would do my utmost to deserve. No, they said, the honour is all ours, Father. It could hardly be expected that a priest would be allowed to participate in the rough and tumble of the ring or soccer field, but my passionate interest showed that I was at least man enough to understand why the boys were devoted to their sports. They certainly were, but they did not expect nor encourage their womenfolk to be there supporting their efforts. Occasionally a gaggle of them would be cheering on the local team for a while in a match, but they never lasted the whole course of the game. Margaret did appear twice with the gang of friends, shouting as loudly as they did, laughing as if she did not have a care in the world. And why should she have? She was a happily married wife and mother. Did she ever notice me other than the man who baptised her babies, blessed her and the congregation at the end of Mass, and once shook her hand at the garden fete held in the convent grounds every August Bank Holiday weekend?

That was the only time this town took on a semblance of carnival. Each year there was a fancy dress parade for the youngsters. One or two of the costumes showed some imagination in the thronged ranks of cowboy hats and holsters, the girls in their mothers' dresses, trailing after them down the town street. But one year Margaret's daughter won a prize. She and a friend, a curious misshapen child, they came as Fred Astaire and Ginger Rogers, the deformed girl with a top hat on her head, the other in some sort of petticoat, wrapped tightly about her. When I discovered who Ginger Rogers' mother was, I made a beeline to congratulate her. Her cheeks were beaming, more happy than I had seen her ever. I longed to take that handsome face in my hands and kiss its kind mouth, but of course I didn't, content to shake her hand instead. She was so happy for her daughter and wasn't it a pity there was no camera to take a photograph of the pair of the girls? It was great for wee Mena as well to be the centre of attention and all the people clapping her – it was the best bit of news she'd had for ages. Who is Mena – your daughter? I asked. Good Christ, no, her little girl was Eunice, the other one was Mena, so I knew that the strange-looking child was Mena. But tell me, Mrs O'Donovan, do you enjoy looking at pictures? And she said she did, but it was a bother getting them developed and all in the chemist's. I said no, I meant paintings. Did she like them? The Sacred Heart, you mean, Father, that kind of picture? I said yes, that's what I meant. She had been given three as wedding presents, two of them still wrapped up under her stairs because she thought it bad luck to give them away. Was that wrong, Father? Not at all, I assured her. But I said it was a great pity we did not have more paintings in our chapel, wasn't it? She pointed out there was a crucifix, and statues of Our Lady, St John and Mary Magdalene. There was also a statue of St Theresa in the side chapel, that her mother, God rest her, had a great devotion to. But statues are not paintings, are they? And she had to agree with that. Do you know you've given me an idea? I said. What better way to fill our church with art than to commission a new Stations of the Cross? That would be lovely, Father – but how did I give you the idea? You said you liked paintings, and I thought you might wish to see more, I flattered her. She assured me she would, and I said she would get her wish, because any lady's wish is my command. She burst out laughing and told me she would make sure her husband Malachy would follow my example.

That is how I came to write the letter to Italy. A priest I knew from Rome had stayed in contact. We exchanged news once, twice a year. As students we shared our passion for Renaissance art, and he, the lucky man, eventually was appointed parish priest in Arezzo where he could stand guard over the very best frescoes of Piero della Francesca that adorned the walls of the church of St Francis. Each year I would promise to visit him, and each year I would send my apologies. He would dutifully extend his invitation, fulsome and insincere as only the florid Italians can be, and as the years passed, he grew more and more confident I would not be coming, so his blandishments became even more intense, safe that they would never be taken seriously. It was to him that I made my request, hoping he might be able to help me.

My dear friend, I wrote, I send you good wishes from Donegal, and I hope this letter arrives safely to you. As always, I thank you for your warm offer to come to Arezzo and stay with you, but once again I must decline. How I long to feel the heat of Italy on my face, to share good food and wine with you, to see the superb art of your city, especially your beloved Piero's frescoes, and to talk and talk and talk with you into the dark night and see in the glorious morning. But perhaps you are a lucky man and can sleep when you go to bed. My eyes do not shut in sleep for more than a few restless hours – and that has been the case since the terrors of the past war have afflicted my mind. But let these nightmares pass, though I must tell you one grievous piece of news. My mother has died. She gave up her brave fight for life and has gone to her reward in the next life. As I am an only child and my father died suddenly many years ago, I do miss her dreadfully and I have been looking for some way to commemorate her in a manner that she herself would approve and would enjoy. I have racked my brains for what would please her, and it has come to me in a blinding flash that all her life she drew great sustenance from the music of Bach, and in particular his 'Stabat Mater'. The image of our Blessed Mother Mary beneath the cross watching the death of her son – this was to her the central truth of her faith. The religion that could weep for a woman's broken heart witnessing the death of her broken son – that was what convinced Mama to believe with all the passion she could muster. To ask our local choir to perform Bach would be to squander money – not something Mama would encourage – our own singers could not rise to the complex demands of Johann Sebastian! But I have had another thought. Why do I not commission a set of paintings on the Stations of the Cross for our church? Why not ask the best to carry out that commission? And we would, I know, both agree that the best must be Italian. Is there a painter you could recommend – a painter you know – who would be brave enough to venture to this northern town at the edge of Europe and do us the honour of accepting this work? I have the money to pay well, and I will tempt you by sending a sizable amount to your church if you can help us find a suitable artist. Please, do your best – as I know you will. I look forward to hearing from you and I send warm regards and prayers to you, hoping that Christ will bless you and your work in the town of Arezzo, that I long to see as much as I do to shake your kind hand again.

There is a man I do recommend, he wrote back. His work is of superlative quality. But I do stress that I have some doubts. You will take a chance if you hire Signor Cuma. Since he came home to Arezzo, he has barely spoken to man or woman and he has painted very little. Something he has seen in his past has stopped his hand. But his is a gift too great to be lost entirely. I have believed for some time that if Gianni could leave this town, leave Italy, go away and live quietly in a country where no memories haunt him, where he sees no ghosts, he will create again. I ask that you trust my imagination here. I feel too that this is a man who understands suffering. He is ready to do what he must if he is to record Christ's passion, and that is to tell his own sorrows in the form that you have chosen for him. This may be a nonsense, but I believe the man will do what you request, and save himself as well. I place you in a difficult position. Forgive me. I do long to see you here in Arezzo, and to shake your own kind hand. I wish the blessings of Christ and his holy mother on you, and on Gianni Cuma.

And so he came here. I put my trust in my fellow priest. I knew the O'Donovans had a spare house, habitable, and with a large empty room suitable for a studio. Yes, there were children in the family, young children, but they would not be there to annoy him and disturb his concentration. He could eat his meals with them, but his time was his own. I would pay him a part of his fee on arrival, the remainder on completion of his work. I would also take responsibility for paying the cost of his lodgings each week to the O'Donovans.

While he was handsome, I admit the first sight of him shocked me. His thin body looked as if he had not tasted food for a long time. His hands were steady enough, but they were wrinkled as an old man's, and rough as the bark of a tree. I spoke to him in what broken Italian I could remember – it had been a long time since I needed to use that lovely tongue – and to my surprise, no, to my horror, he came into my arms and embraced me. I'm sure he felt my shock, through my stiffness, but he continued to hold me, murmuring words that I could not decipher but I nodded all the same, hoping he might soon release me from my embarrassment. In this country men do not touch, but he was immune to our coldness. He would learn.

He knew precisely what he had agreed to do. He carried in his luggage all the materials he would need to execute the paintings. I was impressed that he had come so well prepared. But I was deeply upset by the physical intimacy of our meeting. It surely did not augur well for his sanity that he should be acting in so odd a manner. I am well aware that Italians show their feelings more than we Irish do – I did live there – but this lack of restraint was a source of immediate worry. Did I have a madman on my hands? But no, he soon proved that this excessive behaviour was out of character. And I did feel more than a little ashamed of myself. The poor man surely was only reacting to my sad attempt at his native language. He had been travelling so long that the sound of Italian excited him into this demonstrative behaviour. How long had he been without meeting a soul who knew him? It was myself who was behaving in a ludicrous way. So worried over what was really nothing to be worried about. My lack of warmth in the welcome I showed him was a disgrace. For this I blame my mother. Neither she nor Papa ever lifted a hand to me – they did not believe in beating children – but she certainly did instil fiercely the ability to control my emotions in the company of my equals or my social superiors. Tradesmen were a different matter, and the lower orders respected the occasional fit of temper. That is why she behaved as she did in the shops of Coleraine. Why she got away with it. Why I despised her while she lived, and hated her now she had died. Why I brought a man from Italy to construct her memorial, a man she would have wanted arrested on sight and sent back to his own tribe as fast as the holes in his boots could carry him. But no, he would not be going anywhere. He would stay and he would paint – he would finish what he set out to do – come hell or high water, come what may, let whatever would happen happen.

Chapter Five

Martha

I don't belong here. I was always made aware of that. And it has never troubled me. It pleases me, in fact. I could not care less that the people of this town persist in treating me like a stranger. That is why I take a deep interest in any visitor that comes here. Not that there are many. But this select few – they are my people. If they stay here any length of time, I believe in making them welcome. If anyone had made the slightest effort to make me feel at home when I arrived here ten years ago, in 1940, escaping Hitler's bombs, I think it would have made a wonderful difference. It is not as if County Donegal was swimming with evacuee children. I was the only one. You would think that at the beginning they might have made a semblance of a fuss over my novelty value, but no, I was simply another enemy, another Protestant to add to our dwindling number, and with an English accent to boot. Their favourite trick was to get me to repeat everything I said three, four times and then they might deign to comprehend me. You speak wild funny, that was the local cry, and it took me a considerable amount of time to catch on they were attempting to insult me. I played them at their own game. Whenever I said anything to them, I would do so in triplicate, to drive them mad. The speed with which I delivered even the simplest piece of information confused them further. If my London vowels were so problematic, then I could clip them within an inch of audibility. And strangely enough this linguistic game made me much more acceptable. I fitted in very nicely now – the odd niece of my odd uncle, the Church of Ireland rector. A chip off the old block. By and large, he was harmless, so must I be.

And harmless I suppose I was. Harmless I was reared to be. So much so – so unobtrusive a child was I – I think it's fair to say my mother barely noticed me. To her credit she barely noticed anything, cultivating instead a permanent air of boredom – when she was in a good mood – and disappointment – when the moods were bad. And bad they mostly were. Her sulks could last an eternity. Sitting looking out of that window in the house at 22 Bartholomew Villas, at the streams of rain flooding the gardens in Kentish Town. I remember that impassive stare and now I think I realised what she was doing – praying for escape. It was not a prayer to God, no fear of that – when roused to mockery she used her savage tongue against the piety of the Sewells – no, I think she was beseeching the rain itself to wash her clean away from the filth of family life that was the stain of her existence. It didn't answer her. It just kept cascading from the heavens, mocking her despair.

Now, as an adult woman, I do believe she was in despair. She didn't hate my father – too simple an emotion for my mother. She didn't despise him either. She was simply indifferent to him and all that touched him, and I'm afraid I was included under that heading. From a very early age I realised there was absolutely no point in crying for her attention. She was deaf to such pleading. She could endure the most piercing of screams without flinching. They did not trouble her. They certainly did not arouse her, as she sat at the window eating squares of raspberry jelly, flabby, unmelted, straight from the packet into her belly. This was the delicacy she chose to feed on, and her breath smelt of something resembling fruit. I don't recall ever seeing her eat anything else – she must have put something more nourishing into her stomach – but I make no connection between my mother and food. She has passed on that lack of appetite to her daughter. Even now, I never remember how to spell the word and must consult a dictionary before writing it down. The double 'p' is somehow beyond my memory's retention. Surprising because it is from her also that I obtained an excellent vocabulary and a sturdy grasp of syntax.

As she chewed, she did read, frequently out loud, but not children's books – never, never. That was a literature she loathed, reserving a particularly murderous hatred for the tales of Beatrix Potter and their author. I do know this because it was only in my teens that I discovered Peter Rabbit had not met his fate being scythed down by raging farmers nor did Jemima Puddle-duck have her throat cut and blood sucked by ravenous relations. These were the few bedtime stories my mother invented to send me shaking to sleep. She believed in fear. It was good for the character. That was almost certainly why she kept my father in a state of perpetual terror.

That timid Irishman adored his sullen wife, content to serve her as she pointedly ignored him, having time only for her dreams before the window, interrupted only by the books he would bring home and that she took with no word of thanks. Thank you were words alien to her. A waste of time. I once did a childish drawing of the tree – a laburnum – growing solitary out the back and presented it with due solemnity as a gift to her. Was it her birthday? Or was it Christmas? I cannot remember. Anyway, she took it, looked at it for an age, and then she burst out laughing. I did not know what to make of that, for then she said, I shall treasure this, and her voice was kindness itself.

But she did not treasure it. Not at all. When she bolted, it was found thrown on the floor of their bedroom, along with every piece of jewellery, the wedding ring included, that my father had ever given her. For such a thin woman she must have possessed hidden reserves of strength; she had pulled the necklaces, the bangles, the bracelets to pieces, dislodged the clasps from the broaches, and even gouged out the cheap glass and stones from the hatpins. They all lay there, a broken rainbow, on a piece of paper, and sketched on the paper was my laburnum. I had been walking through Camden Town with my father on our usual Sunday stroll – a bit of air to clean the lungs and do us all the world of good, that was the motto he'd recite after lunch, get your coat and best shoes, Martha. We would walk hand-in-hand through the silent streets and he would tell me stories of when he was a boy back in Ireland. When his feet touched the soil there he grew into a giant and could rescue maidens from fierce dragons breathing fire all about them. That was how he'd met my mother. She was trapped on an island called Valentia in County Kerry and there was a castle manned by all different kinds of monsters, but none of them was as big as my enormous daddy, so he beat them all off, lifted Mummy from her prison and brought her back to life with a kiss on the lips. Because she was a princess she had one magic wish, and she used it to make him the same size as herself, so they got married and lived happily ever after.

I believed every word of that story, forcing him to tell me over and over. I wanted more than anything to be taken to that island and see where my mother had been held captive and my giant of a father had rescued her. But I couldn't tell anybody about that, especially her, because he had sworn me to secrecy that the stories we shared would never be told to anyone else. I was an obedient girl. I did what he told me. But I did ask him where in Ireland Kerry was. It's at one end of the country, he explained, and where I come from is Donegal, which is at the other end. And if you're good, and your mummy's health allows, one day the three of us will walk the whole length of the Emerald Isle and see where your mother was born and where your father was born. How long will that take? Days and days. Will we take a picnic? We'll take loads of picnics. What will be in the picnic? Sandwiches and tea and lemonade and cakes and ices and custard and jelly.

But we never went on picnics. We never went, the three of us, to Ireland. When she disappeared he kept her picture in the living room. He would come back from the office, pay the girl who minded me after school, and start to get the dinner ready. One day as he was cleaning and chopping carrots, I asked him what cannibals were. He said what an unusual question, why do you want to know? I told him that Lydia who, I suppose, counted as my nanny – she had told me that Mummy had turned into a cannibal and that she would come back for sure to find me, and then she would – she would – Lydia couldn't say it out loud and I mustn't try to find out from my daddy what she meant by repeating what she'd said, because nobody, but nobody, likes a girl who repeats things. Still I really wanted to see my mummy, and if she were a cannibal now, I was determined to know what that meant.

He stopped the chopping. He said Lydia was a strange girl to come up with that type of story, and he told me it was time I knew what happened to my mother. She had left us to go away to Africa. There were lots of poor black babies there, and she must have wanted to help them learn or get better from their sickness. What kind of sickness? I demanded to know. All kinds – Africa is full of germs. You can catch anything there. Do they not always wash their hands? Daddy said, well, yes, they did but there are always naughty people who do just as they please and you can't force them to do what you know is right. But what is a cannibal? A cannibal, he replied, a cannibal is someone who falls madly in love and the other person does not want them, so the cannibal, greedy thing, starts to eat himself up, then he'll disappear completely and in that way he will stop loving. How does the cannibal disappear completely? I was intrigued. He dies, he answered.

He did die in the African campaign. Body was never found. We were informed by telegram in Donegal a few years after I was sent here for safely. I could never get out of my head it was not German artillery nor a bomb that put an end to him. No, I thought he had gone to that continent to search for her. Search through the deserts and the million miles of rivers with lovely names like Zambesi and Congo, over the tumbling Victoria Falls, all the way up the Nile or down into Boer country searching for his wife in the diamond mines, fetching her a whole treasure chest of new jewels, so she would love him and love me again. But she could not be found, and he expired in the long trek to return to her arms. Just when he thought he glimpsed her jet black hair or heard a syllable of her pure Kerry voice, it would all be a mirage – nothing there but air. Sometimes I could see her and hear her in that way, but it was never her. After word came about him, I kept dreaming she would come to fetch me, eaten by remorse for how she'd hurt my poor dear daddy, and determined to make amends by bringing me with her forever and ever till death do us part and not abandon me with my uncle Sewell. For I was abandoned, and I knew it.

Everyone else might not think so. I was soon mistress of the house, expected to see to its smooth running, which really meant only that nothing should bother the Reverend. And there was much to bother him. The too loud ticking of the clock. Insufficient soap in the basin in the lavatory. He had seen three magpies rather than the two he desired for luck. A book he desperately needed had gone missing from his library, as had his spectacles. When they were found lying by the bread bin in the kitchen, I was told to take more care when I was putting things away. I bought the wrong choice of bread. The eggs I selected were too small to scramble. The bacon was a fist of fat. The tea was weak. The litany was too long to recite in all its demanding glory but it dawned on me I was in the position of my mother, in prison and waiting for her giant to rescue her.

No giant ever came, and my father was dead. Is it dreadful to say I did not lament? His name was added to the many on the family tombstone, though his body turned to bone and dust in the earth of Africa. My uncle made quite a to-do of this business, but I could not enter the spirit of grieving for the only man who loved my mother and myself. Now I can admit it, his love for her prevented me from returning his sentiments. I was then a deeply undutiful daughter. In danger of coming to a bad end.

But there seemed no sign of it in this town, where I taught school for the dwindling number of Protestant children. I was not alone in my task. There was a sort of headteacher to keep me company, a certain Master Espie. He lodged for years before I came here with Betty Cooke, a washer woman. Suffice to say she didn't scrub him hard enough, but he was a decent man. He did get us out of one particular fix. Betty was sending our clothes back to us dirtier than we sent them to her. My uncle's temper might ensure the entire town knew she could no longer do her job, but Espie saved the day when he announced Miss Cooke need no longer work, he would be more than happy to provide for his old landlady as a thank you for her many acts of kindness to him. Poor Betty was overwhelmed by this generosity, but she was in a panic that she would be letting down all the good people who'd given her employment. We couldn't tell her the inconvenience was, in fact, a relief. I had no fear of rolling up my sleeves to start scrubbing in the roasting water, but Betty did come to see me and in a near whisper suggest Margaret O'Donovan as her replacement. The secrecy was naturally due to the fact the new woman was a Papist. There might be items sent to be cleaned from the rectory that no Catholic should set eyes on. Why, Betty, I asked, do they think we do not shit? The poor woman nearly fainted. She had, I believe, never used the word before and she had certainly never expected to hear it uttered within the walls of the minister's house. It was almost as if I had done the deed in front of her, and I was immediately eaten by remorse. I regret the tendency in myself to resort as my mother would, shockingly, suddenly, to foul language. She claimed it was a trait of the people from Kerry. Filthy words sprang from their lips as readily as the fuchsia that thrived in red and purple swarms all over her island home. Take me back there, take me back, that's all I ask, all I ever ask, she would sometimes break her silence to shout at my father, but he never did. He would never explain why we did not go to see relatives there – there must be some – and when I used to bring up the subject with my uncle, he would simply say, savages, all savages down there – they eat their young. Still, I was, as they say in these parts, starving for news of the place, and I did ask Mrs O'Donovan early on if she had ever been there.

–Me? In Kerry? God love you, miss, but I like to sleep in my own bed. Our honeymoon, even – we were supposed to stay with friends of Malachy's in Dublin. I cried that much to get home after the second day he put me on a train and we travelled back to Donegal. That was the last time I went further than the Iron Bridge out of the town.

–It's Victoria Bridge. The Iron Bridge as you call it, it is really Victoria Bridge. I found out when I was teaching the children about the local landmarks they see every day. It's in the council records they were kind enough to let me consult. That's the proper name.

–Well, there you go. They say you learn something every day. Still, I've always called it the Iron Bridge, and I'm not going to change now.

I stood corrected, reminded I was a stranger – a foreigner,

even. This happened all the time, even in the school room where it seemed all too often I was the one being taught. The children were civil and polite, but I was shown nothing like the instinctive deference they displayed to Master Espie. From him they even learned a smattering of the Gaelic language and seemed to enjoy it, defying their parents' insistence that its Fenian charms be kept from seducing them into the pit of nationalism. It is part of the curriculum and I must teach it, whether you like it or not, he announced at a meeting hastily summoned by one very agitated father who discovered, to his horror, that his son had come home happily declaring that he and the other pupils had Irish language names as well as English. Master Espie had taught them and for fun they had been calling each other Sean and Seamus and all the other blasphemies of the day. The teacher curbed that particular religious riot, but he said let it be a warning to me that anything could cause offence. He said many things that were in his gentle way warnings to me, for he really never let me forget that in the school I was there strictly on sufferance. Not merely had I no formal teaching qualification – I finished at boarding school when I was sixteen, time enough to leave, my uncle declared – but I was of course only there because of who I was. Espie was instinctively fastidious about everything, apart from his appearance. Everything I was assigned to do in the classroom he checked and double checked to make sure I had hammered home the required knowledge. It did not upset me at the beginning – only to be expected with a novice – it would stop after a while. But it didn't – for months, for years. It was part of the pattern of repetition that afflicted me since arriving as a young one in that town. And I suppose it affected the way I approached people. I found it hard – in fact impossible – to make friends of my own age.

This led to my reputation for being a bit stand-offish. A downright snob, I'm sure some were certain. I don't mind. If I inherited one thing from my father and my uncle, if there was something shared in the blood that flowed through the veins of all the Sewells, it was that people, friends, partners even, let you down. We must keep our distance, so it came as a surprise when of all people, the Catholic priest made genuine attempts to know me. Perhaps that is putting it too familiarly. But he did arrive at our door to talk and asked me, almost immediately, if I could oblige him with a favour, an unusual and very large favour. I told him if I could I would be delighted, but do tell what it could be?

It concerned his mother, his sick mother. He hoped I would be sympathetic, knowing I'd lost my own – but I immediately corrected him. My mother was not dead, she was in Africa, and had been there from before the war. Health reasons needing heat, constant attention and nursing that relatives there, coming down with servants, could best provide her with – that's where she was recuperating. Africa? He was intrigued. It was a continent he'd longed to visit, knowing missionaries who were serving Christ there. Which part? I asked. Uganda, he replied, for many years since their taking Holy Orders. My mother is in Rhodesia, not much chance of her having bumped into them, I smiled, but he said you'd never know, Irish people keep coming across each other, no matter what part of the globe you find yourself in. How did he know my mother was from Ireland? The question flustered the poor man. He stammered a little telling me he must have heard it from somewhere – you know how people talk in this town, no secrets here, I'm afraid. There's no secret about it, I insisted, it's just that nobody here had met my mother and I would have loved to have a conversation about her with anyone who knew her, even by sight, even by the merest glimpse, but it was not to be. He was sorry that he could be of no comfort to me in that respect, but I laughed off his apology and told him that my only interest now was in finding out what he wanted.

A nurse for his mother, and here's the strange thing, the old lady is demanding it be a Protestant nurse. He saw my expression quiz him and he explained that she was a woman who would not be defied and who prided herself on being totally unpredictable. It was at this point I realised I had not offered the poor man some tea, and no sooner had the words come out of my mouth and he accepted, there was a knock at my door. When I opened it, there were two little girls standing, one with red ringlets whose father's face I saw in her features, and the other a pitiful shrivelled type that in previous centuries they would have put down at birth in cultures more callous than ours. I do not often sing the praises of this place and its population, but I must say that we foster the feeble in mind and body with some care and consideration. When I think how strange my parents both were – and my uncle, as for him – how rare – that was their word for him – how rare he could be, I know how close I am – how close we all are – to being defective in some physical or mental capacity. To put it bluntly, if I am not now nor will be in the future considered raving mad, would it surprise me?

Did those two children think me mad? They certainly had the fear of God on their faces, standing hand in hand, their blue eyes almost crying with terror. I broke the ice, smiling, and saying to the gingernut, I think I know who you are – one of the little O'Donovans, aren't you? I'm the biggest, Miss, she corrected me. The other one butted in now, to tell me she was nearly twelve as well. And she had five other brothers and sisters, all older than her. Well, I said, two grown up young ladies like yourselves must be here on an important mission. No, young O'Donovan corrected me, we're here on a message. What is it? I asked. My mammy told us to tell you she would definitely be coming to clean today but it was a bit rainy earlier so it took her a good while for the washing to dry on the line, so she was longer at the ironing than she thought, and that is why she'll be thirty minutes late or so, she said to tell you, thank you very much, Miss. I offered them a biscuit, and a look of savage hunger – no, maybe it was greed came into the misshapen one's eyes, but her friend was pulling her away saying, we have to go on home now, come on, Mena, come on. Mena held her ground, however. A biscuit would be lovely, Miss, and if she doesn't want her one, I'll take it. This affronted her little friend, who asserted that Mena had no manners at all, they really didn't want biscuits, honest to God. I heard the priest's voice call from the living room, and at the sound of him, the girls went white as sheets. I could tell by the sheer horror they showed that the last person they expected to find in the rectory was Fr O'Hagen, and it was clear that they believed for this trespass into Protestant territory they expected him to send their damned souls to Hell. Mena was the first to crack.

–It was her brought me here, Father. Euni O'Donovan brought me, I didn't want to.

–I was only here for my mammy, she sent me here to say she would be late. I didn't take their biscuit, but she wanted to, Mena wanted to. Did you hear her, Father?

–I would have spit it out because I don't like biscuits any road.

–She's telling lies, she's telling lies, she loves them. She wanted to take the one that I said no to, that's how big a liar she is.

–I'm never speaking to you again, Euni.

–God forgive you for telling lies to a priest.

–But you took me into a Protestant church, you did – tell God you're sorry–

–It's not a church, it's a rectory, so it's not a mortal sin, is it, Father?

Nobody has committed any sin, he calmed them. No need to tell God anything, but maybe you should say sorry to each other, and to Miss Sewell, for this unseemly quarrel. What do I hear from the both of you? Sorry, sorry. Now go home and tell your mammy you've done what she told you. Run along. At that they scrammed like the hammers of hell, leaving us in fits of laughter. Such a pair of innocents. He accepted the cup of tea, and I promised to help him find a suitable nurse for his mother. Uncle would have plenty of good contacts to meet her strange requirement. He then asked would it be useful to meet the lady herself, and see what the volunteer who undertook this challenge would be up against. I accepted.

It's fair to say I regretted that. When I entered her bedroom, I thought she was asleep, in a bright pink bed-jacket, propped on pillows white enough to match her hair, her smooth hands folded before her, her eyelids closed, her breathing distinctly audible. I stood and watched her, taking in this vision of repose, when out of the blue she barked, I do mean barked, like a dog. I jumped and she said, good, good, I see you are alive. Your senses have not been dulled to death living in that large morgue where your uncle installs both of you, calling it a rectory. My years here have taught me that the subject of my relations is one to be avoided in all quarters of this town for we seem to inspire only jealousy of the most ridiculous order. If we can number among our ancestors two archbishops of Armagh, more than a few surgeons and successful medical men, scholars of the ancient and sacred languages, scientists who have contributed to the geological study of this island, chroniclers of the more esoteric realms of our history, and women who have charmed kings and conquistadors of commerce, then forgive me if I do say we have not fared too badly in our worldly progress from cradle to grave. But the prophet is not recognised etc... etc, and so in this backwater where we now find ourselves, the last surviving remnants of our lineage, we receive no credit but instead must expect to face ridicule and abuse. Me, I've known nothing else, so it's water off a duck's back. I am twenty-two years old, I am ready to bolt like my mother and get away from here. I will not give this hole or anyone in it a second thought, but the question is how do I achieve that ambition? And it was as if this strange, dying lady saw that instantly, out to unsettle me immediately, yelping as she did, like a Pekinese. Then it hit me that this was precisely what her little face resembled, a curious twist of the canine and the Chinese. Again it was as if she read my mind. She asked if I'd ever been to Hong Kong? When I said I hadn't, she asked did I want to go? I told her travels abroad, especially as far as Asia, were well beyond the stretch of my pocket. She then said she would give me the money.

I laughed. She wanted to know what was so amusing? Was her slow Catholic brain missing some point? She would be grateful if I were to use my intelligence and illuminate what it was that had occurred in this connection that was a source of such hilarity to myself. She did not give me time to lie, for she rattled on, declaring there was not a drop of Fu Manchu's blood in her body, coming from wholesome County Tyrone farming stock on her father's side and her mother was an heiress owning most of the land on which the town of Lisnaskeagh in County Fermanagh is built. That side of the family defied the Penal Laws against Catholics. They had used their brains, run rings around their English tyrants of masters, and kept land and power safely ensconced within the family by the simple expedient of becoming fervent atheists, making the choice of any religion a matter of utter irrelevance. My breed, the Sewells, they had tied themselves in knots taking the whole ecclesiastic malarkey too seriously. She, on the other hand, had retained a genuine sense of the ludicrous. Could I say the same?

I answered that I had probably not, I did rather stick to the straight and narrow, and her contradiction of that took my breath away. She didn't think that was an entirely accurate description of my behaviour. Certainly not of my excursions at break of day. Not when I cast my shoes aside and walked like a tinker feeling the dew of the grass seep into my feet. I was up to something then that was far from the straight and narrow, wasn't it? What could it be? She explained she had seen me at this unearthly hour, for it was her misfortune not to be able to sleep. This, she assured me, was not how she always described her affliction. Sometimes she maintained it was a point of principle on her part not to be so vulgar as to doze off, even in the privacy of her own company. It was not that she regarded a nightly slumber as bad manners, it was more that she passionately disliked dreams. They came unbidden, and they left unrealised – a perfectly ghastly combination, didn't I think? She would be very interested to hear what I thought on a whole variety of subjects, for she was quite convinced I was an intelligent girl, deeply intelligent, sufficiently intelligent to seduce her son, if I wanted to, if it was worth my while, yes?

I nearly fell out of my chair. She continued to lie there, unblinking, the hands steady, at ease in front of her, as she repeated her offer in a slightly higher voice to make sure I absolutely understood that she absolutely understood what had just happened.

–Well, what do you think of that? Are you game?

–I have heard you correctly?

–You know you have.

–He is a Catholic priest.

–And you are a heathen, all the more attractive to the devout soul, all the more worthy of inspiring their great sin. Please, do not force me to go into theology, such scholastic shenanigans unsettle me. Will you or will you not give my son a taste of what it is to have sex with a woman? His chastity reeks. And I want grandchildren. Will you oblige me?

–Why didn't you think of this when he entered a seminary – you must have known all about the vows of celibacy. I barely know Father O'Hagen, but what I do know is that he is a very honest man and he would not break an oath. It is a bit late to try and change his character now, why do you try?

–Because I am on my deathbed, you foolish girl. And we are as families, yours and mine, in a remarkably similar pickle. We are almost at the end of the line. The two of you can replenish us both. Have a child. Have two. Go away, rear them. I have plenty of money. All yours to waste as you like once you do the dirty with my boy.

–Mrs O'Hagen, I have to say–

–Call me Freda, like a good daughter-in-law.

–I am not your daughter-in-law, I never will be, I can only assume you are on serious medication for your illness and it is making you hallucinate in this manner. I think the effect of these drugs may be infectious, for I do feel I am hallucinating as well. Have we really had this conversation, or am I dreaming?

–I have already told you I dislike dreams. Do you not listen?

–I have been listening too long. Good afternoon, Mrs O'Hagen.

–Then you will not do as I tell you?

–I most certainly will not.

–Then I regret to inform you there will be consequences, tragic consequences.

–Which are?

–I will die shortly. And you will be one of – no, the only cause. An old woman asks a young woman to save her family name, and she says no. I must say I am shocked at this squeamishness. It certainly did not stop your mother doing what was necessary for the Sewells. I believed she might have set you an example to follow. But no, you turn your back on her too.

–She turned her back on me. She ran off to Africa.

–No, she didn't.

–What do you know about her? How could you know–

–I made it my business to know. And it really wasn't that difficult. Did you say she's in Africa? I'm afraid not. The wilds of Kerry beckoned her home. She's now running a draper's shop in Tralee. Don't ask what alias she lives under. She wants no contact with any man or woman bearing the name of Sewell. That she made unmistakably clear. That was her warning. I'm afraid she doesn't care to see you, my dear. And I hope this breaks your heart, for you have done the same to mine. Get out.

I did so, and she did die within days of her revelations. My mother was alive, but had disowned me. I received in some form or other a proposal of marriage, but I rejected it. I knew if I stayed there was nothing for me in this place but more of the same that I have lived with since arriving here so many years ago. Yet I had glimpsed a way out, and turned away from it. It is fair to say that I had made my bed and now I must lie in it. But I had stopped lying there at night, waiting for dreams to come in tormenting sleep. Instead, I took to sitting up through the early hours in my most uncomfortable chair, looking into our garden through the window, as I had watched my mother doing – my earliest memory of her. It was only now, as an adult woman, I realised what she was hoping for – that the window would shatter, that the room would be suffused in golden light banishing the night's – the day's darkness – that a flash of divine fire would illuminate my world and that I would receive a charge of life to transform me entirely. The Annunciation was the doing of God the Mother. She was filled with longing for a man and she called that longing Gabriel, his wings corresponding to the beating of her heart, seeing in his own shape the reflection – the distortion of herself. And that vision she called angel, most pure, most obliging servant of the virgin Goddess. So it was in the strange blaze of pink and blue that is the sky on May mornings in Donegal, I saw for the first time the Italian painter.

It was jolly useful that he was staying with the O'Donovans. I had access there that I had to no other house of that order in the town. From time to time I'd seen the husband on my morning travels, walking his greyhound. On one occasion he smirked in my direction and I bowed my head to avoid his most insolent gaze. I was sorely tempted to give him a blast of my mother's choicest abuse, burning his ears, ridding them of filthy wax with the ferocity of my curses. But as always, I kept myself under restraint. His wife was an excellent worker. No, I would mind my manners and my indifference to him would, I hoped, dispel any illusions he might entertain as to why our paths crossed so early in the day so often. But he would say hello, so I was forced to return the greeting. Then I would stare straight ahead and continue my walk.

I did begin to think though that his wife suspected me of being up to something. Twice she mentioned he'd seen me and twice I'd cut her dead on the subject. My reticence clearly was a mistake. It increased her suspicions. After all their years of marriage she was still besotted with him, which was really rather sweet. There was only one subject I longed for her to mention, and on him she kept her silence, other than to say he had taken a shine to Euni, her only daughter. I remembered the child who called at my door and decided she was unquestionably the most adorable, most fascinating prodigy ever conceived. My interest in her now knew no bounds. I wanted to know all the ins and outs of her development. I could not be satisfied. She backed away a little at the scale of my questioning, but she clearly felt a pang of sympathy for me, interpreting my hunger in a strictly maternal way. Don't worry, Miss Sewell, she would reassure me, you'll have a houseful of youngsters time enough – my Euni won't be such a novelty to you then. But more than that I could not get – on the matter that I longed to discuss she remained tight-lipped. All I knew was what the entire town knew. Fr O'Hagen had used a substantial part of his mother's considerable inheritance to bring this man all the way from Italy to paint his church's Stations of the Cross. I had no real idea what they were and when I asked my uncle, he was vastly entertained to tell me.

–In so far as I know about that exotic faith and its many mysteries, the Stations of the Cross are fourteen in number. I believe they are meant to be scenes taken from the Passion and Death of Our Lord. They take you on his journey from Pilate's house, when he's condemned to death right up to the end at Calvary. Again – this is only to the best of my knowledge – they are hung around the walls of the church. It's centuries old, the custom – you're meant to visit each Station and meditate on each scene. It might even go back to the first pilgrims to Jerusalem, following the actual Way of the Cross. When they came back, they wanted to continue the practice. I believe there might once upon a time have been considerably more than fourteen but now it's pretty well established. Does that answer your question?

–Absolutely, yes.

–Why do you want to know?

–Our local priest – he's brought an Italian over to paint them.

–What part of Italy?

–I haven't met him. I don't know.

–Perhaps we'll bump into it. Small town, bound to. Do something with those apples, will you, my dear? Be inventive this year. Something other than baking them. Perhaps that cleaning woman–

–Her name is Margaret, uncle, Margaret O'Donovan. You really should remember it.

–Yes, I should. Bring some over to her.

Hallelujah. The plan presented itself. And what should I do about the Italian? What about him, my dear? Do I say anything to him? About what? About being a guest in our town, so far from home, what should I do? Uncle Columba told me I had now lost him entirely – what was I looking for? Should I invite him around for a meal? I explained. Aren't the Italians very hospitable? Columba didn't know for sure, but if I thought it the done thing, then by all means have him over here. Cook, cook something special, something with apples.

All the way there I rehearsed what I would say. A gift to be shared – charmed to meet the stranger – my uncle fascinated by Renaissance art – would he care to call over for a bite – a great pleasure for us all – dear God, how formal it all sounds. But what did it matter? My mind goes blank as I knock at the door, and Margaret O'Donovan answers, deep shock in her eyes, wondering what it was I could want.

Chapter Six

Columba

He arrived on time which threw us a little as I'd always remembered the Italians were remarkably cavalier when it came to punctuality. And for some reason I had it in my head, he was bringing someone with him. Who that could possibly be, I have no idea – he was a complete stranger to this town and its people – but I was under that impression. I said to Martha when I saw how she'd set the table for three, aren't you missing someone? She asked, who? I know there is a tradition in some castle or other, she added, where an empty plate is always ready for the family ghost to feel free to sit and dine, otherwise there will be hell to pay, but to the best of my knowledge this is not a haunted house. No, we are three this evening, and I assure you this Italian is flesh and blood.

I was glad to hear it. I have as I grow older begun to miss the company of others. At one time, until quite recently, I was more than content to abscond into my study and enjoy the fruits of my reading, immensely happy to be left to the pleasures of my own thoughts and terrors. Yes, I do very deliberately entertain my terrors. I believe in not merely confronting them but in entertaining them. Refusing to banish all that frightens me to the marrow. That way at least I know them better than they know myself, so they cannot slip into my head and steal my sanity like a thief in the night. Night-time is, of course, when they pay their longest visits, but so successfully have I accustomed myself to their little ways that nowadays they have the temerity to call before I have said morning service, accompanying me even at breakfast, encouraging me to choke on my daily soft-boiled egg, spilling the salt for bad luck, threatening to take my finger away with the sharp knife that cuts my bread. But so familiar now are these blighters, I refuse to allow them to confine me to my bed, too petrified to face the challenges of the day.

That is why I have come to welcome any change to our routine, and why this young man was certainly a worthy candidate to avail of our hospitality. I only hoped that Martha would not monopolise the conversation and she'd allow me to get a word in edgewise. Mercifully there is not much to connect my niece with her mother, but what I can detect does trouble me, as indeed it should.

There is a marked physical resemblance – that perfect figure, the jet black hair, the somewhat shrill laugh that can still unnerve me when it arrives unannounced into Martha's conversation as it did into the Kerry woman's – but I would insist that by and large she is still my brother's, Charlie's, child, and that her nature is his. Their pleasant, indeed pliable disposition, their extraordinary powers of memory, their generosity towards animals and strangers – they share these traits. But I have noticed one appalling link between the two women. And thank God, it is not the drink.

His wife always blamed my brother for the scale of her boozing. When I'd stay for a few days in that dreadful house in Bartholomew Villas, she would hold my hand and weep sour gin tears, saying over and over and over, he is dull – dull – dull – he is driving me mad with his dullness – I will go mad and kill myself, if I have not killed him beforehand. Then they can lock me up properly, as I am always locked up in this hellhole of a house. I hate Bartholomew Villas, I hate Kentish Town. I hate Camden. Take me home, to Kerry, take me home to Kerry.

I knew better than to remark, you couldn't wait to be out of Kerry, Freddie. In fact you were more or less run out of it. If poor Charlie had not been hoodwinked into marrying you, I dread what the hell would have happened. Who else would supply you with the comfort and booze, would nurse you back to health, would take the time to talk you out of suicide each time you threaten to do yourself in? Locked up, you say? You should be, Freddie, for your own safety – and no man is safe near you. Never has been, never will be. You must be hidden away to protect your name and ours as well, and what is more, this is how you want to live, my good lady, waited on hand and foot, spoilt to the point of insanity, neglecting your only child, a self-pitying, self-loving lush keeping a hold of her beauty by some diabolical deal you have done between yourself and whatever minion of Satan that serves you. Yes, I knew better than to say that, as I knew better than to warn Martha that when it came to men, she had the unfortunate tendency to let their passing interest, if even that, grow into her obsession.

Because she would not have believed me. Not have listened to me. Been utterly appalled by me. Shattered by my referring in any way to the well forgotten Freddie. I did not even let slip my last communication from that dreadful mother. You will be surprised to see the postmark on this, she wrote to me, yes, I have returned to Ireland, to Kerry, where you believed I would not dare set foot ever again. Wrong again, Columba Sewell – wrong again. I abandoned Africa before it abandoned me to its darkness. Yes, my dear reverend, I am quite the reformed character. Your news of Charlie's death shocked me into sobriety. I joke, my dear – I'm sure you've dropped this letter with shock at my grieving for that useless bugger. He would have been so much happier as a bugger, but that's another story. I do take some solace from the fact that he died in Africa. Searching to find me, perhaps, daring to desert his regiment, at long last doing something that required a bit of daring. No, I suppose not. He would have done his duty, and if he could have been in command of a ship crossing the desert he would have sunk with it. Well, God rest him, as they say in these wild parts. You will be delighted that I am writing to tell you I married again – a decent Catholic draper who knows a tenth of my story and is sufficiently male to accept the challenge. I help him manage his thriving shop. But I do ask you not to reply to this letter. Above all, give no information to my daughter, Martha. It is absolutely for the best she believes me languishing under the African skies, frying with the heat of the sun. I'm sure she is like her father, and like yourself, certain to remember me in her prayers. I suppose you have made a virgin of her and will do your damndest to keep her in that nun-like state. This is a pity. Like yourself, she would benefit from a rough fuck. But then, look what that did to poor Charlie. With that in your mind, I leave you now and forever. You believed I was a woman who was over-indulged. So be it. Indulge me now and forget this letter.

But I could not do so, especially as I saw Martha grow into a woman. She was not an animal to be kept on a tight rein, so I gave her the normal freedom that a girl of her age and background could enjoy, and she was really not the rebellious sort, being quite content to knuckle down and do an excellent job in the school. Even that ridiculous idiot, Espie, would have to agree with me on that, although I ask that he agree with me on nothing else. He did not, again to his credit, allow our antipathy to damage how he treated Martha as a colleague. He was, she assured me, respectful and helped her enormously when she first began teaching. I expected different, but said nothing, for I sensed that my niece took a certain element of delight in being able to contradict rather than confirm my suspicions. This disappointed me a little, but I accepted it without comment, because it did betray some independence of spirit, and one shouldn't quash that easily, for it is both a rare and invaluable quality.

I appreciate it in particular, for I have so little of it. I suppose if truth be told, yes, I was delighted to be meeting the Italian painter, but I dreaded it also. I am always reticent in articulating my opinions in the company of artists. They tend to shame me, the opinions that is, not the artist. Even craftsmen who work in the medium of stained glass, they can baffle me with their proficiency. How do you do it? That is the moronic question I always tend to put, and they inevitably sense it, regarding me and my ludicrous ignorance with the contempt it deserves. From my limited knowledge of that race, the Italians were not noted for their patience, so I did expect he would ignore me entirely, consume in silence the food Martha would prepare and probably insist that not a word be spoken to disturb his concentration as he pondered the whole tradition that he was now enlarging in a simple Catholic church in the northernmost part of Donegal, stretching back to the sublime masters of Medieval and Renaissance art, selecting what to include and to discard, far more interested in the perplexities of his composition than in the banalities of a Church of Ireland cleric and his over-enthusiastic niece. But if I dreaded this encounter, I was also grateful to the fellow. He was passing through and would depart when he had finished his work. There was no danger here, as there was serious danger with the O'Donovan man and her infatuation with him. My niece believed, as the young always believe, the older generation notice nothing when it comes to the workings of the heart and the stealthy manner in which it seeks to obtain its ruthless ends, but I have eyes in my head and ears that can hear, and I knew why she left the house at the unearthly hours she did, hoping to catch a glimpse of the man she could not, she could never win. It was also the reason, paradoxically, I strengthened the ties between our families, very happy to hire his wife as our cleaner and laundry maid. The proximity of Margaret O'Donovan would be a constant reminder that her husband is seriously out of bounds. I know my niece is, like myself, a determined person, but she is not stupid. The sheer strength of that working woman – and she is strong in every respect – that might put paid to her chasing of what was an impossible desire. She must leave that man alone, and by hook or crook, I would see to it she did so. Then the good, stalwart, innocent Fr O'Hagen provided the perfect remedy. He hires a fine-looking man – they are all, Italians – and she forms an immediate and comparatively safer attachment to the new arrival. Let him come to dinner. Let him make of us what he will.

His posture surprised me – he had the bearing of a military man. And I was a fool to imagine he would be dismissive of our efforts to show an interest in his work. On the contrary, he tried with all his might to tell us what precisely he was doing. He took it for granted, I suppose, we would be well acquainted with each of the separate Stations – I am willing to assume he had never eaten with Anglicans before – and we bowed as he tried desperately to let us in on the pictures he was creating. We nodded enthusiastically, sipping our sherry while he slugged his glassful back in one go. Good man, I heard Martha compliment him and pour another glass that again he finished without stopping. My uncle has been to Rome, she informed him, haven't you, Columba? Many years ago, I replied, before the dreadful war, and a thoroughly good time was had by all. Do you know Rome? Roma? he shook his head and then pointed at himself, Arezzo, Arezzo, he explained. Ah, your home place, I gather, no, I've never had the pleasure of visiting that town, which I'm sure is delightful. My travels in your country are confined to the capital. Very impressive indeed. Would you believe we managed to get a glimpse of Mussolini?

At the mention of that name his eyes turned directly to mine. I was furious with myself for not realising how damned rude it must have seemed to barge so crassly into that damned sensitive subject of politics. If I had offended, he gave no immediate sign of it, but there was no disguising the power of the silence that had now fallen on our little company. Martha had the good sense to do the necessary and offer another sherry which against all my habits I accepted, as did our guest, again downing it without hesitation. I knew it was now up to me to change the subject rapidly, and so I told him why primarily I had longed to go to Rome. It was to see Keats's grave. Did he know Keats? Keats – he repeated the name – Keats – a painter?

No, I explained, a poet, who died young. Died young – how young? he asked. Twenty-four, only twenty-four, and it was in Rome, suffering from consumption. That means he could not breathe, there was no breath in him. Yes, consumption, Keats's whole family suffered from it. And it killed him in the end. He died in Italy, in Rome? That is where he passed away and is buried in the Anglican church, outside the city walls. Uncle, do recite one of Keats's poems – do, you recite so well, Martha flattered me. Would our guest not be bored? I smiled. No – no, he is a man of great sensitivity, he would wish to hear the poem, would you not like to hear a poem by Keats? She turned to asked him. He gave no answer, and that silence was sufficient for her now to insist I do my party piece and trot out the only part of the 'Grecian Urn' I could remember.

> Who are these coming to the sacrifice?
> To what green altar, O mysterious priest,
> Lead'st thou that heifer lowing at the skies,
> And all her silken flanks with garlands drest?
> What little town by river or sea shore,
> Or mountain built with peaceful citadel,
> Is emptied of this folk, this pious morn?

He listened, and then said, say it again. Say it again. I did so, and I watched his face hear what his mind, logically, could not follow, lacking the language. Again, he demanded, say it again. Taken quite a shine to Keats, I remarked but he was insistent

– quite rude even – brushing aside my attempt at pleasantry. Again, and again, I wish to hear the dead man again. I thought of varying the lines – racking my brains to recall bits of the Nightingale or a snatch of a sonnet, but I thought the better of it when I saw how serious he was about hearing this specific piece of verse. So, for what seemed like the umpteenth time, I gave him the necessary, and this time when I finished he said very quietly, indeed I'd say rather threateningly, Mussolini is dead, this man who wrote the poem is dead, Mussolini would not write this and he is in hell. Do you think Mussolini is in hell? he asked me. I replied it was God who would decide that, but he shook his head. No, not God – not Christ, not the demon, Mussolini is in hell because that is where he wanted to go. Is this poet in hell? I shook my head, and I actually heard myself say, Keats is in heaven, he had a streak of the angel in him. What a foolish thing to admit – in some quarters it would be considered blasphemy – and I wished to apologise for making such a sentimental statement when out of the blue he repeated exactly, word by word, what I had quoted from the 'Grecian Urn'. He burst out laughing, seeing our open mouths, and then he started to applaud his wonderful achievement. And we followed suit.

The clapping continued through the meal. He drank the brown soup and at its end licked his spoon with great appreciation. The salad he ate with his fingers, touching them gently with his red tongue as he finished rubbing his bowl with the delicious white bread. The liver cut in thin strips, doused in strong dark gravy, flecked with the pink of bacon, its sweetness cutting through, he ate it with relish, downing serious quantities of the golden carrots and potatoes roasted to brown perfection. We opened bottle after bottle of stout for him to drink. And they went down the hatch without any sign of drunkenness. He greeted each course with loud approval, and Martha was beaming with pleasure, for she knew the best was yet to come – an apple pie flaked with cloves, that scented the kitchen for hours after leaving the oven, opening to reveal its goodness. Having cleared the dishes, she was ready to present this final triumph when there was a loud banging – no, it was a kicking at the door.

What in the name of God was Betty Cooke, that poor soul, doing standing there, obviously in great distress? Betty had been a wonderful asset to the running of our house for many years, and we did value her very highly, but by the time she departed it is only fair to report that things had got a little beyond her. She would clean the kitchen three times and ignore the bedrooms. The hall floor would be scrubbed clean of the linoleum's pattern, but the bath was filthy. She had even started to forget Martha's name, and the day she locked her out of the house, refusing her entry after she'd come home from school – that was when we knew she really had to go. Espie proved invaluable, solving the problem of how she would cope without the wage we paid. I could just about rise to a small annual stipend that would help keep the wolf from the door, yet we did feel rather bad that we couldn't do more for the old girl and left the brunt of the responsibility to Espie, but he did say he was willing to do it and we let him.

The ferocious kicking made me think that either she had completely lost her marbles or in her dotage she had acquired a serious financial acumen and was now demanding a fortune in back pay. Neither of these possibilities was to my satisfaction, and I prayed that Martha might deal with the mayhem. She went up to Betty and took her into the kitchen, holding the now weeping woman in her arms. The Italian painter gestured to me, obviously inquiring who this was and what was the matter? He did not seem to be unduly perturbed, and then I realised that these violent manifestations were par for the course in the streets of Rome, or Arezzo, or wherever you choose to stroll in his country. He was not remotely fazed by it, nor by the uncontrollable sobbing coming from outside the room where we sat listening to the commotion. So, tell me, I attempted to start a conversation, what do you make of Giotto? An Italian bastard, a dirty Italian bastard, Betty's voice was roaring, why is there a dirty Italian bastard in a Protestant rectory? Do you believe the extraordinary legend of the circle? How each of the artists in Italy was to enter a submission for the Pope's private chapel, I continued to divert him away from the torrent of accusations spewing from the crazy woman's lips. They murdered our men – they put them up against the wall – they hung them without mercy, there's blood on all their hands. And Giotto, I continued, refusing to acknowledge the clamour outside, Giotto, he took his paint brush and drew a circle –

infuriating his Holiness whatever his name and number, until he measured it and found that it was perfectly executed. Is that legend true? Do you believe that story about Giotto?

But he hadn't time to answer or even to tell me if he understood what I was blathering on about, because we were now confronted with the sight of this tiny grey woman, who had never been in a fight in her life, there she was in the dining room she had swept and kept spick and span, standing – no, shaking like a whirling dervish, brandishing a fruit knife, screaming she would cut the stranger's throat, blaming him for the bloodshed that had drenched all of this soaking continent with the dry exception of the neutral little island on which we stood. But Betty's family were the last remnants of the Irish still loyal to the British Empire, determined to do their bit for its survival. So two strapping nephews, Billy and Alan, had joined the air force and both had died too young, too cruelly, in the early days of the conflict. The bother. Or as we Irish referred to it, the Emergency. And now she wanted revenge. Pigeons had come home to roost. An eye for an eye, a tooth for a tooth, as if the bible was being written in my house. For one terrible moment I felt my old weakness creep over me. And I thought I would burst my sides laughing at the sheer ridiculousness of my life – my faith, my family, my fatherland, all one ridiculous failure, one long chain of failure connected to failure – and all that stopped me from hurling the lot of them out of my home and onto the street was the sheer weight of pointlessness that was the sum of my days, my past, my present, and what little time that is to come. Then he did something, the Italian, that I could not have anticipated. Nobody could.

He stood and faced Betty, blue in the face with her diatribe of abuse. He held out his hand to her and now Martha had joined in the melee, screaming Betty would cut it off – he would never paint again. In my head I blamed Espie – he had put the mad old fool up to this, biding his time to be revenged on me, grasping this opportunity. We were all immersed in this melodramatic scene when with great fortitude the Italian simply reached out and took the knife from the harridan. The shock of this, the courage – the bravery – stopped Betty in her tracks. Rather shamefaced, and rightly so, I thought, Martha too ceased wailing her warnings. We all three of us watched him, wondering what he'd do next.

And then he did it. He simply lifted the knife, held it poised in his left hand over his right wrist and asked her silently, eloquently, should he cut it? Would that please her? Would it avenge her? There was not a move out of any of us, not a move except that knife hovering over his flesh, threatening to tear it to ribbons, red ribbons. Of course it would be now that Espie arrived, too late to have put a stop to the pantomime. It must be played to the bitter end, and I knew – I absolutely knew – this man, if push came to shove, would carve the blood from his wrist and feed it to the dogs if the mood was on him. But there was no need for such melodrama. Betty took the strange matter in hand. She went to the Italian and asked him, are you my nephew Billy? Or are you Alan? Have you come back to us? Have you come back from the war?

This was when Espie moved. He held her hand and spoke gently. They're not going to come back, Betty, the boys are not going to come back, he whispered. They've gone. She shook her head. Why will they not come back? she demanded. Who took them away? The Germans or the Japs or the Italians? Was it this boy, this stranger? No, not him, he reassured her, sure he wouldn't harm a fly, he's only here to paint pictures for his kirk. We'd better let him go on home now and like the rest of us have a good sleep. Come on with me, Betty, come on. Aye, I'll go, I'll go, she agreed, but I want Martha to walk me. I've walked her often enough when she was a wee girl. And I want you men to leave us alone. We can manage on our own. She held out her hand to Martha who took it. And as they were leaving, Betty turned to the Italian to ask him a last time, are you sure you're not one of my nephews? If you aren't, have you seen them? Are they hanging about the town street? I hope yous are not turning into corner boys. I'll go home with you now, Martha, I'll take you home. Are we wrapped up nice and warm? Safe and sound, we'll all be safe and sound.

They were gone, leaving the three of us men to stare after them. And with their dismissal, I decided it was time to deal once again with Espie and his many shortcomings. I gave him to understand that there was no need for me to blame that poor ancient and demented lady for this terrible outburst. She can hardly be held in any way accountable for the dreadful show she

151

has just made of herself. It was down to pure luck that nobody was hurt. What did he have to say to defend himself? It was accepted that he had taken on the task of minding Betty, surely he could do a better job of calming her, and if circumstances dictated it, restraining her. Had she anybody left belonging to her, they would have had no hesitation in doing that to spare the family the utter embarrassment of the scenario we had just witnessed in this house. There was not a peep out of him. He turned from me to the stranger, eyed him up and down, but still said not one word. What is the matter with you? I asked Espie. Has the cat got your tongue? Are you so ashamed of what you've failed to do that you can't even have the decency to answer my charges? With that said, he lifted his finger and pointed at me. He spoke directly to the Italian, saying, do you see this fool? He is what we call in these parts a clergyman. What you might know as a man of God. And here is what puzzles me. Here is where you might be able to help me find an answer. How can this fool be called a man of God, when the same God has deserted him entirely, deserted him forever, is dead to him as those two nephews are dead to their demented aunt. And since that is the case, this is a man who had no point in existing, none, nothing – nothing whatsoever. And with that he left us. How much did the stranger understand? I will never know for sure, nor will I understand why he said, yes, I do believe in Giotto's circle. Or did I simply, in my rage, in my confusion, in my anger that I had let Espie have the last word in our argument, did I alone simply hear him say it?

From that night on in my head I kept hearing him say things, and I enjoyed what he had to tell me. Enjoyed it almost as much as Martha was enjoying her walks with him, telling each other the secrets of their lives that I had no wish to be given access to, not in a million years. And I would live a million years before I had anyone to tell that to. It did not trouble me. It was what I was used to. So when they asked me to walk with them one Sunday after lunch I hesitated. I was quite tempted to stroll at our leisure through the dense woods at the Milk Town, but this was my own haunt away from the world's prying eyes. No one could find me there. It was where I could reflect on what decisions I had made about my life and why they had led me to this point of my existence, a man ageing faster than he had ever believed could happen, staring when he ventured to look into his mirror at a face he no longer recognised, to lines and stains as if a thousand birds had scratched their way across its red fall of snow. My hair too was turning to white ice. Everything about me seemed in imminent danger, not so much of collapse, but of disappearing. Walking through those trees, hearing nothing but the incomprehensible language of the forest, all its sorrowful sibilants, I took to wondering not *why* I had been, but *if*. And death then seemed not a release nor a relief, but something that had already happened and never ceased to happen each instant of our being. Was I a corpse carrying my own coffin in the shape of my flesh? As a young student training to be a minister I would look at my thin ribs countable beneath my skin and imagine the skeleton that I would eventually make.

These were ill omens I kept from my fellows – I was considered odd enough as it was, I may have been allowed to stay there only because of the Sewells' ecclesiastical history – but at night when, as always, I dreaded sleep, I would stare with sufficient strength at my hands and will the bones within to break free from the prison of my body and take on a life of their own, committing unspeakable crimes against my own sex, or performing miracles of construction to aid the welfare of the human race, particularly the deserving poor.

They were a particular bone of contention back then – the poor. What made them deserving? What did they deserve? I instinctively argued for generosity to be shown to them, because against all obvious odds I numbered myself amongst them. Perhaps not too surprising when one takes into account the normal lot of almost all second sons. I must pay second fiddle to my older brother, the scion of our noble line, and marvel at his tales of derring-do, his monstrous squandering of our resources and his last-minute conversion to the ways of sobriety and solvency, keeping us all above water, not sinking the illustrious ship of Sewell and all who sail in her. Sadly, poor old Charlie was not familiar with the chosen destiny of many a Regency or Victorian hero. Perhaps it was his tragedy that he shunned the three-volume novel, preferring in its stead the penny dreadful of his own pathetic life. This was a man who if left to fend entirely for himself, really would have had difficulty cleaning his own arse. His list of occupations matched his enthusiasms, and his enthusiasms were many. They ranged from tightrope walking – why could he not have broken his miserable neck? – to cattle farming, an exploit that came to dust when he hit on the marvellous idea of abandoning beef cattle in preference to concentrating on the production of squirrel meat. Where did he get, or more precisely who fostered, the illusion that what the Irish peasants needed to transform their meagre diet was a dose of squirrel? He had been assured that this meat was delicious and easy to prepare. I would not insult my own intelligence by arguing against him, for this was quite simply a catastrophic choice too far. No, I watched him waste what little money was remaining, turning himself and us into the laughing stock of the whole county.

Then he married, and they laughed even more heartily. His great strength was that he did not hear them. He listened only to what suited himself, and what suited himself had the consistent advantage of draining the family dry. It was a great good fortune that our record of service secured for myself the living in this town, where our connections stretched back even before the Famine. If the local populace had not shown any great desire to convert en masse to the true Protestant faith, in this Donegal hamlet they had still sufficient powers of survival to start speaking English, abandoning almost entirely the old Gaelic tongue of their ancestors. To the Church authorities this act of cultural treachery made them ripe for the propagation of our faith. Largely to no avail, but God loves a trier.

And try my side certainly did, pouring money into the effort of conversion. A pier was constructed, the pride of the parish.

Fleets of boats might arrive, bearing fish of every description, fetched from all the waters of the Atlantic. There were plans to employ an army of women gutting and cleaning the myriad creatures of the deep, earning a respectable living, helping to turn the town prosperous, less dependent for its economic and moral survival on the tantrums of fate and the sway of superstition. Ah, the foolish plans of humankind. Fate was waiting with a razor in its fist for the milk-white throat of all our hopes.

Accidents happen, and in the building of the pier several did. None too serious, minor breakages of limbs, grazes, bruises, sporadic fights breaking out, and occasional duckings in the always cold waters of Lough Swilly, the Lake of the Shadows as the English called it, the source of all our financial dreams. But the gods that dwelt therein had other futures in mind, and in one particularly terrible mishap two men and a boy lost their lives, falling from some rickety construction into the sea with no chance of survival, since it's said one banged his head on a rock where he fell. The boy it was who went in first, and the next his father who jumped after. This was not the wisest of rescues, since the older individual, like most of his neighbours, could not swim. It was a skill believed to be unlucky, indeed downright insulting to God. Their stoicism – and it's one I share – is that if you're lost in a vessel off the coast of this county, better go under and get the suffering over than expect you could ever rescue your miserable hide tossed and turned like a melodeon into the air and spray above and below the fierce ocean, from which we come, they sometimes say, and to which we return, if the humour is on the water and your number is up. Well, for those three lads, their number was definitely up – the third leapt into the fray, seeing his brother and nephew lost and damned sure if he would surrender his own family so easily without a fight against the waves. They took him, and all three were swallowed and stripped bare before being delivered back to the White Strand at Fahan for burial. Well, two were washed ashore – the brothers. The boy was never found, and that was the cause of the crisis.

The drownings had inevitably led to murmurings against the whole pier project. Was it not the will of God that it not succeed? Could this dreadful loss of three lives not be taken as a sign to stop the whole enterprise? Rumours abounded, but the job was done, or as I've heard them say, it was all out of our hands. The prospect of earning a few bob was sweet. Roll your sleeves up, ladies, and start to work. They did so and for a time the gutting business thrived, fattening the prosperous seagulls gorging on the entrails so magnificently discarded for their pleasure, stinking the shore front, emptying the Lady's Bay of any gentlemen or women rash enough to fancy an invigorating blast of sea air. The workers now had the strand to themselves. But not quite.

One woman, a Fullerton by name, saw something late one evening. At a bit of a distance from her – and she swore to Jesus the knife in her hand nearly cut her thumb off with the shock – wasn't it the spitting image of the boy – the little Toland fellow, wasn't his name John? – wasn't that him a wee bit further up the road, looking at her and waving? At first she had no notion who it was. Indeed, she believed it was a girl, for the child was wearing what looked like a white shift with white ribbons in its hair, but when it started walking towards her, it had the gait of a boy and when she could discern the features on the face, it was the youngster we all believed lost beneath the flood. Dear Jesus, she blessed herself, and that's when she noticed a dark cloud forming in the sky above her, is the boy alive – and she called out to him, John, is that you? Are you young Toland? No sooner had the words left her mouth than on this fine summer's day the heavens opened in a downpour the like of which was never felt before, drenching her to the bone, leaving her nearly blind, and the wee boy, hadn't he vanished when she dried her eyes to see him again?

The story spread like wildfire. Celia Fullerton was plagued by people wanting to hear the ins and outs of the apparition till she was sick telling them. But naturally she made an exception for the boy's mother. Rita Toland had never been the same since word was brought to her that accursed evening she had lost a husband, a son and a brother-in-law. Three taken from the one breed in one day – was ever woman so unfortunate? All thought better than to tell her that for the love of Christ whole generations of fishermen have been swallowed together – there was always one case worse than another – but there was no point offering rough comfort to this widow when her heart was sore with breaking. It was still sore, still breaking when she came to see Celia. Tell me everything, Celia, tell me, she begged her. God love you, spare me nothing. There wasn't much to spare her, Celia thought, for by now the repetition of the tale had taken much of its wonder from her, and she was a sorry woman not to have saved it until she met the grieving wife and mother first, but it was Rita who deserved more than most to hear what had happened, and to her Celia gave every detail she could recall.

–White, did you say, he was in white? None of mine – I never sent any of mine out in that colour. How could he be my son if that's what you saw him wearing? No, you're wrong – not John, it's not John, his mother insisted. Wasn't it the hand of God guided Celia Fullerton when she decided she was going to stick to her guns and keep repeating the boy was in white. A shift, you say, and ribbons in the hair? Sure what kind of young fellow would be seen out like that? Mrs Toland mocked. Aye, you're right, Rita, it could not have been your boy, Celia admitted, knowing this was the only way to stop this demented creature from turning into a living ghost herself and haunting the pier. That was that, whatever Celia saw wasn't the innocent child, so let this be an end to it.

But it wasn't. There was a move to say a Mass on the pier for the repose of the dead soul, whoever it might be, and bring it to the peace we all long desire in this life and the next. But the authorities said no. They didn't spell out in detail that while Catholic labour might have built this pier, Protestant money financed it and no Papist service would be held on that territory. Ructions ensued. The parish priest, a tartar of a fool called Jessop – his grandfather had converted as atonement for some misdeed or other – he could match the bosses in bigotry at any time, so he decided the sacrament would be celebrated on the rocks of the beach itself as they had done centuries before during the Penal Laws when the brave Irish defied the redcoats and the British, one holy priest having his head cut off, bouncing seven times on the ground, grass never again growing where it landed. So they had no fear on their side from any prohibition the Protestants of Donegal could devise against the native people practising the one true faith of their ancestors. And just to show who really did rule the roost, Fr Jessop issued a holy writ. No Catholic man or woman would toil on that pier ever again, no matter what blandishments were hurled at them. They had gone hungry because of their religion many times before, they could go hungry again, for the bread that truly nourishes us all comes from the hand of the Lord and His divinely ordained priests. And they did as they were told. They each and every one left their employment, not caring for the consequences but saving their immortal souls, come what may.

And what came was really the end of prosperity for all, but Protestants especially, in this town. The pier now was cursed – an unlucky kip – an unfortunate diversion that was the ruin of many a good man and woman. My kind started to leave. Not in droves, not immediately, but in dribs and drabs, declining in numbers until we reached the sorry few that waited for me to bury them, and the fewer still that braved the cold, even in the height of summer, to put on a good show and hear me preach and take on the other side worshipping across the road, another side sufficiently wealthy to bring an artist all the way from Europe, giving him a free hand to adorn the walls of their sacred temple with icons lamenting the loss of Christ's life. The present curate, Fr O'Hagen, seemed a decent chap – he even asked me to help find a nurse for his mother – but I couldn't help feeling that there was a little element of rubbing our faces in it – who now had the money to throw around? I didn't know where his family money came from – I thought it impolite to ask – but he certainly had the look of someone who never knew want. He was also a gentleman, and in so far as I, held captive in this town, enjoyed anyone's company, I enjoyed his. But I was decidedly taken aback by his next suggestion.

The highlight in our social calendar arrives on August Bank Holiday Monday. The shirt factories close the Friday before, and the girls get their holiday pay. Three weeks' money, and they felt like rich women. That weekend the streets are best avoided at night, thronged as they are with drinkers, the gangs of them including hundreds of Scotch workers, here for the fortnight, escaping the streets and smells of Glasgow or Paisley or whatever hellhole they are sentenced to slave in for the year's remainder. I have always been grateful our Unionist brethren tend not to cross the border into this town, but are content to breathe easily, and spend their hard-earned pennies in the resorts of Portrush and Portstewart, neatly contained within loyal Ulster. We need have no fear they will descend amongst us, stirring up trouble, ready for the big fight. No, this is all peace and harmony, and the wild Saturday and Sunday lead into the genteel pleasures of the garden fete, held with the good nuns' permission in the grounds of their convent. They tended to shun the celebrations, and one year tried to have them cancelled, because there was a rickety wheel offering prizes for the lucky owners of the winning tickets. Did it smack of gambling? Well, to my eyes, yes, it did, and to some of the stricter sisters, but it was pointed out that proceeds went to the parish building fund, and it would be bad form to stop the whole show because of a little bit of fun – which is all it was. And might I be willing, Fr O'Hagen asked me, might I join in the fun? Might I help judge the fancy dress parade?

You could have knocked me down with a feather. The request stunned me. With raised eyebrows I read out the note he had sent me to Martha, expecting her to be equally aghast. But no, she thought it a super idea. Do, Uncle Columba, do oblige them. The whole town comes alive on that day. The parade is splendid. And we have never been part of it. Who would want to be? I asked her. When I was a little girl, I wanted to be in the thick of it more than anything on earth, she confessed, so please, do say yes. What harm can it do? And it will not take up too much of your time. It will all be done and dusted before you know it.

It took longer than we had anticipated. The procession of children wound round the streets, a marvellously convoluted, dazzling snake, inching slowly towards their destination, awaiting the judgement of our eyes. We have been told that this year we should try to avoid awarding prizes to those in the parade who are Hollywood film stars. So many are now resorting to the bad example of these immoral individuals. Heaven knows there are better ways of enjoying themselves than matching that type of nonsense. So this year they are allowing the children to use their pets and other animals as part of their costume. I prepare myself to encounter a veritable Noah's Ark marching through the town streets, fouling the grounds of the holy sisters' convent. But word reaches us that there is a limited collection of beasts on show – a donkey, two small dogs, and a sheep, albeit a rather large sheep, accompanying the Bo-Peep.

It is not often that I long to hear the marching noise of an Orange flute band, but this is unquestionably one of those singular occasions. I have rarely in my life felt so out of place as I did on that August Monday, left alone, a cup of tea – weak, milky tea that I abhor – in my shaking hand. Why was it shaking so? I looked to find Martha in the throng of anonymous faces, but my niece had disappeared with what I now must call her young man, Gianni, the Italian painter. With a deadening thud in my prick, against all that I had ever believed of the girl, I knew without doubt she was definitely her mother's daughter – that she would be the last, the ruination of us all – as if there was anything left to ruin. I admired her gumption in choosing him to destroy all vestige of our respectability. And I hoped they were fucking, preferably in a sacred place, to their groins' content. Better that than to end like me, an ageing man in black, observing a chain of children, sucking on sticks of rock – a prize for everyone – waiting to hear if they'd win the prize of being best in show, heifers up for slaughter, Christ – pass me the knife, I'll do the job myself, and end their and my own misery. But before the bloodshed, photographs must be taken. Would the Reverend Sewell oblige?

Of course he would. He would always oblige. A mother wants the photograph taken. It is her daughter who is dressed as Bo-Peep. A dark-haired girl, leading a sheep that is definitely mutton and will never again be lamb. I can hear the donkey bray. At the horrendously ugly sound, the dogs – barely more than lapdogs though I doubt if people in this savage town possess or would admit to possessing a lap – the dogs start to yelp. Their barking brings me out in a sweat. I remember my sister-in-law, screaming she is now only a bitch on heat – for fuck's sake, come and give it to her. My brother has brought this lady home as his fiancée. They are to be married. He refers to her as squirrel. She calls him shit, bag of shit, piece of shit not worth scraping off her shoe. But me, I am worth the ride – for Christ's sake get into bed, you Donegal arsehole, do you have a cock between your legs, can you use it more than your eunuch of a brother, too little of a man to even fuck his own kind – come on, come on, come on. She hauls me onto her, her kisses like wine pouring into my mouth from broken bottles, drowning me, leaving me drunk with her tongues of fire after tasting which I began to speak in sounds that all men understand – the lost language of – the lost – the language of – the damned – what I feel, what I see, what I sense, what I am – damned. And I ask her is she damned with me? Damned for what we've done. And she replies, done what? I've forgotten.

The face of Bo-Peep's ram, it has not forgotten. It looks at me and says, I have come to collect you. I try to charm the evil beast. I sing a long-forgotten hymn under my breath.

> Loving shepherd of thy sheep,
> Keep thy lamb, in safety keep;
> Nothing can thy power withstand,
> None can pluck me from thy hand.

> Loving Saviour, thou didst give
> Thine own life that we might live,
> And the hands outstretched to bless
> Bear the cruel nail's impress.

No one has heard me but Margaret O'Donovan. She tells me she is glad somebody is enjoying himself. There is a tone to her voice I have never heard before. She has now entirely lost her servility. I hold out my hand to her, although it is untouched by the marks of the nails. I sing a little louder.

> I would praise thee every day,
> Gladly all thy will obey,
> Like the blessed ones above
> Happy in thy precious love.

Loving shepherd, ever near,

Teach thy lamb thy voice to hear;

Suffer not my steps to stray,

From the straight and narrow way.

Her little daughter is now looking at me. She has the same look as the ram. It is accusatory, and I agree with their judgement, the sentence passed on me. It is death. I am the sacrifice. The throng, the happy throng, are feasting on my agony. I see Martha and her sweetheart sweep through them. Is that a heifer in her hand, garlanded and lowing to the empty skies, or is my niece simply carrying a red balloon and wailing, fetch a doctor – for the love of God fetch a doctor. I could make the theological point that whatever God may or may not do, love is not within his power, being as he is a selfish destructive shit in whom I have made my image. But this is no time for metaphysical niceties of debate and instead I whisper the last verse of my hymn.

Where thou leadest I would go

Walking in thy steps below,

Till before my Father's throne

I shall know as I am known.

Martha is in the arms of her lover. The red-haired child is in her mother's embrace, her father standing helpless as I am helpless in the face of death. The red from my mouth is the red of the head of the girl who is weeping in fear, as is Martha. The lamb of God is now a full grown ram and it aims its head in my direction. I must go where it shunts me. The crowd continues to snake round my throat. And it squeezes the life from me. My hand is being held. Who by? It is Margaret O'Donovan, who is carrying her grave in her belly. But I do not have the heart to tell her. Her daughter I hear shouting, is he dead, Mammy, is he dying? And I whisper, as best as I can, yes, I am, child.

Chapter Seven

Gianni

The streets were deserted. Those not at the carnival, they were drinking in the taverns. This was a day no one worked. I did not like the quiet. Silence is dangerous in public places. It is always there before there will be terrible trouble. Somewhere in the corner of a street, in a shop, out of the corner of a mouth, word is being passed. Today is when – tonight is when – tomorrow is when – every minute of every hour is when the time will come and we will be ready. Ready to avenge – ready to do what is necessary to remove the rotten smell in our midst. Clean away the stain. And I was born in a room that my mother had purified according to every known law and observation laid down in every book as the proper way to bring a son into the world, for she was convinced that I would be a boy. Perhaps that is not right. Not fair. That woman in all her life never really insisted on anything. It was my father, I am sure, who had determined what I would be, and she did as she was told by the man for whom love was the deepest form of obedience. She did obey always, without murmur, without any idea that there was another way to deal with his demands which were always made gently, courteously, but with absolute conviction that they would be followed to the letter by all who were answerable to him. And answers were what my father was after.

They were what we could never give him. And I think it is correct to say that for this reason we did disappoint him. Each and every one of his many children. None of us measured up to what he was expecting. My mother felt this keenly. At each new arrival she would sit, her face beaming with pleasure and accomplishment, waiting for him to look at the baby and, for once, pass favourable judgement. That never occurred, and yet it did not stop her desiring that this time he would look into her arms and not baptise the infant with some scurrilous but, it must be admitted, usually accurate, indeed predictable, term of abuse. My eldest brother was Hairy Arse, my eldest sister Pig's Eyes, my second sister Elephant Ears, my next brother Rhino Snout and my unfortunate youngest sister was immediately referred to as Scaly Skin. It is terrible to say this about one's own family, but they were a distinctly odd looking bunch. My father's insults spat at them in the cradle did have one good consequence. Being well accustomed to his loathsome names from when they first could hear, they were ready for the world's mockery. No one could possibly match him in the ferocity of his physical disgust at his offspring.

My mother would never, ever cross my father. The nearest she came to doing so was when they were discussing a baptism service for Hairy Arse. Please do not call my first born that dreadful name, she pleaded. We must stop or the whole world will soon hear what his father calls the baby and there will be no other name we can give him. My father defended the title as a noble one, of honoured lineage, claiming his inspiration stemmed from more than the alarming down on the poor mite's buttocks. He had in his youth mastered the complex rigours of the Icelandic Sagas. In Old Norse the hero was frequently complimented on outstanding physical attributes, such as excessive growths and alarmingly oversized limbs. If it's good enough for the great warriors of the Viking era, then it is good enough for this puny example of manhood, and let that be an end to it. For once, my mother was determined that that would not be an end to it. She took no consolation from the precedent of these warriors' names being suitable for a growing child. She was scandalised by this example. She, in so far as she ever would do so, castigated my father for allying himself with such pagan habits and insisted her boy be given a proper Christian name. I know what I will call him, father said, you do as you best please and humour yourself, but I will have no part in this baptism business.

And he kept to his word. Every other birth provoked the same response. The girls may be called Caterina, Rosa and Arianna, but that was not how he recognised them. Often the poor little angels would weep, begging Papa not to give them such cruel nicknames and to address them properly. His defence was that he could only speak as he saw, and so that was reflected in what he had decided to call them. Strangers on the street or visiting the house thought he was being playful, a little too near the knuckle perhaps, but that's families for you, they'd say. When they realised that his youngest girl really did respond to his shout of Scaly Skin, and that Elephant Ears was Rosa's other name, when they discovered he was not being a funny papa but an alarmingly honest one, they tended to get out of his company and avoid him strenuously from then on. This worked to his advantage as he found the common lot of humanity an ignorant battalion. He would bombard them with questions referring to their family history, the geography of Italy, the idiosyncrasies of Latin grammar, the dominant rock formations of the Americas, the precise details buried in the stories of the Bible or in Homer. Receiving only baffled stares, he'd dismiss them completely from his company. You are too hard on people, Cosimo, my mother would sigh as yet another relation was sent packing from our door or from our table even, the meal half eaten, the wine glass still in the hand, head reeling from the barrage of questions aimed at them as the price of their dinner, running for cover from the intensity of my father's accusations of their inferiority. No better than beasts – the beasts cooked and brought to my table for you to devour, he would upset our guests, you are devouring yourself, you are cannibals. And so they would flee from this monster, this beast of all beasts, this greatest of cannibals whose heart, hungry for love, and whose head, hungry for stimulation, could only be calmed by one person, and that was his last born, the son he adored, the child myself, that my father for fun called Giotto.

You can imagine my surprise when the old Irish gentleman asked me about the legend of Giotto. I had lived with that story about the perfect circle since I had first started listening to stories. My father would present me with a pencil and numerous sheets of paper and instruct me to do as I pleased with them, for he was quite convinced I had the face of a Giotto Madonna, and that the artist himself in some supernatural manner had used his brush beneath my skin to shape the bones that were my body's structure. He would look at me on my mother's knee and he would whisper my nickname, Giotto. In her way my mother was as frightened of this infatuation as she was of his disgust with my elder siblings. Perhaps she was more frightened, because whatever remote inkling of power she had over Papa up to my arrival, after my birth that evaporated entirely and, in so far as any man like him could be described as besotted by anything other than his own learning, my father idolised me.

I recognised that too in the old Irish gentleman. I did not know nor could I ever guess what his life was like prior to the arrival of his niece, Martha, into his existence, but she certainly moved into its centre, and he welcomed her warmly. I cannot think of many things I share with many people, but I felt so at ease with her because at some stage in our young lives we knew we were adored. I do not mean we were spoilt. That was not the case, I felt, for her. It was definitely not for me. In many respects my brothers and sisters had it much easier than myself for they were not subjected to hours, days, weeks, months, years of rigorous exposure to the whole history of art in Italy, studious exercise matched by Papa's determination that I would master each and every technique necessary to draw and to paint in the most exquisite, the most accurate, the most sacred, the most profane, most beautiful and grotesque forms of expression. I would be Giotto, reincarnated, and I sensed that the greatest task I could perform, the ultimate task awaiting me would be to paint my father, the reward for his enthusiasm, the thanks for his investing in me the hope for his whole family – the answer to his prayers.

I was wrong. And I tell you how I learned that when I was very young. I fell for a trick perpetuated by my sisters and brothers. I include the brothers in the scheme, but I am sure they did not have the brains to be in on its devising. No, this bore all the marks of by far the brainiest and the ugliest of that brood, Scaly Skin herself, Arianna. She had a marvellous idea for Papa's birthday gift, and it was to be a secret, our secret, a big one to be kept from Papa obviously, and also from Mama, who would have known better and put a stop to it. But I was a fool and I was flattered and I listened to my sister's wicked ways – we should get Papa a portrait, and Gianni should paint it, after all he's Giotto.

How would we go about keeping it under our hats with

nobody knowing? Arianna said she had an idea, but I was sworn to complete secrecy, and if I spoke about it, the devil would cut my throat. She ran her finger beneath my chin, not touching me because that would bring Satan into the garden where she had managed to get me alone. What way was I planning to draw Daddy? I thought he would look nice in his favourite chair. That was too ordinary. Daddy should be greater than a man sitting down. She had another idea. Who was the greatest man who ever lived? Garibaldi? Greater than him. Michelangelo? Even greater. God the Father? At that suggestion she hit me for being so stupid. God the Father was not a man, was he? So who was the greatest? She did not wait this time for me to reply. She said it is Adam, of course, Adam who is our first parent from whom we are all descended. And that is who you should paint Papa dressed as, she said, he should be like Adam. But Adam is always naked, I pointed out, he doesn't wear clothes, have you ever seen him in a suit and shirt and shoes, have you? I challenged her.

She conceded she had not but said I was being stupid again, for this solved the problem rather than creating one. If Papa were to be Adam, then he should have no clothes on either. I burst out laughing, saying now she was the stupid one, how could I paint Papa naked? I would never see him like that, no one would be able to, but she said, hide. Where? Hide in the wardrobe – the big fat one with roses on the doors in their bedroom. Peep out when he doesn't know you're looking and is getting ready for his evening bath. Papa did steep himself in roasting water twice, sometimes three times a day. Mama would make sure that it was perfect for him to climb into, and we all did know when exactly he would wash himself. But will he not be angry if I sneak in on him with no clothes on? She assured me he was so proud of how I could draw he would be delighted I had been so clever to find a way to celebrate his birthday by honouring him and making him the greatest man who ever lived, Adam. Do it, she demanded, and so I did.

To this day I am terrified of naked men. The blacksmith I lodge with, Malachy, he has asked me often to take part in sports like boxing and football and I decline for I have no wish to strip to my bare flesh before complete strangers. A male body I can paint with no revulsion, provided I can avoid the gaze in his eyes and the creases in his cock and above all, the hairs on his arse. I do know why this is so. It goes back to my attempt to glimpse my bare father and the consequences that came upon me after I was caught.

He had removed his heavy boots and was sitting on their bed, the smell of his flesh still sweet from the morning wash. He raised each foot and with a little effort removed his socks, lifting them to his nose and sighing. Next he removed his white shirt, taking an age to unbutton it, suddenly seeming very tired and older than I had ever noticed him to be before. It was the first occasion that it had ever dawned on me that my parents were ageing, not growing old but not as young as I'd always seen them. I got a strong feeling growing in the pit of my stomach and I closed my eyes to say a prayer for it to pass. When I opened them again, my father was bone naked, reaching for his dressing gown and I could hear Arianna's voice calling Gianni, Gianni, where are you, Giotto? I heard her banging at the bed-room door, and the pain in my stomach grew even worse. He is not in here, Papa roared back at her, stop that racket. He is there, Papa, he is in there, Arianna squealed, he's hiding in the wardrobe, he told me he was going to and not to tell anyone, but I have to tell you, Papa.

He flung open the wardrobe doors and for some reason all I could do was smell the rosewood of the press. Now it was so strong that I thought I would vomit but instead I started to peepee because I was holding my stomach and forgot to put my hand between my legs to hold it in. By now my mother had burst into the bedroom, along with my treacherous sister. Mama was crying not about me but about the beautiful press, full of their best clothes – a family heirloom she had brought to Arezzo as part of her dowry, made many years ago by her uncle Tomasino, and here I was doing something unspeakable in it. I never knew my mother had a temper before, but now she was like a dog set on a stranger, and I saw the stranger in her too. Still in his dressing gown, my father watched the proceedings and said nothing.

From that day silence has been the sound of my father. For many years he never again spoke to me. He no longer looked at me. I was like a dead thing to him that had ceased to be in his existence. My mother's rage abated. She even pleaded my case before that implacable judge, but he maintained that he did not know what she was talking about. He could recall no such incident as she referred to. He had no memory of that individual or individuals involved; he must admit he found the details of what she was asking him to remember so distasteful that he would be obliged if she could restrain herself from talking of such filthy matters again. And I, his last-born son, was now soiled in his eyes, to be washed forever from the cleanliness of our family.

He began to call my brothers and sisters by their Christian names. Hairy Arse was Pablo, Roberto was no longer Rhino Snout, and he started to dote on his three Graces, his beautiful daughters, Caterina, Rosa and little Arianna, poor scarred Arianna, touched by God but loved by him also, having been given the joy of a beautiful nature, one that loved and honoured her father above all others, devoted to preserving his good name, and not mocking him in his prime as she would not in his dotage. She was the light of his life. The apple of his eye. A wise girl as well as a good girl, whose advice he now sought and followed, particularly when it came to disobedient children, intent on evil. Should he take away all that allowed me to do badness? Yes, she cajoled. My pencils and my paints, my paper confiscated. Should I be sent where temptation would be forever removed from me? Yes, it would be wise for me to do my penance, and to do it in a place where I would be watched like a hawk for any sign of my sin reappearing. And so it was I was banished to the mountains beyond Arezzo, sentenced not to return home until I had learned the prudence of never looking where I should not look, never saying what I should not say, never touching what I should not touch, never tasting what I should not taste nor smelling what I should not smell, a place to purge the senses from me, to do what my father now desired for me – to kill his Giotto.

❀ ❀ ❀

When I think of my years in that wilderness of a village, I can hear bells ringing. It is why I came to love that town in Donegal, that town without bells, where people tell the time from the sun, from the watch on their arms, from the cries, happy cries of children, released to play. Euni and Mena, they play so seriously. Sometimes they like to ask me what games did I play when I was a little boy? I shake my head and tell them there were none. Then they want to know how many toys I had? Again, none. They do not believe me. Was I very, very poor when I was a boy? Not always. My father was a teacher. Were you his pet? And again I shake my head. Was he very cross? They have a teacher, Miss Curren, and she is a terrible woman, slapping their hands with the leg of a chair, even their faces – she did that to Sarah McKinney because Sarah never knew her multiplication tables. They wished they had Miss Sewell in their school and not in the Protestant one because she was beautiful and smiled at you and said hello even though she didn't know you. So, was my father a crabbit teacher? They explained that crabbit meant being in a bad mood – like a bag of cats, Mena elaborated, and I could see my father tied in a sack fending off tigers ripping him apart, but it was all so long ago, the life he drove me to in that lonely place, I expelled such bad dreams immediately from my mind. And yet they would return, dreams of those days, in my exile from Arezzo.

My mother's eldest sister, she was a nun, a holy, strict woman. I was placed for my sin against my father under her care. She brought me to their isolated community where I was sent from my father's house to do what I did not know, in a place I had never been to, controlled by an aunt I had never met till she agreed to take complete charge of my life – work my fingers to the bone and work the badness out of these bones. Then I would be fit to be sent back, penitent, cleansed of evil, to where I belonged.

Again the girls interrupted my unhappy thoughts to know if I had any friends when I was little. This time I could tell them I did, and they wanted to find out were these friends boys or girls? When I said neither, they accused me of being a big fibber. What is that? I ask them. A liar, they tell me, how can your friends not have been boys and girls? Because they were sheep! This causes great excitement. Could they not have been boy and girl sheep? What colour were they, black or white? Did I eat any one of my friends? And why were my only friends sheep? I reply that when I was a child, I had to work in the fields with the animals. Mena says I was like Mary, who had a little lamb, it followed her to school one day and that's against the rule. Euni told her she was being silly, I was not called Mary, how could I be? But Mena said lots of boys have Mary as their middle name out of respect to the Blessed Virgin. Euni said it was still stupid – no, I was like Bo-Peep. And who is Bo-Peep? I ask. They squeal with joy because I do not know and speak in unison.

> Little Bo-Peep
> Has lost her sheep
> And doesn't know
> Where to find them.
> Leave them alone
> And they'll come home
> Wagging their tails
> Behind them.

That's who Bo-Peep was. And did I ever lose my sheep? I say no, but do not tell them that if I had done so, then I would have lost my life as well.

My aunt, Sr Magdalena, informed the village that indeed I may be her nephew, but I was not to be shown any favours. Keep his nose to the grindstone, never give him an idle moment, do not let him talk to you unless you talk to him, and above all never believe a word he says. More than that she would not say, and so naturally, I, the stranger, I became a curious topic of pro-longed conversation. I had been warned that on no account was I to confess to my original crime, for the shame of it wounded my whole family on both sides. Neither was I ever to give my name, for it would harm my father's reputation that the son of a respectable teacher was now in such a demeaning position. So what on earth could I have been? What could I have done to be driven here and punished like this?

The mountains were a place of many rumours. So little happened there that even the smallest incident needed much investigation and interpretation. The people here thrived on contradicting each other, for at least in argument they had something more to say to stretch out the long evenings and nights when hard work was complete and rest was needed. For some time after my arrival I was the great spur to their imaginations and they devised many stories as to the origins of the crime I had committed to drive me here to be punished. The first story was that I was a priest's son – or even a nun's – that's why I was under the control of the convent, but when wind of that fantasy reached the ears of my Aunt Magdalena, she loudly let it be known that if such a horror were true, I would have been put down at birth and she would have done it herself, safe in the conviction that heaven itself would forgive the extermination of such an abominable thing. So that was ruled out.

If the Church was not the agent of my wickedness, then perhaps it was the state, and even the very highest echelons of state were being referred to when the puzzle of myself was being debated. One woman who had been to Rome twice in her life fancied she saw a resemblance between me and the king himself. The others in that back-of-beyond had never seen his majesty, so what could they do but believe her? I might not be his son, but I may be of the royal blood, in which case was it possible that some great lady of a noblewoman had given birth to me and, when I came of age, I would come into a fortune and, in my kindness, if they showed me kindness, I would share this bounty and make the whole village rich? Hopes were being raised daily – raised to a frightening degree of probability. The woman who'd identified my similarity to our sovereign, she suddenly had the good sense to have second thoughts and spare herself the retaliation that would have taken place when these hopes of regal bounty were inevitably dashed. I was then no relation to our beloved monarch.

And yet there was something about me – the question persisted, what was it? I was good-mannered, thanking all who set me before the slop I had to eat. The cook in the convent, Sr Bonaventura, she said that I was a kindly boy, helping her do the dirtiest jobs of scrubbing pots and floors when I was allowed into the kitchen. I came obviously from a good family – Sr Magdalena was my aunt – but what could it be that made them want rid of me? Bonaventura took it on herself to discover precisely what brought me here amongst them and why I was, to all intents and purposes, abandoned there, for no letters ever arrived for me, nobody ever called to see me, no one seemed to mind if I lived or died. What could be at the root of it?

Though she may only be in charge of the food and have no teaching duties, Bonaventura prided herself on her sharp intelligence. When an entire cheese disappeared for the third time in a month from a larder, she sat up three nights in a row to find the culprit. And she did, despite the ludicrous jokes that it was a whole family of gypsy mice storing up provisions for their long trek back to the family den deep in Transylvania. This actually cut her to the quick more than anyone could know, for she suspected she had Roma blood in her veins from her jet-black-haired grandmother's side. But so deeply concealed was that stain that she was certain no-one on earth, and for that matter in the heavens, could detect the connection. This was why she had stopped including as part of her prayers to God a wish to forget she had ever heard so harmful a rumour. Still, she had an excellent nose for smelling out how people managed to survive and that could well have been down to the instincts of the gypsy in her soul, instincts that ensured she would never, ever go under without the fiercest of fights. And perhaps I too was part of her abandoned tribe?

No, she would discard that. Impossible to imagine that snobbish bitch Magdalena having even the whiff of the smell of the camp fire about her limbs. And what was even stranger was that her pride seemed not in the slightest bit diminished since I had arrived to the community. If anything, she seemed to be radiating even more rays of her self importance. It would be so lovely to discover something against me and bring my arrogant aunt down a peg or two. That woman treated the kitchen staff like dirt, for all the vows of poverty she professed to take. She knew for a fact that Magdalena made a point of washing her plate before putting her morsel of food on it. At one time her refusal to tuck into the plain but well cooked bill of fare seemed as if she were on a permanent fast, offering her hunger as a gift to Jesus, but now Magdalena's near starvation diet smacked to Bonaventura of one-upmanship – a display to all and sundry that she was above such mundane matters as eating. She refused all offers of another helping with a smile and delicate wave that made Bonaventura want to break her fragile arm. But this was no way for two nuns to behave, and she disciplined herself by eating as little, if not less, than her frail enemy. Perhaps it was the deprivation of food that brought on her suspicion – maybe even her hallucination – that we were all on the wrong track in finding out what badness had brought me here. Maybe it was something the opposite, something good, even perhaps something holy?

She started to watch me shepherding the lambs in the fields and grew quite convinced that I had more than a mere authority over these creatures. I appeared to understand what they were thinking. They would do anything for me. And my way of communicating with them was music. I first became aware of her when I was sitting on a rock, playing the pipes of Pan to my sheep. I had mastered the simple instrument quite easily, and since all drawing materials, paints and crayons, pencils and paper, were removed from me, my fingers itched to do something beautiful with my hands. The animals loved that strange sound, grazing or sleeping at my feet. They would follow me with such trust in their eyes that I came to love and recognise each of their faces. Sr Bonaventura listened to me playing my lonely laments and said nothing – nothing – just walked away, looking back at me. She was now convinced she knew what had happened.

I had witnessed a miracle, that was one possibility she rejected. The light that seemed to circle me demanded more. No, it was not a miracle, but a vision I had seen. And to protect me from the marauding hordes of sightseers and well wishers, I had been packed off into obscurity where I would be subjected to the harshest of treatment so that my piety would not be tarnished. I would avoid all the attention showered on those whom God had honoured with an apparition of himself, his mother, or his saints. My sad face was the clincher for Sr Bonaventura. I had glimpsed something of the next world, and that would haunt me for the rest of my days. But what could it be? She was determined not to rest until she had investigated this mystery down to its last detail.

To do this she would, like all the best detectives, need an assistant, and her chosen ally was the young scullery maid, Claudia. Her teeth had made that unfortunate girl a suitable candidate for the nunnery. They were the colour of spinach and the size of bent fingers. Her mouth resembled a green claw and she didn't so much enter the world of the convent as charge in uninvited and adamantly refuse to leave. The devout abbess, Mother Clothilde, for the first and only time, was heard to utter an unkind word when she suggested – it was, in fact, a demand – that Claudia never, ever be let work anywhere but in the scullery and on rare occasions the kitchen. Never, ever, no matter what illness might befall anyone, was she to be allowed to serve in the dining room. The sight of that face only God could love, and for all her piety, Mother Clothilde was not God.

Claudia, being grateful for her life of refuge among the sisters, took each and every one of her appointed tasks with the utmost seriousness. This meant that she watched me at every available opportunity. It happened with such regularity that most of the time I forgot about her eyes boring into me. If I had been a truly wicked boy, I would have tormented the girl, dashing here and there about the fields, but I was content to play my music and let her rest, now that she was under special dispensation from Bonaventura to do next to nothing other than to have me constantly in her presence. When she finally spoke to me, it was to ask how I had learned to play such lovely tunes? I had been taught never to answer questions, so I simply shook my head as if I had not understood her and continued to delight my flock. I was taken suddenly aback by her scream. Dear God in heaven, I was deaf, she cried, and yet there was no doubt that I could make these magnificent melodies. This was a miracle, and she had been granted grace to hear it. God had granted me a wonderful gift, poor wretch that I was. The news was too good to keep to herself.

Soon they were arriving in droves to touch me and pray with me. Mother Clothilde put a stop to this nonsense. The boy is not deaf – he hears as well as you or me. He had no special powers whatsoever – he is simply a poor relation of one of our sisters and we give him food and shelter as our order obliges us to do. He is an ordinary boy, so please, go home now, good people, and say your prayers that you may always be wise enough never to fall for the tall stories of fools and liars. Claudia did not like to be included in the class of fools and liars, but this was Mother Clothilde speaking and what she said went. She did, however, manage to get word by hook or by crook to the abbess that she was not the only one to believe strange things about myself. Sr Bonaventura started it.

Of course I knew the child wasn't deaf, Sr Bonaventura defended herself, I knew that physically there was nothing wrong with him. But there was something else, something not quite right. What would that be, pray tell us? my Aunt Magdalena, who was in on this interrogation, demanded to know. There was between these ladies a hatred quite shocking in women of the cloth. I would prefer not to divulge that to anyone but Reverend Mother, Bonaventura simpered to her superior. Bonaventura was a large peasant squeezed into the habit of a refined order, and simpering did not look natural to her. The sheer grotesquery of this behaviour enraged my aunt and the attempt to exclude her from the discussion shocked her so much that she was sufficiently silenced for Mother Clothilde to suggest she leave them. For once Magdalena did as she was bid without complaint.

–Well now, the floor is yours, what is it you find strange about this boy?

–May I answer that question with another question? Why is this child here in the first place?

–He had been seriously spoilt and was misbehaving at home.

Sister Magdalena asked could he come here to work as a shepherd boy far from the bad influences that were shaping his character. She feared for his nature, as did his family. They wished to remove him from the luxury of his life in Arezzo and sent him to this village where he would learn that in this world we survive only by the sweat of our brow. I believe he has learned that lesson.

—With due respects, Reverend Mother, you may believe so, but I do not credit a word of this whole story.

—Are you telling me I'm a liar?

—No, I'm telling you you have been lied to. By Sister Magdalena.

—Why would she dare do such a thing?

—Because that boy has some power, some extraordinary divine power, and she alone wishes to know of it and to use that knowledge when the opportunity presents itself.

—Opportunity for what?

—To depose you. Now I've said it, and if you wish, I will defend myself.

—You had better.

—Then I will. You know that woman is as proud as Satan, disagreeable to everyone, looking down her long nose at us all.

—She is good to the poor.

—She hates the poor. She hates every single other person, except her family. And she brings one of her own here to use to her advantage.

—What advantage is that?

189

–He has powers, the boy.

–What powers?

–He plays music to the beasts of the field, and they understand him. He looks into their faces and reads what they have to tell. He knows the secrets of animals and of the birds in the air. His song is their song. The whole universe is chanting in harmony with his playing. It comes through a divine being, and he is Sister Magdalena's nephew. She hides him away here until the opportune moment when all will be revealed. The boy will be venerated. Then you will be answerable to her, and she will have the revenge on me that she's long plotted. We have to act fast and stop her plan. Our best means of attack is the boy himself. We must let him know we know what is going on.

–I'm still not sure what is going on. These powers you claim he possesses, where did he get them?

–He saw a vision – an apparition.

–Of what?

–If I can put two and two together, and I do have a logical mind, there is only one possible answer to that.

–Which is?

–Francis of Assisi. He saw Saint Francis of Assisi. That's why he has such power with animals.

There are times in one's life when choices, stark choices, must be made, and they will dictate the rest of your existence. Mother Clothilde knew this was just such an occasion. She could expel Bonaventura from the convent, from the village, if necessary from Italy itself, or she could believe this dream. Crossing herself, falling on her knees, she chose to do the latter, and my penance was ended, for she was devoted to that saint of Assisi.

And for that I gave thanks. Thanks to anyone who'd listen to me. Unfortunately my aunt was not in a position to receive it as she was moved overnight to an enclosed order somewhere in the Alps and no one heard from her for many years. But if Magdalena had vanished from the scene, Mother Clothilde took her place as my new tormentor, only now it was done in the form of kindness. She confessed to me that when she was at the beginning of her career, she would have chosen Francis as her nun's name had it been up to her. But the family expected her to honour a grandmother on her father's side who had died recently and whose dearest wish was to see one of her children's children take the veil. So Clothilde it would be. Did I think that was sufficient reason for St Francis to forgive her?

I knew nothing about Bonaventura's speculations. I had no idea why I should have access to St Francis, but I liked this new regime of flattery, so I told Clothilde what she wanted to hear and reassured her she had acted for the best. I was inclined to believe, such was the good turn my fate had taken, that everyone everywhere was acting for the best, but things were beginning to puzzle me greatly. Why were gangs of villagers starting to arrive at the convent door carrying sick animals? Why were they asking me to bless them and the little creatures in their arms? The nuns in the know realised word about me had spread through the community and soon the source of the information was all too obvious.

Claudia again was the culprit. She had now her moment in the sun. She had been right all along about me, and even if she got it wrong in the detail, she still was right more or less in the essentials. There was something miraculous in me, and she was one of the first to notice. Even in my darkest days of deprivation, she now claimed, she'd slip me an extra slice of meat to supplement my meagre diet. She knew the want I was kept in but she tried to do her best and feed me up a bit so that I would not perish from the cold on the mountainside where my only companions were the sheep I minded. Now God had been good to her and rewarded her munificence towards me by allowing her to see how he blessed me in my tribulation. What this meant was that she had to blab what she'd found out to everyone who crossed her path in the village.

For once nobody noticed the green teeth, so keen were they to hear the wonders pouring forth from her mouth as she told them of my many marvellous abilities. It was from her that they heard about the visit of St Francis and when asked if, like that particular saint, I shared the stigmata of Our Saviour, how could she resist holding her tongue and saying she didn't know? Instead she let it be known it was more than likely I had, she could not say for sure, but in not saying for sure she strongly hinted that indeed I did have the marks of Christ's wounds imprinted at the appropriate spots on my body, my gift from the man himself for receiving his vision. She couldn't – she wouldn't swear to it, but she did know for certain that he had given me the power to heal sick animals.

Imagine the effect such an announcement made on a population of country people. There was the good news they had long been waiting for. A miracle cure for their beasts of burden to undo the toil of ages they had beaten them into performing. A remedy for what might ail their most treasured livestock to get more milk, to live longer, to thrive better, and all to put more money in their always empty pockets. There were some amongst them so sure of my sacred status they said they could no more look me in the face than they would raise their eyes and gaze on the host at the point of consecration come Sunday Mass. That was how much faith they'd put in me and my workings, and that was why it was decided by Clothilde and Bonaventura that they would deny all access to me. The early decision to shield me from the world, now they could begin to see the wisdom behind its cruelty. Not that they would sentence me to return to the fields – no, that was the punishment passed onto Claudia for shooting her mouth off so easily and bringing this unforeseen trouble on the convent and its inhabitants.

But something had to be decided one way or another. What were they going to do with me? A decision was in a strange way made for them by one of the consequences of Claudia's loose talk. It involved the village blacksmith. When I first arrived in Donegal and that priest let me know I would be lodging where he'd arranged with the O'Donovans, the sight of the forge – how can I describe what it did to me? That trade had such a powerful impact on my life; in many ways it was the saving of me as a painter, and here is why.

At that time in that part of Italy, that savage time, that savage part, the blacksmith performed many functions. He did much more than shoe horses and weld irons for gates and railings. He was for many people, because he worked with fire, a kind of magic man – these were a primitive people – and as close to someone with some knowledge of medicine as they would ever meet. Not everyone trusts such a man to deal with their own aches and pains, but they did certainly go to him when their beasts needed healing hands laid upon them, or skilled eyes to see beneath their hides at what was the matter with them. And even if most of them couldn't rise to a small payment for these services rendered – some considered it positively unlucky to offer money – they still could leave on the anvil – always on the anvil – gifts of cheese and honey, a wife's best beautiful pasta or good socks knitted for a wedding, perhaps a piece of meat or the ripest, tastiest vegetables growing in their garden. Always a thank you for what the blacksmith, called Bruno I recall – for what Bruno had done for them. And now I had come along and threatened a substantial part of his livelihood. He must fix me right and proper.

Bruno was a drinker. The dogs in the street knew this. He was decidedly the worse for wear when he staggered around the village, cursing me and all my doings. We got warning of it first when Claudia tore into the kitchen, screaming Bruno the blacksmith was going to kill me. Mother Clothilde remained placid in the face of this panic, and calmly ordered that some cakes and some wine be placed in the room where she received callers. If the gentleman causing this upheaval should chance to drop in, he was to be greeted warmly and fetched into her presence. There should be no attempt to manhandle such a large individual – this was directed specifically at Bonaventura, whose muscles we could feel being flexed at the thought of knocking the drunken sot into a corner. But this was not Clothilde's way. She maintained things could be better settled through peaceful means.

Bruno did not expect Claudia to open the doors immediately when he came shouting, looking for the little bastard whose neck he would wring. He did not expect to be greeted politely as he was led roaring down the corridors past smiling nuns bowing sweetly to him while he still continued to issue violent threats against my person. He was in a state of deep shock when he found himself in an airy room full of white curtains blowing gently in what seemed like a scented breeze and was told Reverend Mother would be with him shortly. His reply was that Claudia had a face that was made for a good hiding and he would do it only she might bite him and give him rabies. Claudia gave him no back-answer, but said she would bear the warning in mind and if he would excuse her she would find the holy sister, please help himself to food and drink.

When she left, Bruno took a deep slug of the stuff and was delighted to find that it was as good a wine as any he'd ever tasted. He even had the unusual sensation of wishing he had imbibed less on that day so his palate could enjoy the savour of this beautiful vintage more. The second slug confirmed the excellence of the first, and it was when he had the bottle in his fist lifted to his mouth that Mother Clothilde entered to greet him by his first name, embracing him, scolding him for not giving her a little advance notice of his visit so she could have prepared something more substantial for him than this paltry fare, for which, nevertheless, he expressed his thanks. She shrugged it away and immediately asked after his mother, inquiring how she managed since the death of his dear father whom she remembered in her prayers each morning. Bruno told her that Mama still pined for Papa and how she only wanted to die and be reunited in Paradise with the husband whose life she had – it was common knowledge – she had made a hell through most of their marriage. Ah, Bruno, my dear child, Clothilde sighed, we suffer – women suffer, but we must cope. But what am I thinking of? She chastised herself, where are my manners? That foolish girl, Claudia, she has not given you a glass nor a plate. Here, let me feed you these morsels, let me pour for you.

He said he could not intrude any longer, but she would not hear of him leaving without a little hospitality. Wine, wine, drink some wine. He still refused. Cakes, cakes, eat some cakes at least. There was now a plate in his hand. Sit down, she commanded, and tell me all your news about yourself. You are still searching for the right girl to marry? He blushed and nodded. She smiled gently, saying she understood, it was hard to find a wife when Mama was bad with her nerves and needed constant attention. Especially as she had taken – so Claudia had informed the convent – to wandering naked through the forge looking to have her feet shod, but Clothilde decided this was not the time nor place to entertain such delicate issues. She did feel she should point out that years were pressing on and he should not leave it too late to find a suitable girl. But he was hardly likely, she joked, to find such a creature in this convent, unless he wanted to take Claudia off their hands. All she had to bring with her as a dowry was the excellent set of gnashers, but Clothilde felt sure a big fine hardy man like Bruno might want more in a bride. Clothilde knew when to appeal to the common touch, and gnashers seemed the right touch to describe Claudia's monstrosity of a mouth. So, to get to the point, why was he here?

I myself was the cause and the culprit, he informed her. I had the cure for sick creatures, he'd heard it claimed. I would be taking the bite from his mouth. It was hard enough making ends meet with a sick mother to tend to, without this on top of all the hard struggles in his life. And he was here because he wanted to know what Mother Clothilde was going to do about it? She said she was now all the more glad to see him – wasn't he always an intelligent boy? Didn't his saintly father have the wisdom of Solomon to pass on his trade to his son and wasn't he proved right once again from beyond the grave, God have mercy on his soul and on all our souls. At this she held out her thin elegant hand to Bruno and he took it in what she noticed was his surprisingly small and shaking grip. She assured him that there was nothing to worry about. But Bruno asked what exactly was she going to do with this miracle worker that could put him and his to the side of the road? Well, first she was going to call Sr Bonaventura and the boy, and if he would be so good as to excuse her she'd ring the bell. She paused before doing so to look at and comment on its exquisite workmanship. Do you recognise the hand that crafted that? she asked Bruno. He nodded, and started to weep. Yes, this was made – this simple bell – by his dead father. A gift to the nuns for the safe delivery of a son. And that son was – well, wasn't she looking at him in front of her? Bruno was now cradling the bell at his breast, whispering Papa, Papa. Clothilde let him have his moment but then said they really should get this matter with the boy settled. But it would be nice if Bruno rang the bell and summoned us to the reception room.

That was when I first set eyes on him, as I stood hand in hand with Sr Bonaventura who was shooting daggers at him, reminding him that if he made one false move she might have any assortment of blunt instruments about her person to flatten him like a pancake should she feel the need to. But Bruno was now meek as a lamb – a rather large, unkempt, wine-sodden lamb admittedly, that would never frolic too freely in its pastures but might even run into the slaughter house to escape the weight of itself. There you both are, Clothilde declared, and must be wondering why you're here. Well, I didn't ring the bell – Bruno did – he called for you – so I'll let him do the talking and shan't interrupt.

Speak up then, Bonaventura snapped, I haven't got all day. Get to the point – why send for us? Bruno explained his respect for nuns, but she said that was irrelevant. She had respect for the birds of the air, they were all created by God, but she didn't go around demanding that they come to her beck and call as if they owed her an audience, so he could stop the flattery and spell out what he wanted and why he was here. Was it her tone that turned his temper so quickly? Was it something she said? Did he have an aversion to the birds of the air? Whatever it was, he changed in the instant from a docile and obedient man, full of respect for the reverend sisters, into a demon possessed by hatred of humanity in general and of me in particular, because it was on me he leapt – the whole bulk of him – me, a boy that he hurled to the ground with the full force of his fist. I was too winded to cry, too frightened to scream, already too much in pain to curl up in a ball and protect any part of me from the blows raining down on me, delivered with all his grown man's strength. He is a child, a fragile child, Mother Clothilde was pounding her fists against this madman, you will break him in two. That was the last thing I heard before my head received the point of his boot, and I now knew he would either kick me to death or leave me blind in both eyes. In that instant I also knew I would prefer death to darkness. If I by some chance, some true miracle, survived this onslaught, I would draw again – I would paint no matter what hardship that meant I'd face, or what obstacles were put in front of my ambition. It would not be fair to say that since arriving at that village I had not been allowed to make art. I had instead stopped myself from doing so, but now the instinct returned to me, and I will always maintain it saved my life, for in that extremity of this murderous attack on my person, it was as if my spirit stepped outside my physical body and from some strange height in the ceiling of this room I could observe all that was happening to and around me in that torture chamber of perfect architectural proportions, its cream walls, its magnificent windows looking into the gardens of the well-run farm, my sheep gathering in its peaceful lush meadows, perhaps still waiting for their lost shepherd's return, but he was delayed, having fallen at the feet of this bull of a man, breath steaming from his mouth in a shower of filth, obscenities hurling from him as rapidly as the blows of his boots on top of the soft boy, two women in black suspended in shock, sensing that they were seeing a child being beaten to death, lamenting their lot to the god they believed in, the god they had given their life to, and if he had not quite deserted them, I could see from my vantage point above this fracas, he had certainly deserted me.

It was then I saw the bell in Mother Clothilde's roaring hand, and the bottle swinging down on Bruno's head, breaking in the rampant fist of Sr Bonaventura, the bell cascading in torrents of sound right through to his brain, cracking his skull and pealing as it killed him, re-echoing like mad through the convent. Then it was over as quickly as it had begun. He and I lay still on the ground, me feeling its coldness against the bloodied heat of my wounds, him dead to this world and now awaiting judgement in the next. The women held each other and wept tears of relief. They realised that they had done what was necessary. There was sufficient of the knight in courtly Mother Clothilde and enough of the peasant in Sr Bonaventura to know that this man was an animal no longer in control of its strength, and needed to be put down. This they did without regret, and after their embrace they stood above the creature they had felled with two blows. Ever practical, Sr Bonaventura wondered who would tell his mother. Even more practical, Mother Clothilde said that the old lady was now in her dotage and would not take it in, so it didn't matter who told her. That was that problem solved. The much more pressing one was how to save my life. They felt that must be their urgent responsibility, for they vaguely accepted that their enthusiasm for my sacred vision had placed me in this jeopardy and it was therefore essential they, and no other nun, nurse me back to health.

They did this with great solicitude, and my heart was sore because these good women did not know the source of my great shame, shame that should have prevented me from receiving such duteous care as I was receiving. It was time to tell Mother Clothilde what had happened to bring me here. I tried to explain I had never seen any vision of St Francis. I was just an ordinary boy who had deeply upset his parents. This was my confession to her, yet she stopped me as soon as I said that word. Hearing confession – that is a priest's job, not for the like of her, a mere sister. No, such sacraments are best left to men, but she could do one thing – she could partake in what she considered women's work – and the greatest act any lady can perform is to forgive. The first sign of forgiveness is a gift. What did she have in her power to grant to me?

So it was when I made a request for drawing materials, it was instantly granted. And they beamed with maternal pleasure when they saw the portraits I could so quickly provide for them. Coming so near to losing my powers of vision – that concentrated the eyes marvellously, and the hand did as they bid it do. Bruno may have threatened to punch the daylights, literally, out of me, but I had hung on to fight another battle, and the proof of that was my pretty sketches now being hung all over the convent walls. And seeing them sketched there, Mother Clothilde had a wonderful idea. Each nun slept in her separate cell, a plain white walled room, with no ornamentation other than a prayer book on the wooden chair, a brown slab of table, a crucifix on top of it, and the only colour the shafts of light whitening the gloom, catching the showers of dust that evaporated from the ancient furniture and decaying flesh of those who slept there. Why not decorate each of these bare chambers with a scene from the life of each sister's favourite saint as an aid to devotion? Who better to do the necessary than myself, the brave little soldier whose life they had saved for the glory of the faith? This was to be my mission, having cheated death and come back to them to complete this great task.

That is how I started what was my first commission. I was so small I had to stand on a ladder to reach the most suitable part of every wall on which I was to execute my painting. My limited skills could not really rise to a whole series of different episodes from the lives of various saints. So it was confirmed I would paint over and over again Mother Clothilde's idea of how St Francis looked. Each cell would be unique only in so far that I would include a different animal or bird, beast or insect, flower or tree as a tiny detail on the separate walls. And since Francis was always to be portrayed according to her instruction – looking remarkably like the Reverend Mother with the notable addition of a beard – I took greatest delight in the diversity of the detail. The sisters loved to gather unusual flowers and plants, mushrooms and feathers, even dead birds, their wings stretched out in pitiful colours, frogs the cats deposited at the kitchen doorstep, all were delivered to me and I would breathe them back to life on the walls. The most unusual demand came from Sr Bonaventura.

She did not want anything from nature in her cell painting. She demanded instead that in its topmost corner I place a map of Africa. I now had sufficient confidence in myself to ask why. It was on that continent she had first heard the call of her vocation to enter the sisterhood. Hers was a military family. Her father had entered that profession at its very lowest ranks but worked his way up, and her brother had followed in his footsteps, becoming a general, a very well known and powerful general, much respected by all who served in the army, well known and well liked by Il Duce himself. She provided me with a model of all the countries of Africa and I copied it dutifully for her. When I asked if she would like some fierce beast from the jungle to stand within the map and frighten Satan away, she told me she had never any fear of that individual. There was the best warrior blood in all Italy racing through her veins. She would tackle the Prince of Darkness any day and send him packing, for she had learned, as her brother had learned, at her Papa's knee that the only way to deal with a ruthless enemy was to exterminate him ruthlessly, absolutely, with no hint of clemency.

Clemency was the motto of the order she belonged to. It was, she knew too well, at the very core of her Christian beliefs. But there were times when it was absolutely necessary to turn a blind eye to the demands of the meek if they were to inherit an earth that was worth having. This was what her blood connections with the best soldiers in Europe had opened her eyes to – sometimes to be kind one had to be cruel, it was time I began to appreciate that. I was no longer a little child. I was growing into a young man, and when I lost the innocence of childhood, she was certain I would lose my divine protection and so need to defend my own corner.

How could I be divinely protected when Bruno had nearly battered me to death? The fact that she and Mother Clothilde were there to save me, to her that was sufficient proof the Lord in his heaven was minding me well, but there had to come a time when this would stop and now I must make my decision in what way I would earn my living, for the time was soon coming when I must leave the sanctuary of the convent behind me. I was far too puny for my own good, she claimed. She knew the best way to toughen me up, I had spent too long in the company of women. She would write to her brother and see to it that I would be well looked after when I enlisted. And she knew the man to convince me why. I was a lucky lad. Her brother the general was due a visit. He would tell me all. And he did.

The general sat surrounded by the adoring nuns. Sr Bonaventura was in pride of place, her red face a match to the balloon of her brother's. No one dared interrupt his sagas of the most recent campaigns in Africa. Every so often she would applaud, and the others, with the exception of Mother Clothilde, followed suit. The general would eye her, and she would smile sweetly at him. That was sufficient encouragement to continue telling his glorious tales. He stopped to gulp down his coffee, and before resuming his hymn to the worship of Italian bravery, Sr Bonaventura was pointing at me and saying, Ricardo, this boy – he is the future of our beloved country and the empire she shall build to last a thousand years in Africa. Tell him, my dearest, bravest brother, tell him what is Africa to you? He breathed deeply, taking me in, and then he started.

–Africa is blood. An ocean of blood. The body of Christ risen on the cross, shattered, pouring, the River Jordan baptising every man, every women, every child of that till now cursed continent in the torrents of their own blood. Swim through it, young man, and it stains you forever, steeped in the stench and sewers of blood. When I close my eyes, I am always there. When I open them, I am always there. I have Africa now in my bones and in my blood. You must dare to go with the flow of blood. Dare to march into battle with me in Africa.

–Tell him about Cyrenacia, tell him, Ricardo, what you had to do in Cyrenacia.

–With pleasure. They are vermin who live there, rats and lice, no homes to go to, wandering through the sands of Libya, and with the most almighty notions about themselves, considering us their inferiors, if you please. Led by a barbarian, Omar al Mukhtar. Remember that name, boy, fear that name, dear sisters. All good women should tremble at that hellish name. They are a people without culture. They have no idea of a civilised life.

–What did this man, Omar– Omar–? I stammered.

–Omar al Mukhtar.

–What did he do? Is he like Il Duce?

The good sisters rapidly fingered their rosary beads, offering hasty decades to the Virgin, pleading silently that the general would not shoot me where I stood for making such a hideous comparison. But the general burst out laughing, reddening his face even more, slapping his thighs till I imagined they too were red beneath his trousers.

–Is the child simple-minded? Mussolini is a military and political genius. The saviour of our race, the triumph of our people – he will lead us to the greatest glories our beloved country can imagine, and he will be as good a father to his little children across the waves in Africa, if they are not naughty and disgrace themselves with their bad behaviour. So concerned is he for the welfare of these people that he had me organise them to march into safe compounds when that revolting Al Mukhtar creature was urging them to revolt. Imagine the difficulty of shepherding one hundred thousand beings, none too marked with intelligence, across the Libyan deserts. And of course when we do get them safely ensconced, comfortable and ready to avail of the best medicine, the most efficient and hygienic way to live, they are too stupid to appreciate our efforts and soil the splendid places so badly that inevitably diseases run rampant. I call myself chosen by Our Blessed Lord himself to be spared the epidemic of typhoid that struck because of their ignorant ways. The same typhoid took forty thousand of them, and between us and God's good grace, they deserved it.

–Did they not try to escape? Mother Clothilde asked, and she had now stopped smiling.

–Sweet Mother, did I not describe them from the first as vermin? As rats? That was how they attempted to swarm to safety. There was only one way to stop them.

–So you built a wall, a high wall to keep them in? Sr Bonaventura asked to help her brother out.

–No, more a fence – I would describe it as a fence.

–What was it made from? I asked.

–This little soldier wants to know the ins and outs of everything. I admire that thoroughness. It shows a fine logical mind. A military mind.

–It does nothing of the sort, Mother Clothilde contradicted him, and the general's face showed he was not a man used to contradiction, so, in the manner of such men, he ignored her completely to continue telling us about his fence.

–Barbed wire. Kilometre after kilometre after kilometre of barbed wire. Four metres deep. Fancy falling into that, young fellow? Not like scratching yourself on the thorns of roses to give to your little sweetheart. No, there was so much barbed wire Il Duce himself joked to me that I was keeping that industry going, just to supply my needs in Africa. And it did the job, I maintain. We had them isolated. But there was more to be done. We called in the bombers to give our boys on the ground a bit of support. And in the end we got our man. Old Omar walked into our trap.

–What did you do to him?

–We did what should be done to all traitors. He was sentenced to death. He had insulted and betrayed the motherland.

–Not his motherland, Mother Clothilde pointed out.

–Libya is a colony of the motherland. We hanged him in the camp in front of his followers.

–And so you made him a martyr, Mother Clothilde concluded, a martyr to his own people, a martyr to his entire race of Arabs, a martyr to the whole world.

–I recognise no martyr except those who have bathed in the sacrificial blood of Christ. I have no truck with infidels and heathens trading under the holy name of martyr. No, I let him swing, and I let the rest of the vermin see him swing, and I won the war.

—It has not started yet, this war, and when it does, fools like you will make sure it will spread everywhere and come to destroy us all. Yes, Bonaventura, you did hear me. I called your glorious general of a brother a fool, and in that I am restraining myself. He drops bombs and worse on innocent families. He slices them to death. He leaves what precious little they possess in pieces. He hounds them into camps where all they can look forward to is the release of death. And what does the fool expect in return? I do believe it is gratitude, it is loyalty. He expects they will be true to an Italy that does nothing but devour them. Thank God they are not as big fools as this nincompoop is. Thank God when the time comes they will know what to do to rid their land of his kilometre after kilometre after kilometre of barbed wire. You speak of vermin, great general. Yes, there is much of it in Libya, but it is us, the likes of me so ashamed to be Italian, and the likes of you and that other greater, more dangerous, that truly suicidal fool, Il Duce himself, who will not be content until he is shot down in ignominy, and brings our country with him.

Sr Bonaventura was white as a sheet. It was as if Reverend Mother had somehow borrowed one of the general's bombs and dropped it in that room. She has said the unsayable. And now we waited for the reply. When he spoke though, it was not to Clothilde. It was to me.

—And when do you wish to join the army?

But I could not answer. For I was watching Mother Clothilde, and to my amazement there were loads of tears falling down her cheeks. She was shaking with grief, or maybe it was with rage? For the first time also, she reminded me of my own mother, that woman I had nearly forgotten, when she too transformed herself before my eyes in paroxysms of anger. And my heart swelled to breaking point with my desire to go home, to be allowed to see Arezzo, to talk and touch my own.

−When do you wish to join the army? The general repeated. I have not spared you the hardships a man must face if he follows that path in life. The terrible decisions we face. These shock the good ladies, but they have never had to confront a mob of barbarians determined to drain the blood of yourself and the men you command, the comrades you must save as they would save your skin. It is the roughest of all roads to travel, but it is the best, and if, as this good Mother Clothilde insists, I am a fool, then so be it, let me be a fool who loves his foolishness, who lives and dies by it, for all that he loves so foolishly can be summed up in a single word, and that word is Italy. You are young, but you are of an age when you must ask yourself, would you die for love? Would you die for Italy? Do you wish to join the army?

By this stage of proceedings, Mother Clothilde had stopped weeping and stopped shaking. Her usual calm had returned. She looked not at me nor at the general nor even at Bonaventura. She waited for my decision as if it had ceased to matter, as if it had never mattered to her what I would decide. And so I could think of only one answer to win back her desire that I do the right thing. I said, no, sir, I do not wish to become a soldier. I know what I want to do. I want to be a priest.

I heard him snort with laughter. A little nervously, Sr Bonaventura joined in. And Mother Clothilde, she simply said, a priest, is that right, Gianni? Yes, Reverend Mother, I replied. Then a priest you shall be, she decided.

❖ ❖ ❖

But that was not the case. My father wouldn't hear of it. His hatred had not abated. The years of absence had not softened him. His heart was still stone. He did not melt to the entreaties of Mother Clothilde. At long last I told her precisely why, and the reaction of that wise and gentle woman utterly confounded me. She laughed as if her heart would break saying my family were all mad, from Magdalena down to this idiot who called himself my Papa. I think she expected me to side with her, but it is an old and true saying, blood is thicker than water, and to tell the truth, I was shocked and a little distressed by her behaviour. They may have more or less disowned me for my transgression, but my people were from a distinguished line of public servants, and deserved more than to be ridiculed in such a manner. I was grateful to the nun for all her many acts of charity towards me, and she had proved herself to be a great ally in my painting, but I could not side with her in this ludicrous evaluation of Mama and Papa.

I took courage and dared to write to them myself. I offered sincere and abject apologies for all I had done to offend them. Every morning and every night, I said an entire Act of Contrition to God, begging forgiveness, because I had hurt my dear, loving parents. At Angelus time, when the bells rang, I said my prayers and offered them up in the hope of their happiness. Now all I asked was that they permit me to serve as an ordained minister of Christ, so that I could at last bring credit through my actions to my suffering Mama and Papa and atone for my past misdeeds. When Mother Clothilde read my letter, she advised me not to send it. The sight of my handwriting, the echo of my voice, were sure to enrage their furious hearts even more. She dreaded what their response might be. But I defied her and pleaded that it might be sent to them, telling them of all I had accomplished in my exile.

I was now in my fifteenth year. A boy my age turning into a man could not expect to stay in a holy convent. I needed to know my future. And then came the letter that decided it for me. Not from my parents, but from a priest in Arezzo, Fr Stefano. Mother Clothilde read it to me, and I had to ask her to do so again, as I was so excited to hear my news I did not take in the contents at first. She read it more slowly, and then I knew what was to be done with me. Fr Stefano sent warm greetings and the blessings of God to Mother Clothilde, but on the express instructions of my father, he himself withheld all such pleasantries and prayers from me. The priest though could appreciate something needed to be done about this unfortunate case. The kind sisters had dealt with this dilemma for too long, and now it was time to settle the affair once and for all. Stefano had taken upon himself, with the agreement of the good people who brought this boy into the world, a solution he hoped might be for the benefit of all, not least myself, the source of all this trouble. He was glad that hard work and deprivation had opened my eyes to the reality of my nature and the need to change it. He was also pleased that I had knuckled down and mastered at least the basics of a trade in painting. My parents, however, adamantly refused to countenance any further training in that profession, being of the mind I could encounter the type of creature in that career who would drag me back to my dreadful ways. Nor would they ever entertain my studying at a seminary. They were shocked to the core at such a request and were unmovable on this matter. But they had come to Fr Stefano for assistance and advice, and this is what he proposed, which had proved acceptable to Mama and Papa, and he hoped would be so to all parties concerned. His small church in Arezzo, Santa Maria in Gradi, it was fully staffed. All of the few who worked there had been in the parish's employ for many years. When they passed on, their sons and daughters would rightly expect their offspring to step into their shoes and earn their living, as generations of their families had done before. At the mention of that name Santa Maria in Gradi, I tried to remember where it was and what it looked like, but Arezzo was now so far away from me that even though for a long time in my mind's eye I had walked through its streets, climbed its steep hills, knelt and begged that I might return to its places of worship, I could barely recall where this was located, and I listened to the remainder of the letter.

One afternoon, looking for a way forward, Stefano left the church to get a breath of fresh air and bumped into a pair of fellow priests, Andrea and Bonifacio, in a dreadful hurry. He hoped there had not been an accident, and barely stopping, they replied there had indeed – a shocking one. A young sacristan had shot himself in the vestry of the Church of St Francis where they were curators, and they had been called to go there immediately and deal with this dreadful event and its consequences. I asked the lad's name – they didn't know, he had just started, one of the Morelli family who had always cleaned for the clergy. Why had he done this? They didn't know – how could they – they must be on their way. Fr Stefano followed them in the hope he would be of some assistance, but the screams of the boy's mother and sisters diverted him back to his own church where he entreated the Lord for mercy to be shown to the dead lad who must have acted in madness.

But the family Morelli were maintaining it was not madness. Yes, the boy was crazy, but he had been driven so, and they knew what was the cause. He had seen a ghost in a chapel of the Church of St Francis – the ghost of a man standing in its midst, wearing the clothes of the figures in the ancient frescoes on its walls, beckoning the young man to come to him, touching his private parts. The boy was frozen to the spot. All he could do was cut the Sign of the Cross on himself, and then the man vanished. There was not a trace of him. When the story was reported, no one believed it. They had laughed at him, and his mother even insisted this was made up to get out of the job as a sacristan and go to the big town of Milan where her pretty son would get up to all types of depravity with those no better than himself. She would beat the degeneracy out of him. No more nonsense about ghosts. And now here was her child, she lamented loudly, lying at her feet, his brains blown to pieces and she had done nothing to help him in his hour of need. She had sent her boy to hell and she was beyond consolation.

But one thing she could do – no child of hers would again set foot in the Church of St Francis, let alone work in it. She did not care about family tradition, about them emigrating anywhere, even to America. They would at least still be alive. And she demanded both Fathers Andrea and Bonifacio exorcise that chapel and, if necessary, paint over those accursed frescoes. The two thought she was joking, but no, she was serious. She wished to obliterate from the face of the earth the greatest achievement of Piero della Francesca as revenge for the death of her child. If she had blood on her hands for not believing his story, so too the art on the chapel walls was guilty in her eyes as well. She was absolutely convinced that whatever or whoever the dead lad had seen must have a close connection to the evil monstrosity disfiguring this chapel – it had led her boy to take his own life. Get rid of it.

The priests stammered this was not possible. She was proposing that they would destroy the Legend of the True Cross, the greatest treasure in all Arezzo, possibly in all of Italy, the lovely jewel in the gorgeous crown that was the art of Piero, world renowned, celebrated for the beauty of his colours, the symmetry of his architecture, the gorgeous mysteries and ambiguities of meaning in all his finest work, and the Church of St Francis lay claim to having the finest. Generations had learned from it that the wood of the Cross came from the Tree of Knowledge in the Garden of Eden. It had been used to coffin Adam. The Queen of Sheba found these planks and brought them to Solomon to furnish his temple in Jerusalem. To the Emperor Constantine they were proof positive of God's power and existence. All this the frescoes showed. The very roots of Christian faith on the walls of the church. Money could not buy this glorious mystery. But no amount of lire would bring her son back from the dead, so his mother still blamed this Piero who had come to entice her beautiful child to his doom. She wanted his wickedness erased forever. And if she did not get satisfaction in Arezzo, she would go to a higher authority, high as the Pope if necessary.

There was no need to trouble his Holiness. The woman eventually calmed down. But she did keep her threat never to let another belonging to her set foot in that institution again. And word about the ghost of Piero della Francesca had spread, terrifying the poor townspeople to such a degree that none of them would fill the position of sacristan. With the consent of his parents, this is the employment I propose to offer to your ward, Giovanni Cuma. His special duty will be to guard the aforementioned frescoes. You have mentioned his interest in painting. This may suit him. As his parents still refuse to allow him lodging in their home, I can offer a room – small but clean and comfortable in my own house, that he is welcome to take until he finds his feet. I look forward to hearing the young man's reply, and to him and to you, Mother Clothilde, I wish the peace of God and his blessed Mother.

When Mother Clothilde finished reading me the letter, she folded it, saying nothing more, and handed it to me. I wished she would tell me what to do, but all she did was sigh, saying, what in God's name is there in the air of your home town? I will never, ever set foot in Arezzo, for they seem to be incapable of intelligent conversation if this rambling letter is anything to go by. Your parents will not exchange two words with you, but this chatterbox makes up for their reticence. His proposal could have been suggested in a few sentences. Did we need to know about the unfortunate suicide? Well, it is up to you. Do you want to go and do what he says? This stupid man – really, who are they allowing to enter Holy Orders these days? Perhaps you should go and work there. Study there, if you like – paint there. I have no doubt you will soon run rings around Father Stefano. And if you should meet up with Piero's ghost, get him to sketch a few details for you. Sell them to rich Americans. You will be set for life. The decision is yours entirely. What do you want to do? I would go home, I told her, to Arezzo.

❁ ❁ ❁

That is where I spent the war years, in Arezzo, as the mountains about us opened with fire, and the town lands were bathed with the blood of all races, staining the fields, the sheep and their shepherds forever, while I remained hidden, keeping safe the Legend of the True Cross, as Father Stefano suggested I should do. I now had as my protection the miraculous vision of Piero della Francesca, for I had made this vow: if I am to be consumed by fire from the sky, if the Germans or the Americans, the English or any other army, are to put a bullet through my head, then here is where I will meet my death, choking on my own life – or buried in the rubble of what is left of Piero's art. If his ghost came to take one young man, then I called on that same ghost to save my life. To save the chapel. To save Arezzo. And he did. But I knew that there would be a price to pay for my salvation. It would be my parents.

They had refused to see me from the first. They persisted in that refusal. I was the talk of Arezzo for a time. They knew I had been banished as a boy in deep disgrace. Now I had returned as a grown man, surely Mama and Papa would relent – surely they would send for me – surely we would be reconciled? It did not happen. People marvelled at the strength of their hatred. They wondered if I were such a demon, why did this evil sinner find refuge and stay in the priest's house? Through the terrors of the war I remained a mystery, diminishing in power as it ended and the peace returned. Slowly but surely our life went back to normal, and that great constant stayed constant – my parents would have nothing whatsoever to do with me. I must confine myself to my place of employment. They also made it clear that they suffered deprivation too, prevented from praying before the frescoes because of my abominable presence in that shrine. So it was that I tried to imagine I could find them represented in Piero's painting. Perhaps my father now was ancient as Adam, caught at the point of death, entering his grave, his white hair and beard blanking his face, removing all life, all questions of who he was, now at the end of his existence. But where was my mother? She could not be Eve – that ancient crone, her face a nest of lines and wrinkles. That was not possible – not allowable. Could she be the Queen of Sheba kneeling in homage to Solomon – the blue, the enormous blue of her gown, the blue I saw where I remembered Mama and myself a child, happy in her arms? But even as a young woman, she was never this beautiful. And so I began to sketch how she might look – sketch her again and again. See her as our family once was, loving, arguing, speaking together, until my crimes put them on the cross of my own wickedness and we expired through my evil actions, breathing our last of happiness because I was bad. The darkness within me now took shape in the drawings I'd scrawl on any scrap of paper, as if this was the way to release it and free me from the sin of myself. And these were nothing like my childish efforts on the walls of that convent, doing a favour for Mother Clothilde. Something had broken inside me. Something that could not be repaired. This was a wound that would mark me forever. The mark of Adam, the mark of Eve, our first – our every parent, and their ancient dying flesh Piero carved from the Tree of Knowledge. They had dined on the fruits of good and evil, devoured the serpent, its tooth and skin, and the cost of their perilous bill of fare was death. There was no sacred protection in this place where he had painted. It was instead the home of night itself, disguised as his most luminous light, for everything in the frescoes was a shadow of what it really was. Piero was not preaching salvation. He was showing us damnation, and only I had means to decipher that dreadful prophecy he was now telling – there is no hope, there is only hell, and all faith, all fables are only means to guide us into eternal nothingness through horrendous war. It was as if my hand was possessed as I drew these secrets without ceasing on page after page, seeing in the prophets and the saints and the angels and the servants of the Lord the truly misshapen agents of evil lurking beneath the surface of the wall, pulling me into its very fabric, demanding I disappear into its cracks and lines, crawl through the colours and shapes, let the horses bite and the dragons burn, let it take my life – take my life – take my life – as I whispered to Stefano when he found me weeping in the blackness of my mind and my heart, my soul and myself in the thick night where I could see perfectly the ghost of the dead boy, illuminated all before me, holding in his hands the corpse of Il Duce and his lover, suspending them upside down, hanging them on Piero's cross before letting them drop into the red flames of hell that burned beneath their feet and my feet. As I explained this to Stefano, it was then I knew for sure I was going mad.

In the hospital my mother came to see me. When she was led to where I was lying, she asked if I had been injured in the war, so changed was I from what she imagined I could look like. And she too was a stranger. When she spoke, asking if I could be her son, Gianni, I shook my head. Yes, that was my name, but I did not have anything to say to this old lady. They tell me you are my youngest child, she insisted, but I think they are wrong. Then you should believe yourself and not them, I told her coldly, and leave me alone. Are you a married man? She asked, have you got a wife? I told her in no uncertain terms I had no wish to talk to strangers – would she have the good grace to leave me alone? But this had no effect on her, although it did stop her questioning me. She simply sat like a stone beside me, not moving a muscle, no more than I did, breathing quietly in the near empty ward, bereft of all curiosity now as to who we were and why we were together. The silence brought us to our senses.

Next she told me she was ready to make her confession. I told her to find a priest, I was not one, and she replied, I know, Gianni, I know, we did not allow it. It is a terrible sin we committed, my worst sin. We have driven you into this place, so ill, so very ill, look at you – we took away your childhood, now we have taken your health. Why did we do it? To punish you – for your own good – and look at you – look – what good was this suffering for? You were a little boy, and now you are a ghost. A

221

shadow of a man – I heard you were screaming to Fr Stefano – screaming you could see Il Duce hanging upside down on a cross and that dreadful whore of his – I cannot repeat what you said about her. You are still inclined to impure thoughts and deeds. Our severity has not improved you. A waste, all a waste. That is what your poor father thinks. Fr Stefano asked us both to come and help you get well. Your papa could not bring himself to do it. Can you blame him when we hear what obscenities you are shouting for all to hear in the middle of the night? We can no longer hold our heads up in Arezzo. Perhaps if you married, you would behave for once in a civilised manner. But who would take you? What decent girl would look twice at you? Who in their right mind would marry a madman?

I don't know, Mother, and if I did, I would not tell you. A nurse was passing – a stout woman, well into her thirties. My mother stopped her in her tracks. Excuse me, young lady, I interrupt your work, but I need your assistance. The ludicrous specimen of a man you see stretched on the bed before you, he is my son and he is single. Tell me honestly, are you surprised? The poor woman, who must have seen some horrific sights in her medical career, blushed to the roots of her fat cheeks. She explained she had a fiancé, she was quite happy, she would be tying the knot very soon, she was sorry. Oh, for God's sake, my mother corrected her, I'm not asking you to take him as a husband – I'm simply inquiring do you think any woman would be desperate enough to express even a vague interest – take him off his parents' hands – do something to make him respectable?

The nurse said she must give my mother her humble but honest opinion. And it was no, no such woman existed.

I was surprised that this rather took the wind out of my mother's sails. She castigated the unfortunate lady once she was safely out of sight. Who the hell did she think she was? A jumped up peasant whose father was a poacher. Known never to have the arse in his trousers. Didn't have ten lire to rub together. Now she is a nurse, they have one foot on the ladder, and this class of people did not know their place. She blamed the Communists. Whenever she saw the colour red, she spat three times, for it reminded her of those Stalinists. They would come in the middle of the night and shoot us all in our beds. They would do this so they could steal the sheets from under our sleeping bodies. Then they would send them, still warm with our smell, all the way to Russia where they would be torn and made into bandages to dress the wounds of the millions upon millions of Soviet soldiers who would soon overrun the whole of Italy, slaughtering the Pope and his cardinals, turning the Vatican into a public convenience, looting and pillaging all the bells to melt into bullets that would kill us all.

To put a stop to this, I told her I would like to marry a Communist. You are a pagan then, she declared. And it was then she saw Father Stefano approaching. She began to chide him for sending her to the bedside of a man who could not possibly be any blood relation to her. None of her breed were pagans. And this poor man – is he a pagan? Stefano asked. You would not think so if you'd see how he draws like an angel. Forgive me,

Gianni, he asked, but I have seen all the work you have produced. I have collected it together. You have remarkable skill. More than skill. My dear man, you are an artist. And you have done all this without schooling, without any formal training, how has this happened? You have simply been rewarded for all you have suffered with a gift. You must celebrate it. You must continue. It is in your blood. We must find a way to let you work more and develop. If I have to provide the money myself from Church funds I will do so with a clear conscience. It would be an act of wanton destruction not to let you see what God has given you.

My mother said nothing to Fr Sefano's effusion. He turned directly to her, then said, someday, my good lady, your family's name will be known throughout Italy because of this son of yours. I'm convinced he will achieve fame and honour. You will be praised for rearing such an artist. I didn't rear him, my mother interrupted, I sent him away from me, at the urging of his father admittedly, but I was in complete agreement. You are a fool to think that this fellow will come to anything. I am sorry to call a priest a fool, but in this case I do because that is what you are. I know you are a good man, you give this chancer – artist, my foot – board and shelter. We are grateful you take the waster off our hands, but I'm going to tell you your trust is misplaced and he will take advantage of your kindness, as he did to his mother and father when we thought him an innocent child.

With that she turned on her heel and would be gone, but I stopped her. I rose from the bed and told her in as threatening a voice as I could muster I had no wish to set eyes on her again. She and my father had rejected me, banishing me from them and their home when I had barely attained the age of reason for a ludicrous childish prank, instigated by my sister. Now, so many years later, I would do what I had at long last fully in my power to do, and that is to reject them as completely, as violently as they had done to me. I know that would not destroy them as they tried to destroy me, but they had failed, for I was still alive, I was back in Arezzo, I was earning my living independent of them and I had just been told what I'd always dared tell myself – I am a painter. Now do as you were about to do – do what I demand you do – leave.

She turned on me. You have long broken our hearts, Gianni – it was what you set out to do, and you have succeeded. Whatever else you may do in your miserable life, you have done that, and I would congratulate you, but the words would stick in my throat and choke me. Would that make you happy? Will you finally be at ease when you achieved what has always been your intention – to see myself and Papa finally in the grave? I am not yet ready to go under. I had even hoped to see you changed from what you are – to see you even pretending to a semblance of normality – to see you settled down. That was why I was provoking you out of your stupor. Why I wanted you to marry. So I could tell your father you were not the man he feared you were, before he dies. Because he is dying, Gianni. Your papa is dying. And now he dies, as I will die after him, knowing how you hate us.

I sat back on the bed, holding my hands out to her, but she shook her head, still standing rooted to the spot, never taking me in her arms. There was nothing to say, so Father Stefano broke the silence, advising my mother not to worry about my being single, I would be married to my art. She eyed him directly, saying, I no longer think you are a fool. I think you are the greatest idiot ever to don a collar around his neck and call himself a priest. What god do you worship? The god of stupidity? The god of craven cowardice that lets a man believe such ludicrous ways to escape from the realities – the responsibilities of life? Married to his art? Will his art give him children and me grandchildren? Will his art stroke his brow when fever strikes him? Will his art be there when fair-weather friends desert him for the other friends from whom they seek the next favour? Will his art be there when he dies, as he will die, alone? I leave you together – one as useless as the other.

Mother, I cried after her, may I see my father? She did not answer. She did not look back. Mother, I cried again, my father, may I see him? My dying father, will you let me see him?

* * *

The room where it all happened had not changed. Not a single stick of furniture had been moved. The bed that he sat on that day was the bed that he now lay in. The wardrobe with its flowers, still painted pink on its door, stood there, my hiding place of shame. The smell of its wood still stung my nostrils, and the memory of it and all that happened made my stomach nauseous. They had drawn the heavy curtains to keep out the light of day. The dark floor still echoed beneath my moving feet. They had brought in more chairs than I remembered being in that room, for the five of them to sit on. I found my way alone there, walking up the endless stairway, taking the proper directions, opening the ivory doorknob, revealing myself to my brothers and sisters.

Hairy-arsed Paolo now had a hairy face to match, the black bushy beard in contrast to the bald pate. Rosa with the elephant ears now was the size of an elephant. I had forgotten what name he threw at Roberto and Caterina, but they had grown so alike as to pass for twins, sitting hand in hand beside each other, as happy to be in Arezzo as they would be in Siam. But of course it was Arianna I most wanted to see; had her scaly skin been shed, or did she still resemble the serpent that she was in word and deed? When I saw her I could not believe my eyes. She had not grown a centimetre, but was exactly the same size, the same shape, the same revolting complexion. Somehow she had been perfectly preserved in childhood, but her hands and face had aged more rapidly as if in retaliation for the rest of her body's refusal to obey the laws of human growth and decay. I longed to know if her voice still bore a resemblance to some bird of ill omen taking delight in its shrieks of horror, but that was one pleasure denied to me, for she and the rest of them were clearly declining any attempt to break breath to me.

I would not give these monsters the satisfaction of my speaking first, so I stood where I was in the doorway as no chair was vacant, nor was any effort made to fetch me one or to make me feel in the slightest bit welcome. So we persisted for the best part of five or ten minutes, but I was still damned if I would crack first. Then a loud sobbing could be heard coming from Caterina, and I saw Roberto pat her continuously, gently. I wondered what effect this excess of emotion might have on my father, but he lay there unruffled, as if oblivious to this show of grief at his passing. I decided the best policy was to match his indifference, so I let Caterina cry without any sympathetic inquiry as to whether I could do anything to assist her, largely because I guessed – no, I knew only too well – that such an offer on my part would only have been greeted with the desire that I make myself scarce now and forever. It had taken me so long to enter that house again, to walk into this room, that I would not oblige any of them. Here I am, here I stay, until my father recognises me and speaks.

But he did not do so, either by choice or by infirmity. Hairy Arse now picked this moment to clear this throat and Rosa scowled at him, her whole bulk shaking at the moving of her mouth, the arching of her eyebrows. He shrugged an apology but it was deflected by a sudden violent sneeze from Rosa. This spasm seemed to trigger off an equally alarming coughing fit from Arianna and she was joined almost in chorus by the Siamese twins, who now released their bond of hands to shield their mouths from passing germs in my dying father's bedchamber. What had been peaceful and quiet, if not quite serene – you could, I admit, cut the silence with a knife – it was now a cacophony of human noise, almost – in fact perhaps a little too orchestrated, as if they had long been in the practice of this uniformly distributed demonstration of involuntary tics to unsettle any social intruder. That clearly had been their aim, but I was not going to allow it to intimidate me in the slightest.

I remained where I was perched, standing firmly in the doorway. From my vantage point I took in these specimens of Italian humanity, and I realised why my mother had such an obsession that I either be married or get married, for certainly none of this shower looked or smelt of anything but celibacy. I might be polite and describe them as odd beings, but as I consider myself odd, I would not want to be included under the same heading as these, my flesh and blood. The coughing, the sneezing, the twitching had now passed, and the silence resumed as if nothing had happened. My father continued to lie unperturbed, waiting for death. It was only then I noticed there was one significant difference here to what I remembered. There were paintings and drawings crudely framed on the walls. Not many – but identifiable because they were all done by me. The shock of seeing them caused me to speak. I said the word, Father. My father's voice spoke. He asked who called him?

I answered. I said, it is me, Father – your youngest son. Giotto. He did not reply. The others now were shuffling in their seats. Rosa signalled me to go near to him, but still none of them moved from their chairs. I walked up to the bed and looked down at my father, and for the first time in my life I saw in his face the faces of all his sons and daughters, perhaps the faces of my father's father and mother, and theirs before them, and more before them, until I swear to the Lord I was looking at Adam dying in front of me, prophesising my death and the death of all sitting about me, the beginning and end of our mortal species. His hair had grown long and white around his head like a mad halo. How different from the trim, tight cut when he was younger – so neat, so perfectly groomed, you could have counted accurately each strand on that full head. I longed to touch him but knew it would be a knife in his flesh, so I simply repeated the word, Father.

–Leave us, he breathed, leave us alone together.

–Do you not know who this is, Papa? At long last I heard Arianna speak. The sound of her voice was still like a child's, piping, insistent, whining, demanding attention. And my father did not deign to reply to her. It's him, Papa, she persisted, it's the monster. He's dared to come into our home, into your room, after what he did to you. What he did to all of us. And he's continuing to shame us. I know for a fact that he is painting filthy, filthy drawings and corrupting everyone who looks at them. Even poor Father Stefano, he talked our mother into this, agreeing to let him dare contact us and you, Papa. He tried to kill you before. To shame you to death. Now he wants to finish the job. Send him packing, send him away, don't let him slaughter you and us. That's what he really wants. Believe me, Papa.

–I believed you before, my father said quietly.

—Because I was telling the truth, Arianna stressed.

—She was telling the truth, Rosa backed her up.

—We all believed her, Roberto and Caterina said in unison.

—And now he comes back like an old ghost, Hairy-Arse Paolo sighed, comes back to send you to your grave, Papa. Don't allow him. Don't indulge him. You did once and look what happened. Send him away.

—I send you away, my father whispered, yet the threat was audible, and he, even in that feeble state, was not a man his children could disobey. Do as I bid you. Leave us, leave us alone together.

They trotted dutifully out of the room, Rosa crossing herself, Arianna throwing holy water from a small font – Christ with a crown of thorns sculpted above – and showered its blessings on Papa, on Hairy Arse, Roberto and Caterina, on Rosa and on herself, studiously avoiding me, the werewolf at the wake, ready to howl with anger at the touch of sacred rain, lifting my head to the moon in the heavens, shrouded by sinister clouds.

And now the room was empty apart from myself and my dying father. I spoke first.

—I've come back, I've come to see you, Papa.

—Do you know who I am?

His question softened me. I wanted to take this old man and hold him close to me. To say, yes, I know who you are, the father who turned me away, who took me from all I loved, who sent me far from him, from my mother, my brothers and my sisters, the father that I now forgive. But before I could do so, he had risen up in his bed and was taking a good look at me.

—You are too thin, much too thin. None of the rest of them are so thin.

—I have not had their advantages, I replied. They had home feeding, and I suppose it's stood to them.

—Aren't you better off to be so slender? You will live longer. You will thank me when you are an old man.

—No, Papa, I do not think I will ever thank you for what you did to me.

—And what was that? Did I drive you mad? I hear from one of them, that lizard daughter-

—Arianna?

—Is that her name? Arianna, call her that if you wish. That poisonous tongue told me you had gone completely mad in the church at night, thinking you were Il Duce, or did you see him hanging upside down on a cross? What does it matter? He's dead now, God's curse on him. He nearly took us all with him, you included, my lost son. Tell me, were you mad? For once in her life, was Arianna telling me the truth?

—What do you mean, once in her life?

—Is that her name, Arianna? What a pretty name for such an ugly child. And she has stayed ugly. Is it God's revenge on her, you think?

—Revenge for what?

—Lying to her father.

—You know she was lying?

—I have kept some of your paintings. The one above my

bed, that is of me — my face is like the sun. That was how you imagined your father. A great light in the sky. Too great a light, a blinding light. You should have covered your eyes when you looked at me. That way I might not have harmed you, Giotto, my last-born. I have done you evil, but less evil than I could have done. If I had only loved you less–

–Less than what?

–I still cannot say. Before I die, I wanted to make peace, but I still cannot.

–You knew Arianna was lying?

–I have kept some of your paintings.

–I can see the paintings, Father. Thank you for keeping them. But you knew I was telling the truth?

–I loved you more than her.

–Because she was a liar?

–Because I was a liar.

–What do you mean, Papa?

–I had to send you far away. Never see you again.

–But was I not your favourite? Your last-born child, was I not–

–The child – the son I loved, yes.

–Then why do what you did?

–To protect you. I was your father.

–How did you protect me?

–I knew what you were doing. Where you were hidden. And I wished you to be there. We share a guardian angel that saved us both. He put Arianna up to her evil tricks. We did not harm each other. We let her do it to you. For years you may have seen her as an agent of the devil. But she was a force of light.

–The light that shone from my Papa's face. The sun by which I see, the darkness that is life. The sin that is my father. You may die now, without forgiveness. That is what you wanted, what you deserve, and I give it to you, as you gave me nothing.

–I gave you life.

–And so I'll die. As will you. Before me.

I left him calling my name. Gianni – Gianni – Gianni. But I did not reply, for I did not know who it was he looked for. The boy he desired had died and grown into the man who now walked away from him as he was dying, looking for comfort, a hand to hold, a voice to sooth, a child to destroy forever. When I walked down the long stairway, there they were, waiting, longing to know what could have been said between us, something they already resented, something they had been always excluded from, something they envied, and I would leave them in their envy. He is waiting for you all, I told them, I have done what I needed to do. You should go up to him. I think the end is near. What did he have to say to you? my mother asked. It was more what I had to say to him, I replied. I wanted to tell him myself why I'd never marry – why none of us ever would. How could we match the happiness you shared as a couple? How could we create such a brood as the one now gathered about you? Where could we find such joy – such a sense of accomplishment as that which you must share, Mama and Papa? You have, for all your kindness and devotion, done us a great disservice. We will not find peace in this life or any other. I fear, my dear parents, this is where we must abandon you – looking for our own redemption, finding our way to Calvary.

❊ ❊ ❊

The funeral was well attended. Copious tears were wept. It was not my place to join the grieving family. I sat two rows behind them in the church as Father Stefano preached what was gener- ally described as a beautiful sermon. He singled out my father's civic accomplishments. Whole generations of students owed their proficiency in languages – well, French and English – to his steadfast teaching. Our house was a habitation of many tongues, well trained as we were from birth to revel in the marvels of Europe's Babel. Papa had also kept a dignified distance from the turmoil of our recent past, maintaining Italian civilisation, its subtleties, its secrets, through the dark decade of our expulsion from the Eden of what we were before that apocalypse of war into which we were dragged. My father, he concluded, was a man whose life was love. That is as much a legacy as we can ever hope to leave behind us. To that statement the congregation deeply assented. I followed his coffin, without weeping.

Within days of the burial Father Stefano asked to see me. He had received a letter. From Ireland. A fellow priest, he had almost forgotten him – he needed a favour done. A painter to travel there – a commission for new Stations of the Cross in his church. Would I want to travel there? Get away, far away, for quite a while – away from Arezzo? It might be what I needed.

Who was I to argue? To point out I had never sold one work of art? That I had never been outside Italy? Had no notion of Ireland, what it was, where it was? And so I said, I'll go there, yes. I will do as I am asked to do. And what is it I am asking myself to do? Find the home of night, disguised as luminous light. Find my true cross, paint it, bid farewell to Christ and all his works as he bids farewell to his life on Golgotha.

l

Chapter Eight

The Stations of
the Cross

i. Christ Is Condemned To Death

My Roman general
Bathed his hands of blame,
Shocked
At the rejection of his offer –
The gift of this crown,
Its gold sharp as thorn,
Bestowed on my head,
Heads that come after.

I could not refuse
That expensive trinket.
I must do the deed
And sweat my life's blood.
There was no applause
At my condemnation.
None was audible
To my ears, being deaf
To the Hebraic cries
For Barabbas,
Passing sentence
That neither shocked nor surprised.

Anything else I would regard as sham.
Justice must be done.
Be seen to be done.
I did not flinch.

I knew how this would end.
Standing in red sun,
I was man exposed.

ii. Jesus Receives The Cross

This is the legend of the One True Cross
Fashioned from a tree
In the Garden of Eden,
Tree of good and evil,
Tree of knowledge,
Its planks used to coffin
Father Adam.

Branches that stretched
From hell to high heaven
Brought by its queen
From Sheba to Solomon
Were blessed by that king
With most fertile wisdom –
Through them tribes of Israel multiplied.

I embrace the cross –
A love long waiting
For the shoulder
I lean on that cedar.
Inconsolable,

Lilies of the field
Knew that their splendour
Was a mere shadow
Of the tree,
The branch, the cross I carry,
The stains of blood
On my purple raiment.

iii. Jesus Falls For The First Time

I walked across the Sea of Galilee.
I felt no fear of drowning
In the sway of water,
Obedient to my will,
Doing as my flesh demands
It would do.

The highest peak
Of the highest mountain,
I gazed at the wonders of the wide world
And was steadfast,
Never sliding,
Sure that no temptation
Could seduce my poor soul.

When rock turned into bread
And rain to wine,

I chose to hunger
Than to dine on pride.

Earth gives way beneath –
I see it spinning –
A moon the devil whips
Through the torn sky.

My most solid feet are taken from me.
I taste clay.
It is myrrh, it is aloes.

iv. Jesus Is Met By His Blessed Mother

Dogs in the street are baying at the sun.
Is it their howling that has turned the sun red?

I wipe my eyes
With the sleeve of my cross.

I can see clearly my blessed mother.

She dares to brave
The Roman centurion
Warning he'll spare
Neither women nor children
Begging for mercy
As if it were money.

She blocks his men on the way to Golgotha.

I am stone
In the heel of her sandal,
Bringing her pain
Since the day I leapt forth,
Her belly a battlefield of desire.

Shaking her claw at
The Roman centurion,
My mother howls,
While the dogs in the street
Are licking their lips
And smell what's coming.

v. The Cross Is Laid Upon Simon Of Cyrene

I met a man coming from Cyrene.
He was burned black by grief for Africa.
He asked the crowd,
Where is this man going,
Carting his burden of death
On his back?

Who is it bids me
A kindly greeting?
I ask like a blind man
Hunting for clues

In the hoard of faces
Turning against me.

Who does not fear this suffering animal?

I throw him the cross,
I watch him catch it,
Expert
At shouldering blame and reproach,
Spreading like gorse fire
On Libyan sands,
Parched
From the want of the reddest rain
Pouring in torrents
From the barbs in my skull,
Turning Cyrene into my colour.

vi. Veronica Wipes The Face Of Jesus

I saw a woman searching for her child.
She waved a white flag through dangerous lands.

Or was I mistaken?
Was it myself
Who was the white, the danger, the woman?
As if we were neighbours,
She approached me,
Asking,

This girl, had I seen her girl on my travels
To the ends of the earth
And back again?

She told me her name was Veronica.

Like a man avoiding the charge of a bull,
Maddened by grief
And hell bent on harm,
She brandished a cloth
To wipe my sore face,
Imprinting
On it someone's reflection.

Her own or mine?

I could never decide,
But her voice tasted
Like the quench of wine.

vii. Jesus Falls For A Second Time

Something seismic is shaking the earth,
Quaking its plumage of river and mountain.

It has turned us all
Into prancing clowns –
Emperor, soldier, penitent, beggar.

I took a tumble
For the second time,
Convincing the high priests
My time might come
Before they were ready
For the riot act
They'd read to the wind,
To the seven seas.

The birds of the air
Mocked my lack of grace –
I who once matched them
In elegant flight,
All red and green
As magnificent wings,
Heedless of marble kingdoms beneath me.

A kick in the arse,
I'm back on my feet,
Risen again,
The talk of Jerusalem.

viii. The Women Of Jerusalem Weep For Our Lord

Fetch water from the well for you are dry,
Daughters from the city of Jerusalem.

You will feed your children
Hunger and thirst,
And the stars themselves
Will be plague to you.
Save your tears
For the time of lamentation
When the earth itself,
The ground does not open
To hear you beating,
Mother, let me in,
Save me from the lion,
The snake, the dragon.

Fetch water from the well, drink it dry,
Daughters from the city of Jerusalem.

Do not remember
The swigs of laughter,
The wedding feast,
The raising of the dead,
Full in the belly
From the fatted calf,
The sheep led astray
Returned for slaughter.

ix. Jesus Falls For The Third Time

This country has drunk itself stupid –
Reeling –
Falling to its knees –
In need of a hand
To get back
To the straight, the narrow way –
Draining to the dregs
A fierce alcohol,
Draining my days
To the lees that are left,
Poisonous,
Smelling of sweet vinegar.

Fruit of the briar
And bitterest thorn,
I am the hunger
Of the bare table.

I'd feast on the air
Like mother's milk,
Pouring in streams of ivory,
Rose,
The elephant's tusk,
The perfumed night,

The rip and the shred
Of the scented bed.

There is nothing more left to remember.
There is nothing more left to remember.

x. Jesus Is Stripped Of His Garments

There was a fire for water in our house.
They'd use it to bathe my infant body.

I remember the smell
Of swaddling clothes.
I am standing
Naked on Calvary.
I am ashamed
Of my infant body.
The scourge, the piss,
The shit down my legs.

I am soil
In the night of my darkness.
The River Jordan will not wipe me clean.

I am raw as pelt,
As red as red meat.
I am on fire
Like water in our house,

Boiling

Before the women of Jerusalem,

Boiling

Before the Roman centurion.

They have broken

My clothes in smithereens.

They play dice

With the number of my bones.

xi. Jesus Is Nailed To The Cross

I can smell the wood of the True Cross,

Sweet as cedar,

As the tables and chairs

Carved

From the green trees of Nazareth

I cut and fashioned

Into furniture,

My nails like the teeth

In a traitor's kiss.

Asleep

On that delicate handiwork,

I would take my rest

After sore day's toil.

From this vantage point

I see the oceans

Swarm about earth,
Breeding like the flies
Devouring my flesh –
Deaf, dumb and blind.
A spill of despair
Flowing from my side,
Congealing my blood,
I am my disease,
Crying,
Why do you desert me, Father?

xii. Jesus Dies On The Cross

Humble and chaste
As cleanest rain water,
Ending this life
And sustaining the next,
Sister Death, I am your long-lost brother
In love with your serene peace and madness.

I can no longer bear
The heat of the cross.
It has split asunder
The chain of my heart.

The sinew and limb
Of that broken heart

Give themselves now
To your devouring love
Blinding me
With the light of your darkness,
Piercing my side
With the spear of desire.

I fell upon the cross
Like a bridegroom
Saving himself
For the wild wedding night,
Breaking into songs
Of lonely sorrow.

I am your long-lost brother, Sister Death.

xiii. Jesus Is Taken From The Cross

Friend, have you been to Arimathea?
Did you meet a man there known as Joseph?

He wrapped my dead body
In a white sheet,
My body blue
From the wounds of falling.

The sheet like the snow
That stands for winter —

The sheet like the snow
That melts the furnace
Burning
All traces of the sins of the world,
The sheet I will wear
For all eternity
In the arms of
Joseph of Arimathea,
In the desolate eyes
Of daughters weeping,
In the perfect circle
Of sun and moon.

My dead body wrapped
In the whitest sheet,
I am the colour
Of my Sister Death,
And I drink the snow
From the highest mountain.

xiv. Jesus Is Placed In The Sepulchre

All roads lead to my death on Golgotha.
I've long been walking to that desolate hill.

That was the star
Shone on my nativity.

Why then do I feel
So much the stranger?

The blood in my veins
Has turned to silver.
The bone in my breast
Is turning to gold.
The tomb I lie in
Listens to that stone
Of my silver, desolate
Blood and bone.

Wake me in time for the resurrection.
Wind the sheet from me –
The sins of the world.

I am the god who expired on a cross.
I am the man searching for a story.

The why and wherefores,
The thus and therefore
All roads lead to my death on Golgotha.

Chapter Nine

Arimathea

The day they were going to see the paintings, that would be special. Not special like a birthday or First Communion, but still you would need to wash yourself very clean and dress up. Euni O'Donovan was polishing her boots closely. It was also her job to leave her daddy's best black shoes shining so he would see his face in them. If she did that well enough to satisfy him, he sometimes gave her her pay early, a three-penny bit – an Irish silver one, with a wee rabbit on it. The first time he handed it over to her she called the creature on the coin Mena, for that was her best friend's name and she vowed she'd never spend it ever, but two things happened to change her mind. She saw a paper fan with a red sun and a silver moon in Mausie's shop at the bottom of the street and she really wanted it, but she kept her vow and held on to her money. Then, when she admitted to Mena that she'd called her rabbit after her, Mena got really cross with her. What did Euni think she was doing? Was it supposed to mean Mena looked like a rabbit? Euni knew her friend when she was in a bad mood of that kind, so just for the sake of peace and quiet she called her three-penny bit nothing. She still talked to the coin and told it all about the fan in Mausie's window. To her surprise, the silver rabbit spoke back to her, telling her to spend him. Buy what she wanted and enjoy her money. So she did.

Mena thought the fan was wild looking. If it had been up to her, she would have bought something different. Was there none with flowers? Mausie had a very small selection – Euni should have waited until she went to pick one in the toy shops in Derry. This was such a stupid thing to come out with. Euni didn't have the money for a bus ticket there and back, the fourteen miles to Derry, so how could she get her hands on one with flowers? Was she supposed to walk across the border and smuggle it back home to the town? She only had enough money for this one and, anyway, she liked it, so Mena could take a running jump. It didn't stop there. She told Mena that the rabbit did look like her, especially her big teeth, and Mena squealed she didn't have black teeth. I said big teeth, Euni corrected her and marched off, leaving Mena to roar after her that Euni's teeth were big as well as black, but Euni didn't give her the satisfaction of answering back. She really loved the fan, and it was one of the treasures she trusted to show Gianni, the Italian. At least he thought it looked gorgeous.

He unfurled it very gently. He examined each crease, and he told her it probably was made in Japan. It's come all the way from there to Donegal to be used by a very delicate young lady, he said. Then he lifted it up before his face and waved it swiftly. He told her that in Italy girls used fans to hide what it was they were thinking, and whatever was on the front could give their boyfriends a good idea what kind of mood their signorina was in. What's a signorina? she asked. You, he answered, that is what you are, lovely as the sun, full of secrets like the moon. He laughed, and for some reason she could feel her body softening. Why did that happen? And it happened again once when she dared venture into the big room where he was painting. Normally, he'd just roar at her to get out and she fled. This time he chased her with a brush covered with purple. When she let him catch her, he streaked her upper lip and it looked as if she had a moustache. It looked wild silly when he showed her her face in the mirror and they both laughed like drains. He wiped it off with turpentine and she smelt of it for ages, but she didn't mind because it was funny, the whole nonsense, her squealing, him acting like a child.

Still, she didn't go back in there to bother Gianni again. So she didn't know what his paintings looked like. Mammy asked her. You and your man are thick as thieves, tell us. But Euni couldn't oblige. She wasn't supposed to watch him when he was working, and she was an obedient girl, so she did what she was told. You must have seen even one of them, he must have left the door open, go on, tell us, what is it like? She swore to good God she couldn't tell because she didn't know. Why did her mother not believe her? When it was pretty clear Euni was going to cry if this forcing kept on, her father intervened, saying leave the child alone and stop questioning her. If she didn't know, she didn't know. Anyway, was it their business what he was up to as long as he got the job done? People should mind their own business, and Euni was the right girl to do just that.

But she had sneaked in one day after school when he was out. She still couldn't tell you what they were like. All the paintings were piled face inward against the wall, and the one he was working on, it was covered with a sheet that was stained all colours of the rainbow. Her mother would have a blue fit when she saw what the paint did with her good bedclothes. For sure Euni was not going to breathe a word about that, because Mammy this last while seemed to be losing her temper wild often, many times over nothing. Her daddy could lose the rag completely – everybody knew that, he did it so often – but then just as suddenly he would calm down. His big beating face would lose its scarlet and go back to normal. And he never lashed out at man or beast in the forge when he got cross. Mammy, though, she was a different kettle of fish. You never knew what way she'd turn when she lost control. She started screaming that loud once recently at the wee ones her daddy heard her where he was working and even came in to tell her to take it easy. She used a bad word to tell him what way she would take it easy and that she would do something she'd regret if he didn't move his children out of her sight. Euni made the mistake of saying she had done nothing, why was Mammy annoyed with her as well? Why was she blaming her for what the boys had done?

Get her out, just get her out, her mammy was roaring now, get the three of them out. Where? Daddy asked her, where am I going to put them? In the forge, in my sister's, I don't give a damn, she shouted, get them out. Gianni, the painter, must have been walking down the Pound Lane and heard the noise, for next thing Euni knew he had her by the hand and said he would take her to the lower house and mind her there. Are you saying I can't look after my own children? Is that what you're implying? Mammy was now nearly crying with rage. Gianni did not answer. He just went to the tap, turned it on and walked out. What is that supposed to mean? She called after him. Are you trying to be funny? Answer me why did you do that? He looked back as he was closing the door and said, drink water. Drink some water.

Mammy needed a good sleep, and so the wains went down to play in their aunt Seranna's house. She and Tessie spent a fair bit of time whispering in the kitchen. Euni couldn't hear what they were saying, but she knew it was something to do with her parents and she didn't want to know exactly. She did ask Seranna was her mammy sick? Seranna said it was likely Mammy had a sore leg – our Margaret is always getting a sore leg – be patient and soon all will be right as rain. And to all intents and purposes it was. The house more or less went back to normal, and there were fewer fights.

She knew they wouldn't fight when they went to see the paintings, because they were in the chapel and nobody would be so bold as to have a battle in God's house. Everyone had to hold their tongues there. They all got into their best clothes. Daddy in his suit, white shirt and lovely green tie that he saved to wear on St Patrick's Day usually. Mammy wore her good coat that she got in Bannons of Derry and that she would never tell the price of, although her aunts put Euni under the third degree in the hope that the child by accident might slip out something she'd heard about the cost of the piece of swank on our Margaret's back. Did she buy it outright? Euni didn't know. Did she pay pounds or guineas? Euni didn't know what a guinea was. Who went to Derry with her when she was buying, seeing neither of the two sisters was good enough to accompany her on this expedition? Euni couldn't help them there either. She was pronounced useless and sent out to play with the warning ringing in her ears she was to say nothing to her mother about the cross examination. Of course the child blabbed at the dinner table, wondering why her aunts were so keen to find out everything about the coat. Do you know what you'll tell them, her mother said, next time they ask? Tell them I stole it. Oh Mammy, God forgive you – you didn't, Euni was scandalised. Then her mother laughed and said she might have, so Euni had better not say anything or they'd all be landed in jail. This put the fear of God into the child, so when the subject arose again, she clammed up, and the silence let the aunts know she'd mentioned it definitely at home. Time to let the matter rest, there would be no news out of the mouths of babes. Euni was glad to get off the hook, not least because she thought her mammy looked the last word wearing that coat. As her hair was being combed and curled, Euni told her so, and Mammy did something very unusual. She hugged Euni and told her she was a good girl, the best in the whole town.

❁ ❁ ❁

Margaret O'Donovan took no more enjoyment out of dolling herself up to go down Walkers' Lane and gawk at these bloody paintings in the chapel than she would talking to the man in the moon, but sure, what could you do? One thing she did not need in her condition was to traipse about buttoned up to the nines surrounded by priests and nuns and the pukes of the town — even lasting out at Mass was tight enough — but the man had lodged with them and she would not let him down, seeing as how he had no family of his own here. And it might take the smile off the Sewell one. What was she doing trooping after them into a Catholic church? Margaret had no doubt that Martha would brazen things out and come in amongst them. It still came as a shock the way she was throwing herself at Gianni, and him falling for it hook, line and sinker. And what, pray, is that to you? Malachy demanded.

She wouldn't honour that with the dignity of a reply. All Margaret knew was that it was better for any lady to mind her modesty as much as her manners, and Martha was in a bit of danger of forgetting the first, if not the second. She was of course always sweetness itself – meet her on the street and the girl was as civil to you as she was in the rectory, but something was going on in that quiet head and it did not augur well. There were rumours about her mother – she had been some class of loose woman before being married – and what's in the blood must out eventually. The messenger of this news to Margaret was her sister Tessie – a fount of scandal always delivered with eyes raised heavenward and the impassioned plea, God spare us from harm but I have to tell you this. If Tessie smelt a rat in Martha's background, then most of the town would have smelt it too. When it came to gossip, Tessie was a generous woman.

And so should Margaret be towards Martha, she was suddenly ashamed to realise. Dear Jesus, hasn't the young one recently lost her nearest and dearest, her uncle, the minister? Isn't it natural she turns to another man more or less of her own age? Gianni seemed to be a gentle fellow who'd listen to her sobbing her heart out if that's her way of coping with her loss. And loss it certainly was, for as well as having no immediate family to care about her now, Martha had also to flit her home in the rectory. That would pass on to the next vicar. She might just about hold on to her job in the school, but there was no one to defend her there either, God love her. Margaret did have to hand it to Martha – the girl was genuinely upset that the cleaning job had vanished as well. There was no guarantee the new man would keep on old staff – indeed he may have a wife and daughters to run the house completely themselves. Her mind could be put at rest on that point at least – no sooner was the Reverend Sewell in the grave than Mrs Byres of Mill House was round offering her hours. Margaret took them gladly and would even be earning a bit more. So that was something good she could tell Martha – a big relief to her, a bigger relief to Margaret. With the way work kept drying up at the forge, Jesus, it was just as well there was something for her to do and bring in a few bob.

Mrs Byres wanted to know if Margaret would like to wait until the happy event was over before starting. No – no – no need to delay – she'd begin this very week, and all hands were delighted about that. She didn't know this woman well – in her late thirties, too much powder on her face, hair immaculate, funny shade of lipstick neither red nor pink, and she drank coffee the smell of which reminded Margaret that this is what tea would be like if you could burn it. One Wednesday morning Mrs Byres was talking about sending her son, Tim, to prep school – how would she manage without him, how would he manage without her, he was his mummy's darling. Remembering the necessity for manners, Margaret didn't like to ask what in hell is a prep school, just let her rabbit on and as the talk cascaded, Jesus, didn't it strike her that this lady is bit tiddly. Has she been on the drink at this early hour? Why is she sucking mints to disguise her breath? Anyway, between jigs and reels, the booze had loosened her tongue, and curiosity was getting the better of her, for she asked straight out about Miss Sewell – how was she coping? Grand, as far as Margaret

knew, grand. Tim adored her as a teacher, she was quite jealous of the wonderful Miss Sewell, Mrs Byres confessed, but of
course she would only do while the lad needed to acquire the
basics. His dad had other plans for him once his schooling had
started in earnest, and the lady in question, charming and kind
as she undoubtedly was, had not really got the qualifications to
stretch him as he'd need to be stretched to get where his father
wanted him to be. Mr Byres was also rather upset that Martha
spared the rod. He'd made a point of stressing to her that he
had no objection to her chastising Tim as firmly as he himself
did. She asked if he meant beating the child and was told in no
uncertain terms that he did. She would never, ever strike a pupil
– never. Quite fierce she was too in her answer. Mr Byres was
rather taken aback by this – well – by this display of character.
He had not expected such a determined answer from a young
lady. It was as if the woman turned Turk, he told Mrs Byres, and
she said, you never can tell, there are hidden depths in us all,
and Martha Sewell is no exception. She has her own opinions
and follows her own heart. Had Martha ever given her heart?
Mrs Byres suddenly asked Mrs O'Donovan. So that was where
this was all leading to.

Word must be out among her own kind about Gianni and the
Protestant teacher. What a stupid girl to give them this kind of
ammunition. Well I'm damned if I'll give them any more, Margaret decided, and asked what did Mrs Byres mean, ever given her
heart? Is there a young man – does she have, as they say in this
part of the world, a wild notion about him? Margaret couldn't

answer that, sorry. She just didn't know. She never listened to stories about other people, she had enough to deal with in her own family, never mind the rest of the town. Excuse me, I have work to do, she said. It was best to nip this kind of conversation in the bud. If the Byres woman thought she could get satisfaction out of her on this topic, it would be open season on all secrets, and that was not going to happen. But she had underestimated her boss's tenacity. She was like a dog with a bone. Not giving up, never giving up.

Was there not something between Martha and the Italian painter? Didn't he stay with Margaret's family? This was what the drunken bitch wanted to know. Damned if that would be the case. As far as she knew, Gianni was a decent fellow. He might be foreign, but he was Catholic (and you aren't, Missy). He might not be wearing out the knees of his trousers praying, but if she might be so crude, he still kept his trousers on, so she couldn't oblige with scandal. Sorry. Margaret expected to be given the road for being so cheeky, but the Byres one kept her mouth shut and her face had the look of a slapped arse – deservedly so. If she thought she had soft caramels in Margaret O'Donovan, who might talk scandal about her friends and neighbours, then she was wrong. Jesus alone knows what might be going on between Martha and Gianni, but it was of no concern to this stupid bitch, too lazy to scratch herself and with more money than sense. She asked if she might be excused to continue with her cleaning and that was absolutely acceptable. She didn't get the sack. In fact, there were two shillings extra for her – she'd done such a good job cleaning a circular mirror Mrs Byres' grandmother had left her in a will and it had never looked as well before. Margaret said thanks and left. She didn't bother pretending it was too much. There was a difference between pretending and lying, but at that minute she couldn't give a damn about that.

What she did give a damn about was what the hell was happening in her house. She could not believe Gianni would be that cruel to have taken Martha to his bed – that they would both have been so reckless – the bed that she trusted him – the bed – in Christ's name, why did she keep seeing that bed and the Italian painter in it? She tried to rid her mind of this nonsense – rid it completely. She found herself praying, but not to God. It was to Malachy, to her dead parents, to her sisters Tessie and Seranna, to her three children – praying to stop the thought of herself doing something terrible with himself, the man whose body she could not believe when her eyes got first sight of him, the sight – the body she had denied all this time but now was breaking through her as if her brain would burst at his beauty. Christ, stop her thinking like this. Christ and his blessed mother, keep the husband and children she had to rear, keep them always in front of her. Don't let her fall. Don't let her stumble. Keep her awake to the danger. She was a married woman.

And a married woman she'd stay. Had she'd taken leave of her senses? She did what she had to do to get herself back in line. Work. Work hard. She washed their clothes, the men's clothes, her own, practically to a pulp, beating all sign of stain out of them, the sweat from their shirts and socks, the shit from their drawers, scrubbed them till they smelt like new and as she wrung them dry, it was as if she was melting them into one, draining them together, making them a single long line of white, letting her touch without panic the blouse and the shirt and the long johns, going mad together, fucking in the basin, doing what she wanted to do with the two men, responding to the power and command of her hands, obedient to her desire, Gianni and Malachy, the men of this house. And they would do as she told them. Until she caught herself on. She laughed hard and long at herself. What in Christ's name was she thinking of? The child within her belly was doing funny things to her. This had happened before. She remembered the strawberry jam episode, suddenly grabbing a piece of bread from poor Euni's startled fist. Whether it was the sound of the word strawberry or its sweet sugar smell, she could not resist stuffing the slice of loaf into her mouth, nearly choking with the pleasure of the taste, leaving the poor child screaming, Mammy stole my bread. That brought me to my senses, but it was a crazed thing to do – something though she had to do – no matter what. Of course she didn't see the savage look in her own face when she did it, but she saw it in Gianni's sometimes when he was watching them, and watching them, and she knew for sure that whatever else he was up to, herself and her family would be in his painting. She knew what he was doing. It was Gianni's way of melting all of them together. Let it be so – she wouldn't stop him. Wasn't that what she wanted?

❋ ❋ ❋

It was always this way, Malachy O'Donovan reassured himself, when his wife was waiting for a wain to be born. Always a bit of panic – this time, though, more than before. If the forge had been doing well, he would have said no to the lodger. Put his foot down. They needed the extra money, so they bid him welcome. And as it was the priest who asked, they couldn't very well refuse Fr O'Hagen, could they? He was a decent skin, no airs nor graces, took his head out of the prayer book long enough to be civil to a body, and he could hold his own in conversation with the men of the town, interested in football, not stuck in with the women like some of the yokes you see preaching on the altar, taking too big an interest in the flowers or even, Jesus protect us, the vestments on their back. No, Simon O'Hagen was all right. If he asked you to do him a favour, and if he was willing to fork out for the privilege, then so be it.

Malachy was getting himself ready for this do – could you have a do in a chapel? He'd be careful not to use the word, but that's what it seemed like to him. The Italian had not been much bother, keeping himself mostly to himself, working like a Trojan to get this finished and then clear off home. He did like his grub and tried even to get Margaret to eat mushrooms – more fool him. Maybe he should have warned him against it, but, God forgive him, Malachy did like to see people take the rise out of each other, whether they knew what they were doing or not. In fact, it was better sport if they really didn't know. And if truth be told, he'd enjoyed the Italian's innocence. The man seemed not to have a guileful bone in him. You could take a hand at him from now till Christmas if you were in the mind to, but was it worth it? Was it worth mocking him when there was nobody to join in and when the boyo himself hadn't the English to defend himself?

Malachy had decided the better course was to be friends. Or at least try to gang up with him against Margaret for a bit of fun – two men against the one woman, let the sparks fly. But he didn't tune in to that kind of carry on. He was the first Italian to walk the streets of this town and to kip down in a bed of this family, so Malachy couldn't say if they were all as tight-arsed as this boyo, but if he was what you could expect if you were to walk into a pub and share a few drinks with the men in Italy, then O'Donovan for one would not be rushing there should the chance offer itself. There was little chance. There was no chance of it, and it broke nobody's heart. Travelling was not to his nor Margaret's liking. If she whinged like a cat to get home from Dublin on their honeymoon, he would have shot himself rather than let her know he didn't feel much better, and if she didn't soon shut her mouth and dry her eyes, he would be joining in on the chorus. No need for that – they got home and have stayed put since that very day. He wondered how in the name of Christ Gianni could up anchor and come to Ireland, knowing not a single soul, possessing only a smattering of the language, taking on work that nobody would train him to do, at the mercy of another man's approval. How did a man live like that? He had to admire him. And he had to admire the way the ladies were going for Gianni, who seemed to give them no encouragement.

Clever, clever lad – the best way of having them fall at your feet. He himself had proof of this. The sad bitch, Bid Flood, she was a prime example. Once upon a time, a long while ago, Malachy might have given that game girl the glad eye and she would have been blind to him. Then he set his sights on Margaret and when she had a rival, Bid turned into a raging fury, hating the apple of his eye, practically throwing herself at him. One night he stumbled into her when she was in her cups, and she as good as begged him to marry her as desperately as he would hear from any woman in this life. The unfortunate thing about this episode was that Tessie, Margaret's sister, witnessed the whole scenario, and he was certain there would be hell to pay – that at the very least she would be running to inform on him quick as shite from a shovel. But she didn't do as he expected. She did confront him, but the warning she gave him showed a side to her he would have hardly credited. That poor girl, she said, that unfortunate Bid Flood, she has made the biggest show of herself she'll ever make. With a bit of luck she's drunk enough to forget what she's done – and if you have a heart you will forget it as much as I am going to do.

And he did. Or he tried to. It was not that he was carrying even the slightest torch for the woman, but his heart was definitely sore for Bid when he saw the Scotch lacheko she landed herself with, and the hidings they gave each other when they were full of drink. She still had the worst word in her stomach against Margaret, but that word his wife could well return. Bid's spite spilled over against him as well. She now said she hated the sight of the dirty, ugly O'Donovans. But nobody listened to her – they knew she was a woman scorned, she'd had her eye wiped, and they are the worst on God's earth. But now he had to ask himself, was he a man scorned? That was what for no good reason he felt Martha Sewell had done to him now she'd set her cap at the Italian painter.

There never was much chance of a court for Malachy and her – the walls in this town have eyes and ears – but she was a smart girl, and he longed to learn how precisely she would arrange the tryst, for that was certainly what she had in mind, and she struck him as a woman determined enough to get what she wanted. All changed. She was after the foreigner and he was willing. Free and willing. He'd begun to take his eyes off the Stations at least long enough to notice her. They were bold as brass to be seen out walking together, once sharing an orange. Why shouldn't they? What should stop them? And why was he asking questions better suited coming from the chapped lips of an old woman? He should be ashamed, and he was. He could do little to prove himself when Margaret was in the condition she was. Work wasn't pouring in – Jesus, it was barely a trickle. He'd had to let the young lad go, and that affected him more than the parents of the boy would let him admit. He would have liked to talk about this on a walk with a brother, but no one fitted that bill. You cannot spell out what's annoying you – that's women's talk. You need to rely on saying nothing or saying next to nothing and it being understood that way you're saying everything. Gianni would be useless in that respect. The man barely said a word, but his silence wasn't earned – it was the only way he could speak. Malachy wondered if that was because he was a painter as much, as if not more, due to him being foreign. Did that kind of boy not need to talk? Or maybe he kept what he had to say for the bold Martha?

She was thriving on the Italian's attention. Looking very well indeed. Malachy had her face in his mind, as he fixed his green tie in the mirror, hoping she would like it. Jesus, what a rat you are, Malachy O'Donovan, he accused himself. You would take the bite out of another man's mouth. You would hurl the plate from your own hand and throw what's on it into the face of your nearest and dearest. What is going on in your dirty mind, man? Three children, and another due at any minute. You think your wife is losing the run of herself, what about you? She at least has some excuse for her fits of madness, do you? And as he asked that, he had the terrible sense that something was stirring within him as well. His insides were suddenly churning. A pain shot through his cock as if it were in the grip of the tightest fist he'd ever felt. It was a claw trying to get down from his chest, and he could feel the blood circulating through his body. He could actually hear the sound it was making. His heart had started moving, churning though every limb, pounding till he thought he was either going deaf with the noise or going to die with the fear. The legs were weak beneath him, and he found himself with his hands balanced on the table to support the whole weight of himself, the black-smith now turned into some creature that was neither man nor woman, carrying some kind of child that neither he nor his missus had created but seemed to be planted and growing, and guilt and shame were its parents. He had to snap out of this lunacy. He had to get a grip on himself. The way he'd do it was the way he'd tackle the toughest job he might have to face in the forge. Do it step by step. Be gentle with the animal. Take it easy, and get the work finished through patience. Know where you are by knowing what you're doing. Admit what you are. A married man. A father with three youngsters. A hard-working individual. Jealous of a stranger who's arrived and stolen the young woman he should have nothing whatsoever to do with. He'd said it, jealous. Having said it, he could deal with it. That was always the way. But this was no preparation for the next shock he admitted to. Perhaps it was not him – perhaps it was her he was jealous of? And the pain, the claw, the blood in his belly hardened so inside him he thought he could not breathe – that he was struck blind. Or did his eyes open? He could see Gianni naked and wanted him. He had to get out, out into the air, and never admit this.

✿ ✿ ✿

Fr O'Hagen was as much in the dark as to what the paintings looked like as the next man. Yes, of course he had used a fair whack of his inheritance money to pay for them, but that did not give him any right to interfere with the progress of the work. Gianni said nothing much, but his sternness impressed on everyone he knew what he was doing. Fr O'Hagen certainly hoped so, for if this were not the case he would have to answer to his mother. Yes, yes, he knew she was dead and buried, but dear Jesus and his saints preserve us from all harm, the woman had taken to calling him in dreams. Since the day of her funeral he now had great difficulty finding sleep. Her passing had brought him a powerful sense of his own mortality. All the prayers he had uttered over graves, all the hands he had shaken in sympathy, all the words of condolence that he now realised fell glibly from his mouth as he felt the spear in the side of his own loss, nothing had prepared him for the shock to his system that followed the drenching day when he bid that woman their last farewell. The thought he would never see her again, never hear the sound of her voice – how could he hope to contain his grief? But he did and it surprised him how well he managed. It was only sleep that defied him. He did his best to get it back. Walked for miles, read into the night, wrote sermons of such a length no one could listen to, just for the spiritual exercise that he hoped would exhaust his restless body into submission. But nothing worked for more than two weeks – he lay awake in the black night, listing to himself the possible misfortunes that might befall him – punishments for not being sufficiently dutiful a son. When, at last, he did nod off, the blackness of his visions that night were a comfort to him. Nothing in dreams to distract him – nothing, mercifully, to wake him. But he did hear her voice, and this did disturb him when he remembered it. She was not calling his name nor anyone else's. She was not engaging in any rational conversation. No, she appeared to be barking like a dog. He remembered reading about an old Chinese lady whose mania was that there be no fur around her flesh when they placed her in the tomb. If they did dress her like that, she believed she would come back and haunt them in the shape of an animal. Deprived of rest as he was, he now worried that perhaps he had made this mistake with his mother, but a moment's sane reflection convinced him this was not possible. Yes, she did pride herself on the pair of beaver lamb coats she had possessed, but these hadn't gone to the grave with her. Heartbroken he may have been, mad with money he certainly wasn't. Both garments had gone to a relation of his father's who had long admired them. That was the entire gettings for the O'Hagen side. He was a little annoyed to learn that this ungrateful lady chose to have the furs cut into jackets, despite the near tearful protests of the man with the shears. Such magnificent pieces – a sin to slice them apart like that – but he was speaking to deaf ears. And perhaps it was because his mother got wind of this sartorial outrage, perhaps rumours of it reached her in the other world, that she chose to come back yelping in complaint to him.

Complaint he was sure it was, but he could not check, for that first visit would seem to be the last. The night was innocent again. What little shuteye he now managed to snatch was free of her visitations. And then once, when for some reason he dreamt he was on the boat travelling to Liverpool from Dublin, didn't he glimpse her face on the woman behind the counter serving cups of tea? The sight of a lady like Mama doing such a menial task was enough of a jolt to wake him immediately, and in the cold light of morning he was nearly sure it could not have been herself. But there were no doubts about the other sightings. Her face on the prow of a boat sailing gracefully down Lough Swilly, distinct as daylight, leisurely rampaging through his dreaming mind. And then the one that shook him most. He was digging, rough as a navvy, through the ground of the Church of San Clemente, that ancient haven for Irish pilgrims to Rome. He had burrowed through its many archaeological levels, beneath the medieval chapel down to the pagan place of worship, until finally he was standing smelling the stench of damp in the temple of Mithras, when he felt distinctly the cold point of a sharp knife at his neck. Turning his head, he saw the painted face of the heathen divinity. The god lifted the blade to the priest's lips and pricked them, catching a single drop of blood, spilling not on the weapon but staining the purple tongue of Mithras scarlet, quenching his thirst for human sacrifice, terrifying the poor Christian as to what would befall him next. Strong arms enveloped him, the floor of the dank cave caught him as he fell, and preparing himself to surrender body and soul to the ecstasy of divine power, he felt he was breathing his last. Then the poke of an umbrella in his side shifted his vision away from the underground chamber and its painful pleasure into the open air of the war cemetery beside the church, attended by a thousand widows in deepest black, keeping the graves as spotlessly clean as they did their kitchens, adopting a million cats as the children their fallen heroes of husbands never gave them. And he searched the throng of avenging angels for his mother with her brolly raised and ready for the fray against alien gods and their attendant minions from hell, but he could not see the identifying weapon. Had Mama again simply done the unthinkable? Had she submerged herself into the crowd? He was now in the midst of these women, terrified of their identifying him as not one of their dead, and taking immediate revenge by letting their battalions of wild cats loose on his flesh. But it was then he heard her voice and rather than coming from a human, it was as if it sounded from the very soil of Rome itself beneath his feet. She told him she could see and hear him every instant of every hour of every day and night. That she was guarding him, observing him, protecting him. Now she advised him to wake up and change out of the pyjamas damp from his excavations in that strange place of worship, whose depths should never have been revealed but were best left hidden as the good Lord had intended. Have no truck with heathens, son, she declared, they're all burning in hell, and I should know since I'm dead. Wake up and have a good wash – forget this nightmare.

But he could not forget it. He knew that this was a message from a soul who was restless, and it was his duty to appease it in some form or other. He would have commemorated Mama with a magnificent tombstone that might have dwarfed even Monsignor McShane's, and that had set his folk back a fair bit of their fortune, but somehow he knew another great chore must be undertaken – leave something behind that would speak to generations about their generosity, Fr O'Hagen and his mother. A new set of Stations of the Cross. There would of course be mumblings that they had stretched things too far – over-reached themselves – but he was ready with an answer for that. They had always been servants to the Catholic Church in this town. They had also been patrons of the arts and culture. He'd provided a perpetual cup for the summer soccer knock-out tournament in Maginn Park. Mother had always been a soft touch when it came to sponsoring the piano accordion competition in the Feis Ceoil, providing a plethora of medals and trophies – only for that particular instrument, she was insistent. When he questioned her about her love for this type of music, she assured him she absolutely hated it. If it had to be inflicted on her, why should she not inflict it on others? So, she sat in St Mary's Hall, listening to the beginners' caterwauling for hours on end, third Saturday in June, and those who were courting favour from them in any capacity whatsoever had better be prepared to follow suit if they were to be given any hint of a kind ear. There was then a tradition on their part of benefiting the town, and this new work of art continued such good work. She would be pleased, wouldn't she?

So he reassured himself. He only wished he had got a glimpse of work in progress. It might have been safer to settle for a nice piece of stained glass. But still, he was glad he'd gone down his own road. He just hoped that the job would be Oxo, as the football lads sometimes declared a result that pleased them. The one regret he did have was that the painter really wasn't the friendliest or most outgoing of chaps. Fr O'Hagen would have loved to discuss the intricacies of Renaissance iconography with him and to have been enlightened by the painter's eager eyes. Share delicious suppers and decent wine, pondering the illuminations of Raphael – learning something new every day. He would even have been grateful to practise his rusty bit of Italian, but the man's more than adequate command of English put a stop to that. He did say to Fr Stefano a working knowledge of the language would be an asset, so he couldn't complain if he got what he asked for, but it still might have been nice to speak and share secrets no one else in the town could comprehend. It was not to be. The man was his own master. And he preferred the company of women.

Now of course in a place like this there is tittle-tattle. He himself had never listened to it, knowing too well the danger of putting too much faith in the sniggering reports delivered too often by their housekeepers to priests who should have known better and kept themselves apart from the doings of their parishioners. It was extraordinary how little it took to create scandal. That was why he limited his looks at Margaret O'Donovan to an absolute minimum. Why he made a point of speaking as much, if not more, to Malachy as he did to the wife, removing any hint of suspicion. Still and all, he knew that the slightest slip up, the merest excess of interest, the longer than usual flicker of desire, the word that prolonged a conversation into an act of intimacy – all of these could be taken and used against him in the cross-examination of his daily details that made up too much of the town's conversation. Fr O'Hagen was on his guard and with good reason. He was – he had to be – a careful man. And while he was capable of spontaneous gestures such as this decision to acquire a new Stations of the Cross, he still was sufficiently responsible to hope that the paintings would pass muster among the faithful. He would stress hope here, not insist, for he did passionately believe in the freedom of an artist to create as he sees fit. Rules of some kind must be respected by all parties, of course – he did believe Gianni would keep to that part of the bargain. That there would be nothing too shocking. The world and his wife knew what happened on the way to Golgotha. That story was the one to be told. And yet something in him wanted to be stunned. He wanted to be taken by the paintings into the heart and mind of the suffering Christ, share this torment and sorrow as he'd never done before, stand before these images, and see and hear the mystery of his faith in a manner he'd not yet been able to imagine. A sin of pride, yes, he'd admit that. He'd enjoy that, damn it – he was his mother's son. They had been in their way jointly responsible for this, and he felt now her haunting of his dreams was due to her desire to share in his triumph, for triumph it would be.

Or would it? Why the hell had he not sneaked even a peep at the work in progress? Why was there such secrecy? Could the Italian painter be up to a fast one? Was he, as they said in this town, taking a right hand at him? What if he had contrived to come up with some Picassoesque strangeness? What if the work was obscene in a manner liable to disgust anyone who viewed it? What if these people, used only to the most conventional of holy pictures hanging on their bedroom walls, the Sacred Hearts, the Child of Prague, the Saints Bernadette and Therese, the Assumption into Heaven and Immaculate Conception of the Virgin Mary, the pious earnestness of these icons was all they'd ever looked at – what if these people were confronted by something mad and exotic, the ravings of an artistic temperament that knew no boundaries of religion or taste? What if he had been made a right fool of, spending his mother's money on worthless daubings? Already he was paying for the sin of pride – already he was paying for another sin – the real reason he did not listen to tittle-tattle. The sin of seducing, albeit only in his mind, another man's wife, coveting her as he was coveting the glory of staring at another man's art, and saying I paid for that. By giving him this anxiety God was having his revenge. His conscience now was biting him in the arse. A crude expression, but an accurate one. And he could not rest. He could not sleep. This was why. So, let this day pass – let him see what dreams Gianni had painted.

◆ ◆ ◆

Their conversation now obsessed her. It was flattery to herself to describe it as conversation, for she had sat there, listening to the torrent of his memories, the stories he had chosen to shape with her, with her alone – of that she knew for sure. Martha was equally sure he would never again confess as much about himself to another woman. So often she wanted to stop him in his tracks – to question him more – to look for more details, for elaboration – but she thought the better of it. There comes a time when it is best to keep your trap shut, and this was one such occasion. She did worry that his heart would burst with the urgency of what he had to confess, but it did not. Nor did she feel that telling all of this had brought him any peace. Still, she was glad she was the one he picked to hear all that happened to him, for now she did devoutly believe he would never leave her.

Her life seemed to be one long act of being left behind. Her mother, her father, now her uncle. If there was any pattern, any rhyme or reason, to all of this, then it surely was one of desertion. It no longer surprised her – perhaps it never had – that people simply ceased to be there. She dealt with this by placing herself at one remove from everything about her. That detachment gave her the power to deal with crises and emergencies as she dealt with calmer aspects of her existence. This was how to manage things. Better do so efficiently, and tick them off the list of things done. She could not see any point in panic or pain. That was why she received the news of her dead uncle's letter with equanimity and instantly decided to visit her mother where she was alive and kicking in Tralee, County Kerry.

Trains to Dublin and Kerry took her there. She had no more intention of telling anyone where she was travelling to than she had of blaming Uncle Columba for his refusal to say a dickie bird about the family secret prior to his death. Caution was his way always. No, let's call a spade a spade – cowardice was his way. The man would have eaten a shovel of burning coals before letting this one out of the bag. And really, what was to be gained from blabbing? What good could satisfying her enormous curiosity have done? What more answer could he have given to her inquisitiveness, than what he told her so succinctly in the note? An address, a name, an apology for the lie – the necessary lie – told to spare her feelings until the time was inevitable for revelations. To an outsider it might strike one as odd – ludicrous maybe – even scarcely believable – but they simply didn't realise that this abruptness – it was the Sewell way of doing things. And as far as Martha for one was concerned, a jolly good way of doing things. Minimum fuss – maximum of information, for good or ill, take it or leave it.

She took it, come what may. And all the way there, on that eternal journey through the whole length of this island, she kept imagining her mother's face as it presented itself through the endless rain that seemed to seep through every inch of the soil of Ireland, drenching it, abolishing the sun and its light, shading everything, its mists of grey and dirty silver. Would she still be pretty or worn by age? Thin as a whippet or fat as a fool? Would her voice lilt a welcome or squawk in southern horror at the arrival of this northern stranger, her daughter all the way from Donegal? Martha entertained the possibility that the front door would no sooner be opened than the sight of her would ensure it would be slammed closed in her face. There might be a match put to the welcome mat. Or perhaps there could be the offer of a cup of tea, a sandwich, a drink of sherry – but definitely no more. Could there be a flood of tears, an embrace, a plea for mercy, a vow never to lose contact again? No, there would not be – Martha herself would ensure that. Whatever else would be the outcome of this meeting, there would be no reconciliation. That was not what this was about.

Then what was it? To answer that Martha would have to be a mind-reader, and she did not indulge in such idiocy. Through those years of neglect – the wishful thinking that her mother might one day come back from Africa after all the separation – it was still important to the girl that she actually say goodbye. And that was precisely why she had travelled to this town, walked through its drowned streets, found the house she sought, chose to knock at its blue door rather than ring its bell, rap three loud times and wait for her mother to answer. She did, standing staring at her in long silence, knowing precisely who had called looking for her. It's you at last, the old woman hissed like the green snake she now resembled. I knew you'd be here one day. What do you want? What are you looking for? I have nothing to give you. Nor have I anything to give you, Martha answered her, that's what I've come all this way to tell you – nothing, nothing whatsoever.

At that Martha turned on her heel and was determined to go, when she heard her name being called. She looked back and saw her mother still standing in the doorway. Is he dead? She asked, is old Cissy Sewell dead?

–My uncle Columba has passed away, yes.

–I might have guessed as much. That's why he'd spill the beans. No chance of you turning against him, demanding why he kept mum about me. Ever the weakling, like your ludicrous father. Always running out of harm's way. So now he tells you I'm in the pink. Well, what do you make of your Kerry mother? Do I fit the bill of the wicked witch abandoning you? Yes, I do. Is that any worse than being stuck with the fucking Sewells? Have you enough gumption in you to agree with me on that?

–No.

–No what? Don't tell me. Keep yourself to yourself. That favourite trick of your father. His little girl is a chip off the old Protestant block. Saying nothing. Doing nothing.

Thinking nothing. You even have his revolting colour. It takes away your prettiness. That pale and wan look. I can see your veins through your skin. And to think my blood flows in them. I'm sure you are as disgusted by that as I am. Please, get away from my door. Why did you trek down here? To let me know I'm hated? That is hardly news, is it? Get away. Never come back. Why the hell have you come back?

—I had something to tell you, something specific.

—What is it?

—I needed to say this myself to your face.

—I've asked you already. What is it?

—You will die soon, very soon.

—What?

—And I wished to say good riddance. Goodbye, good riddance.

—Don't turn your back on me like that, don't run away, how dare you frighten me like that, how do you know, who told you that? I warn you. Answer me, Martha, Christ damn you.

But Martha chose to ignore the threats. She was walking away, the woman's curses ringing in her ears. She smiled to herself, gleeful that she had struck the blow. She knew if she couldn't quite claim to have killed this monstrous individual, she'd struck in a way the woman would remember for the rest of her days, and when she was lying on her death bed, those simple words – you will die soon, very soon – would resound through her dying mind, hastening the well deserved end when it finally did come. It brought a smile to Martha's lips, the sheer badness of what she'd done. A shocking, rather dreadful act and singularly appropriate in the circumstances. Martha had at last done something worthy of her mother. It was only right – no, she'd say it – it was divinely right the cruel bitch should be on the receiving end of such a punch. And do I have anything to regret? she asked herself and she answered that she did. I should have killed her at my birth, she reasoned, my world would have been a better place.

❋ ❋ ❋

In his grave the Reverend Sewell listened to his niece unfurl every detail of her escapade, sparing himself nor herself anything, revelling in the details of how she had put her mother in her place – a place Martha could not wait to be gone from. The dead man knew for sure she would be leaving Ireland, having headed far south to Kerry and back again, crossing the whole country, finding nothing to detain her any longer, making ready to flee forever. Where? Italy, likely, with the painter, if he took her. But there would be no guarantee he would. Martha was perfectly capable of irritating him beyond endurance. He only could hope it would occur sooner rather than later. That he would not desert her with a child, or stuck in the wilds of God knows where, destitute, ignorant of all being said about her.

Still she continued to list her trials and tribulations, and what was there left for him to do but listen? The dreams of an afterlife recited before him at Sunday School, and which he had in turn recited to squads of youngsters under his religious instruction, had been proved to be wrong. No hell, no heaven – perhaps the Papists were right, perhaps he was in Purgatory. He had been sentenced to exist like this, neither living nor dead, as punishment for the great crime he had committed against himself. That was to pass into the land of shades and shadows having led an existence which ultimately left no mark of significance on man, woman or child. The sense of futility that had always drained him of the energy to do something – anything – startling – it was afflicting him even now. No, here was not purgatory. This was the way things had been always and now it appeared would ever be. And if this girl did not take courage in both her hands and grab the nearest means of escape, one day she would be lying beside him, rotting into exhaustion, never to know the blissful release of pure extinction.

He tried to speak but the clay in his mouth clogged his words. She had now not so much grown silent as paused for breath. He tried to raise a hand to caress her hair, the soft hair he had loved so much, but the grave was a prison from which there was no release. How could he warn her that this was even more of a crisis than she feared? That she held the future in the choice before her? That the choice came down to herself alone, no matter what any other might do to influence it? So often in this cemetery, subject to the whims of wind and rain, he had tried to control their force to his will, using their power as his language, as his prayer, to be released from this unchanging state. And each time he had failed. As he had expected. Failure was his nature. Now he would try to go against nature. If he could not speak to her, then the whole cosmos must save his niece.

A flock of birds suddenly had gathered about the grave – strange companions, magpies, seagulls, the robin, the wren. She eyed them cautiously. They were utterly still, and then began their song. He could only describe it as if his dead heart had started beating again. This was what was meant by joyous melody. The sky had turned into an astonishing azure, and the sun was golden. If it had begun to spin in cartwheels, he would have believed the miracle, and it was as if Martha had shared in that secret with the dead man, for she next began to clap her hands and shout you're right, Uncle, of course you're right. What good advice as always. I knew what I must do.

With that she raced away, leaving him none the wiser what it was he had advised her precisely to do. All he knew was that she had now abandoned him to the clay and he doubted if he should ever see her again. The mad birds continued in chorus, the astonishing shade of the sky still dazzled him, the sun persisted in its dance till it seemed to him the earth itself was in complete upheaval, shifting the continent beneath him, tearing Ireland itself asunder, the soil that covered him now loosening, and at last he felt his spirit rise from within him, shaped like a dove, the name of his patron saint, the name of himself, Columba. The flock had been sent, he thought, to comfort his niece, but he was wrong. Instead they were waiting for the moment he might choose to release himself and escape. Not Martha – it was himself who was free at last. As usual he had been wrong – gloriously, spectacularly wrong. And with that condemnation gleefully ringing in his ears, with his throat now pouring out a song that had nothing to do with the music of the spheres but stemmed from the sorrow and secrets of the life he loved and lost, he burst forth to meet his Maker, ablaze with light.

They looked at the paintings, and Gianni could not read their faces. The chosen few had the first showing – Fr O'Hagen, Martha, Mr and Mrs O'Donovan, Euni. The crowd would be soon arriving. Why did they say nothing? The child was not even smiling at him, as she usually was. Instead, they walked from one station to the next, stopping, watching, and moving of their own accord led not by the priest, but by their own decision, their own desire to see what follows. He sat in a pew away from them, avoiding their reaction yet expecting Martha at least to offer him congratulations on his work. They were not forthcoming. She was as quiet as the rest. The stillness was broken by a man's tread walking up the aisle. He did not turn his back to see who it was. All he felt were two strong hands pressed on his shoulders. He heard Malachy's voice say, you have done your work. Done it well. And then he was released from the other man's touch. Each of the others came up to him and shook his hand. That was all that was said and done. It was over. He must now go home. That much he had decided as the doors of the church were flung open, and the hoards swarmed in to see his handiwork.

The silence of the first viewing was gone. This shower were keen to have their say. Some were determined to find this set of stations inferior to ones they'd prayed before in Fermanagh and Tyrone. One woman had been to Dublin and visited the Pro-Cathedral, not a hope these could hold a candle to what she'd seen there. And yet this mob too progressively grew quieter. They were taken aback by how the paintings controlled them. The more they saw, the more reluctant they were to speak or to exchange opinions. Then to the shame of everyone, who came staggering in but Bid Flood and her bowsie of a Scots-man, stinking of drink. Jesus Christ, but those two could be relied upon to take the good out of anything. If he was in a bad condition, she was in a worse one, hardly fit to stand. She should have been shown the road out of a public house, let alone a chapel.

Gianni noticed Malachy took guard beside Margaret as if expecting an attack from these arrivals. The drunk woman had tied a white ribbon in her hair, and it had come loose, hanging down her back. Her greying red locks were all over the place. They had long been strangers to a comb. Her nylons were well laddered, and the green dress had seen better days. There was evidence of a fresh tear at the sleeve as if she had been seized by something or someone stronger than herself. The partner was bald and muscular still, running a little to fat, his blue suit neatly pressed but smelling slightly of shit. The congregation moved apart from them, giving them free passage wherever they wished to wander. He noticed the woman bless herself at the first station, and instruct her husband to do likewise. But instead he stumbled backwards, and no one broke his fall. The thud of his body echoed through the church. A volley of oaths shot from his filthy mouth. It was then he started to laugh uproariously, using his hands to help him rise from the ground. Jock falls for the first time, he shouted, and the woman joined in the laughter. For fuck's sake, what's wrong with you, she asked the shocked onlookers, he's cracking a joke, can you not take a bit of sport? Fr O'Hagen knew it was time to act. He placed his arm over the woman's arm and said, Bid, dear, it's time to leave, this is not the time nor place for this kind of carry on. I'll see you and your husband home. Excuse me, Father, she corrected him, but I am home. This church is our home. We are children of Holy God, aren't we? So I have to correct you, with the best will in the world, but you're wrong, Father, you can't see me home. I am already there. I am where I should be. Is she – Martha Sewell? What's that whore doing here?

She had broken free now and was walking towards Gianni, dragging Martha with her. She looked into his face and said, so, you're fucking the wee Protestant, are you? That's the word. Well, isn't that nice? You come to this town at the invite of our holy priest and you do the dirty with one that doesn't even dig with the same foot as ourselves. Christ above, is that not desperate? Would that not break your heart? What do you say to that, Maggie O'Donovan? There's you stripping naked in front of him, leaving last week's washing lying at his feet, and he won't look twice at your old diddies. No, he has younger fish to fry. Poor old Malachy, there — he must be worn out holding his missus down, her fit to be tied because the Italian won't be her fancy man. Or maybe he was — how long has he been lodging with you — could that fat lump in front of you be down to him and not your big man's work? Might that not be the case?

Woman, you have no children, and you will never have a child. Gianni heard his voice speak in the chapel, and the woman shot him a look of hatred. What did you say to me? she hissed. You Italian bastard, what did you say? He said you have no children, Martha repeated, and he said you will never have one. It was as if their words lashed across the drunk woman's face. She now took her time before she'd give her reply and when it came it was a roar of almighty pain. Her body shook with a violence Malachy had only seen once before. It was when the men of the Pound Lane had to catch a beast broke loose from the slaughter house and haul it back to the abattoir. That was the panic he saw Bid unleash from within herself. She shook as if she'd palsy, and it would never be cured.

They looked to Fr O'Hagen to stop this woman making such a show of herself, but he was in as big a state of shock as they were. Gianni and Martha who had started this ball rolling, they were rooted to the spot as well. Having begun this nonsense, the two could not finish it. Malachy knew better than to interfere with this sad specimen but he did guess instinctively who would deal with this, if the spirit moved her. He looked at Margaret and nodded. For a fair while she did nothing, just stared at the sorry sight of her old enemy reduced to this before the eyes of the world. Then she moved. She knelt down beside Bid. She put her arms about her.

A second sound freed itself from within the Flood woman's body – no one had ever heard the like – it was as if she were the banshee lamenting her own death, or another demon coming from inside her to carry her to hell and back. No one who witnessed it would ever forget, and poor Euni was burying herself against her daddy's knees, squeezing hard on her pal Mena's hand, both of them too terrified to cry. They all thought Bid Flood might lay a blow on Margaret O'Donovan that would silence her for all time, but Bid didn't raise a finger, let alone a fist. She even let Margaret ask her was she all right now?

–Am I all right? How can I ever again be all right? I deserve every misfortune that's been poured on me.

–How have you deserved that, Bid?

–Every wain you carried, I wished you and it bad luck. I wish it deformed. I wished the birth would kill you.

–Bid, you're very drunk, you don't know what you're saying.

–I know exactly. I tell you to your face what I prayed on my knees for.

–I believe you hate me, but how could you hate my innocent

babies? What harm did they do you to cause them ill?

–They belonged to you. Belonged to him. That was enough harm for me. Now you know, and I can never show my face to you nor to anyone else in this town again. All I'm fit for is the grave.

–But you weren't heard. Your prayer wasn't answered. My wains were born healthy. So will this new one. God didn't listen.

–He did, but not in the way I intended. He's taught me a terrible lesson, hasn't he, Father O'Hagen? It's not your children he took, Margaret. It's mine – mine that were never born. And none ever will be. I know that for certain, Margaret.

–We know nothing for certain in this world.

–Then why did that foreigner and his fancy woman pass sentence so severe on me? What did they see that made them so sure? What was it in me?

She was pointing at Gianni and Martha. They stood impassive to her accusation. He would not relent and pity her by saying sorry. And where he led, Malachy realised, Martha would follow from now on. People were being eaten by embarrassment at what they'd witnessed between the two women. The crowd was starting to melt away, some of them for whatever reason were shaking Malachy's hand, as if he had done a brave thing when all he had done was the same as the rest of them – watch his wife stop what was clearly a sick woman make a fool of herself. Others looked to Fr O'Hagen, wondering what he'd tell them to do. But they got no satisfaction out of him in that respect. He was as lost as the rest of them, wishing this outburst would be definitely over, not daring to say a word in case he provoked more crying. He felt sorry for the unfortunate lady, but he was also angry. He had more or less spent a near fortune on making this day happen. The Stations of the Cross were his mother's memorial. But it was as if they were forgotten while Bid Flood's agony played itself out in front of them. One part of him wanted to shake her. Another part wanted him to make Jock stand up and order Bid home to her own house. But the main part of him wanted to embrace his beloved, his Margaret, for the wise way she handled this woman and her hatred, calming her, holding her as she wept buckets in her regret and shame at what she had said and done. He heard Margaret say then to Bid, wait till they're all gone. All of them. We'll say the Stations. We'll ask the Blessed Virgin to give us what we want. The two of us, we'll do that, on our own. And he knew he should leave them to it, signalling to Jock and to Malachy that it was time for the men to be gone.

Word soon spread about the incident in the chapel. There was no containing it. It moved liked wildfire, and took as many forms. Nobody could keep track of the yarns being spun. One had it that Fr O'Hagen expelled a devil from the drunken pair and they immediately signed the pledge to abstain forever from alcohol. Another told that the Stations themselves came to life, and Jesus asked all sinners to repent. The word as far away as

Malin was that a woman, seeing the suffering of Our Lord, gave birth to the son she was carrying and didn't the infant know the 'Our Father' off by heart the instant he was born? A few credit that there was an unholy row between a married couple at the unveiling and the good priest trying to come between them got a black eye for his troubles and then sent them packing forever, warning them not to darken the door of a church again. Rumour had it that the niece of a Protestant minister, the one who'd died recently, was supposed to have asked to be baptised in the Catholic faith, so completely swayed was she by the power of what she saw. There was a belief that the Italian boyo who was responsible for the painting, he had been working himself into such a state of exhaustion to finish it, didn't he collapse and die in the arms of the people he was lodging with and was now buried in the local graveyard? Whispers of a scandal between him and the minister's niece were rife as well. Fr O'Hagen was said to have banished him from the parish and refused to pay a penny for his work. Bid Flood was reputed to have looked at the image of Christ crucified and decided to enter a convent. One story led to another, until nobody, including those who were in the chapel and saw everything that happened, could agree on what they actually did witness. Fr O'Hagen decided not to dignify the sillier nonsense with a denial, and that is what he advised Mr and Mrs O'Donovan to do as well. Bid Flood made up her mind that if people were mad enough to believe she'd lock herself in a convent, it was them who should take to the drink as a cure for their lunacy. Malachy and Margaret barely broke breath to each other about what happened, let alone would they discuss it with gossip mongers. Martha was too busy in the clearing out of her uncle's belongings from the rectory to pay much attention to this whole scenario. She was grateful Gianni had a man's strength to give her a hand with the heavier lifts and she no longer cared – did she ever care? – what the town thought of her. All was quietening down till the morning Margaret O'Donovan's baby was born – a healthy boy with magnificent blue eyes and blond angelic hair – unearthly, the midwife, Nurse Kelly, whispered to a neighbour before news of the delivery had travelled around the town.

It had been well known that this was a difficult pregnancy. The O'Donovans were in terror they might lose the child. Her two sisters had walked the leather off their shoes hiking up to the Holy Well on Mamore Gap, risking that wild climb, to stand and pray for their sister and her child, while Urris in its barren stoniness stretched before them. That the lad should come into the world, whole and hale, beautiful indeed, now this was a miracle. His life had been saved, and there was a reason, and that reason, it was decreed, was the new Stations of the Cross. Slowly but surely, pilgrims were gathering, a trickle first, sharing the great secret as to what truly drew them to worship here. The numbers increased, and they grew so bold as to state openly that they believed this newborn infant was in his way as holy as the Stations they wanted to venerate. The sincerity of their faith moved Fr O'Hagen. He would make no attempt to stop the hoards descending on his church, but he did make it clear it was Our Blessed Saviour and his holy mother they should be praying to, and not the innocent baby, so the O'Donovans' house and forge were to be left unmolested. That was fair enough, but Margaret worried just what this attention might do eventually to the wee child when he was man enough to know what was going on about him. Malachy reassured her that by the time this young fella got near to the age of reason, the same gang of holy Joes would have attached themselves to another wonder, and it was best to let things lie.

If the O'Donovans were out of bounds, so too was the Italian painter. In the few days or weeks left to him in the town, he was not to be harassed or questioned, but left to mind his own business, which was of no one else's concern. Fr O'Hagen was a happy man that seeing the work completed seemed to leave his mother peaceful – well, at least content enough to stay put in the grave, for he'd seen neither hilt nor hair of her in dreams, nor had he heard her since the day they'd first viewed her memorial. She was either at rest or so affronted by the escapade in the chapel she'd not deign to show her face again in such a disgraceful kip. No matter, she was gone, he was sure of that, and if he had paid a high price to ensure that – well, it was worth it. He gave the wages due to Gianni, who took them with thanks, but said no more of future plans, and Fr O'Hagen, while fearing for the artist's mortal soul and for Martha Sewell, felt it best to ask no questions. He would have received no answer anyway.

Gianni himself did not know what would come next. The

work was completed. It had taken more out of him than he thought, but it was time to leave it behind him. His mind was straying to Italy – to Arezzo. He was wanting to go home. When Martha told him she would go with him, he put up no resistance, for he was sure of only one thing. Martha would not depart from Donegal. She would not leave Ireland. Why was he so sure about this? When he looked into her face after she announced her decision that they would travel together, he saw in it the loneliness of that desolate place she called home, a loneliness matched by the beauty of the new son asleep soundly in the O'Donovans' bed. No, she was meant to be here, remain forever, grow old and meet her maker, rising from the grave where her uncle Columba lay as well. Martha, when it came down to it, would not live with him as a wife.

As always, she surprised him. She did travel with him. The O'Donovans received one letter from the pair of them. It bore an Italian postmark and contained a splendid drawing of a child. Was it of their baby, or did Martha and Gianni have one of their own? Had Martha given birth? Was Gianni a proud father? They did not spell it out, but Martha called the sketch a nativity and said they were thriving. The family framed the picture. It was much admired, holding pride of place beside their wedding photograph, until both Margaret and Malachy passed away within two months of each other and, as was the custom, the walls of the house were stripped bare for the duration of the mourning. In their fifties – the pair – much too young to leave this earth, it was generally agreed. It was decided Euni should inherit the drawing, as she alone had any memory, vague enough as it was, of the man who painted it. She treasured it more for the association it had with her mother and father than for any other reason.

Wasn't there a knock on her door one summer's day not that long ago? The town clerk stood there. He explained he'd had a request from Italy, from a town called Arezzo. They were having an exhibition of your man Cuma, who painted the Stations of the Cross. They were looking to include some of the stuff he drew in this town. The priests naturally wouldn't let the Stations out of the chapel. There was a rumour Euni had a drawing. Would she allow it to travel? For some reason she found herself lying, saying they'd lost that years ago, sorry, she couldn't oblige. She hoped she'd done right, but she would never let that possession out of her house. A few months later – it was a warm August Monday – she was tending to her parents' grave in Cockhill cemetery, planting flowers to scent the loneliness of the legions of dead, pulling weeds dry as dust from where the remains of her pal, Mena Kiely, were long lying. Draining a sup of tea from her flask and unwrapping the green tissue from an Oatfield Emerald caramel, Euni thought of poor Mena and herself reciting Bo-Peep for the Italian painter all those years ago, watching the sheep graze in the fields surrounding that church built by the starving hands of men and women, their guts rattling, gulping a handful of meal their labour earned, barely sustaining them through the black Famine that took too many of their own – too many of her own, if truth be told. She was getting the shivers, all right, as she always did in this desolate spot, wanting to race away, inclined as she was to panic. In this mood she expected the sky to open and pour dark rain, but it was instead the colour of a blue she'd never witnessed before and, suddenly, didn't Euni hear what sounded like all the voices she'd ever listened to, Mammy, Daddy, Mena, the whole town together, singing – would you believe that? She never knew if any of them had a note in their head. She could not make out what the words were, and then it dawned on her who else was joining in. It was himself, Gianni, and the one who ran off with him, Martha – two she had long buried. They had come back. And what was the song? She wasn't sure but she knew one thing for certain. They were home and they were speaking of Arimathea.